ONLY
WITH
YOU

Dianne Venetta

ONLY WITH YOU
Book #4

Silver Creek Series:
Romantic Mystery/Adventure
NOT WITHOUT YOU ~ #1
BECAUSE OF YOU ~ #2
ALL ABOUT YOU ~ #3
ONLY WITH YOU ~ #4

Other novels by Dianne Venetta

Ladd Springs Series:
Cozy Mystery/Romance
LADD SPRINGS ~ #1
LADD FORTUNE ~ #2
HOTEL LADD ~ #3
LADD HAVEN ~ #4
LOSING LADD ~ #5
LADD CHRISTMAS ~ #6

The Gables Trilogy:
Romantic Women's Fiction
JENNIFER'S GARDEN
LUST ON THE ROCKS
WHISPER PRIVILEGES

Women's Fiction
CONDEMN ME NOT

ISBN 97809977738-0-4

Only With You
Copyright 2016 by Dianne Venetta
ISBN: 978-0-9977738-0-4
Publisher: BloominThyme Press
Editor: Best Foot Forward
Cover Design: Seductive Designs

Acknowledgements

The Rocky Mountains hold a powerful allure for skiers to test the limits of their ability. As such, skiers challenge the mountains every season as they challenge themselves. But sometimes, the thrill takes a nosedive. Enter... Search and rescue.

Search and rescue teams dedicate their time to helping and saving the lives of others. The teams are comprised of skilled pilots, medics, skiers, climbers, rafters—and dogs—who are trained to handle the dangerous conditions unique to backcountry. In addition to rescuing those in need, SAR educates the public on how to "play" safely.

Paul Barth, a friend and professional helicopter pilot well-versed in the operations of mountain search and rescue, provided the essential knowledge and expertise needed to create the realistic scenes in this story. Thank you, Paul!

Dedication

Our duty is not to exist, but to live.

My father was a pilot of both fixed wing and rotor aircraft. His passion for flying defined him as he lived and breathed the freedom of the skies. He continually challenged himself on land, sea and air, never allowing a day to pass when he didn't test the limits.

This novel is for the thrill-seekers of the world, and the dedicated SAR members who rescue them. Courageous, one and all.

Chapter One

Standing atop a sky-kissed ridge in Silver Creek, Colorado, Dr. Hal Richardson gazed down the steep slope. At over eleven thousand feet, this narrow swath of untouched snow was the stuff of heli-skiers' dreams. Dropped by helicopter at the top of the mountain, Hal and his friends were about to ski down virgin terrain. Embedded between walls of sheer rock, it was pristine powder as far as the eye could see offering an experience that was surreal, like skiing weightlessly where no man had gone before him, the air shockingly quiet. It was skier and mountain and nothing else.

The air was crisp and cold, the sky unlimited. As usual, Hal felt a "high" imagining their first run of the day. It was pure euphoria. He and his group planned to hit the back bowls next, and he couldn't wait. Weather was supposed to move in this afternoon and adorn the mountain with fresh powder, but at the moment, it was clear, inviting, and waiting for them to carve their tracks.

Hal inhaled deeply. He never tired of the thrill. It was unmatched, unequaled in the sport of snow-skiing—and today, he was sharing it with friends. Good friends. Grant Powell and his girlfriend Kinsley Fairchild had signed on for the adventure, along with Hal's normal crew—Canyon Laredo, McIntyre Walsh and Lisa Richardson, Hal's daughter. The only ones missing from their group were Hal's longtime girlfriend Adele Simms and Canyon's new flame, Katharine Wainwright. Adele was busy with her restaurant and Katharine was not a fan of heli-skiing.

"It's beautiful, isn't it?" Lisa posed wistfully, tipping her nip of a nose up to face him.

Hal smiled, noticing how the frigid air brightened her faint spray of freckles, the effect accentuated by a fuchsia

turtleneck tucked beneath a turquoise blue jacket. The temperature was three below, but she wasn't deterred. Like father, like daughter, Lisa would brave even the toughest of
elements to enjoy an adventure of this magnitude. Strapped to
her back was a small pack containing essential gear—
avalanche shovel, probe, mini first-aid kit, and spare radio.
They all wore one, in case of emergency.

It was a trip he'd been looking forward to for weeks.
"It's the cream of the peak," Hal agreed.

She dropped her gaze to his leg. "You're certain your
knee can handle it?"

As an orthopedic surgeon, Hal knew better than anyone
the physical stress this ski run posed. And while his recent
knee injury had fully healed, he was only one wipeout away
from another. He cast a glance toward Grant. But that held
true for all of them, Hal mused, especially him. Unlike Hal's
issues, Grant's troubles were cardiac in nature.

Hal chuckled. Nothing a young girlfriend couldn't fix—
Kinsley Fairchild was over a decade younger than Grant and
kept a sharp eye on the man, forever pushing her vegan life-
style and strict exercise regimen upon him. Hal savored a private smile. The formula seemed to be working; Grant had
never looked happier or healthier. Hal paused on the thought.
Actually, the weak link on this ski trip was Kinsley. Dressed
in a black designer jacket with fancy gold adornments and
form-fitting ski pants, a white helmet, a black balaclava, and
shiny black goggles, her long brown hair braided and tucked
into the back of her jacket, her attire shouted fashion, not
skill. Before Kinsley met Grant, she had limited her skiing to
intermediate runs with her parents or his daughter. But once
Grant entered the picture, she took lessons to improve her
skills so that she could join him on the more advanced runs.
Not surprisingly, skiing four or five times a week with a private instructor seemed to do the trick. Add Kinsley's charac-
teristic refusal to back down from a challenge and it was a
no-brainer. She was joining them for the day.

Hal returned his gaze to the mountain, to the layers of jagged snow-covered peaks in the distance, thousands of feet above the tree line—that elevation where trees simply cannot grow. Primarily, cold temperatures were to blame, but sun, wind, and terrain all played a role in limiting growth as the forest crawled up the mountain. The alpine environment was harsh and the sparse tree covering near the top was visual proof.

A sober reality settled in. No matter who you were, or what kind of physical condition you were in, the mountains were humbling. It was wise to remember that.

"We ready to get this show started?" Walsh asked.

Hal laughed and leaned into one of his ski poles. Dressed completely in black, Walsh's attire underscored his personality. The Marine was all business. No fluff, no frills, he was determination defined, making him the perfect mate for Lisa. Determination was his daughter's middle name—especially when it came to chasing those sacred boreal toads of hers during research expeditions. "We're holding you up, are we?"

"I don't see the point in wasting this gorgeous day standing around," Walsh replied. "I'd like to get three or four runs in today."

"Listen to the newbie," Lisa quipped with a cock of her head. "Give a man a taste of fresh powder and suddenly he's a thrill-seeker."

Walsh grunted. "It's your fault."

True, Hal mused. Lisa had introduced Walsh to the sport. When she'd met him, he was an ex-Marine living in solitude on a mountain, doing little more than existing. Now, he was a regular member of the mountain search and rescue team and an extremely competent skier, something Hal attributed to Walsh's supreme physical condition. The man's body was an intricate mass of steel plates honed for battle.

"I feel your pain," Grant said. "I'm ready whenever you are."

Kinsley nodded. "Me, too."

The two were a stylish pair, Grant also sporting the latest in high-tech ski gear. His black jacket boasted red stripes on the sleeves and chest and coordinated perfectly with his reflective-lens red-trimmed black goggles and black helmet. The man wore custom-fitted boots snapped into top-of-the-line powder skis. Specially formulated for deep powder, they were shorter, wider, and waxed to glossy perfection. Between the two of them, Hal imagined they had spent a small fortune on ski equipment. Both could afford it. Grant's jewelry store was a hot spot in town and Kinsley's blog, *Wildlife Neutral*, attracted almost a million visitors a month, commanding top dollar in advertising revenue. She was an animal rights activist of the highest degree and had followers all over the world. Last winter, she had set her sights on Silver Creek—more specifically, Palmer International. They were expanding the ski resort and she was protesting—a conflict that almost turned deadly.

"Count me in," Canyon added, his brown eyes dancing. He stood next to Kinsley with ski poles stuck in the snow on either side of him. Despite the frigid temperature, his navy ski jacket was opened at the top, revealing a white turtleneck. Tufts of blond curls poked from beneath his black helmet.

Hal paused in thought. Canyon's dog Buck had been caught in the crossfire of protest, a fact for which he held Kinsley personally responsible. Luckily, the dog had survived. It was the only reason Canyon had been able to move past the incident and forgive Kinsley. That and her extravagantly generous donation to Wainwright Ranch.

As if to echo the skier's impatience, Jack, the helicopter pilot who had delivered them to the peak, lifted his chopper from the ground and banked west. He would meet them at their rendezvous point, then return the group for as many runs as they wanted to make. As lead guide for the day, it was Hal's decision when to go, where to go, and whether they should go at all.

Moving his gaze back down the slope, Hal worked his mind back through the weather report. Reading the conditions was an important aspect of heli-skiing. Recent heavy snow made for amazing powder, but also carried an increased risk of avalanche. On the flight up, Hal had studied the ridge and consulted with Canyon—the person next most familiar with this terrain and Hal's informal second-in-command—and the two had decided this section would be fine for this morning's run. Not guaranteed, but that was heli-skiing. You never completely erased the risk. Decisions had to be made. And not only based upon conditions, but also upon skier ability— weakest skier's ability. Translated: Kinsley.

But peering down the steep terrain, a thick blanket of bright sparkling snow bracketed by jagged rocks, Hal was confident she could handle it. He'd skied the resort's back bowls with her and Grant in recent weeks and walked away impressed. Impressed enough to allow her to join them today.

"Okay," Hal replied. "If everyone is ready, I say we head straight down from here, then cut a line right, steering clear of that ledge to the left." He pointed to a rock-lined cliff that would drop them onto flatter territory. "That area will be harder to negotiate. It's a narrow channel, not to mention the plunge is almost one hundred feet, and littered with rocks. Bad news if you hook an edge."

"But if you do, lean forward and hang tight for the flight," Canyon quipped.

Kinsley's face turned upward, as though trying to decipher if he was serious or not.

"How about we stay right," Hal suggested. "Everyone agreed?"

Canyon lowered a pair of mirrored-lens goggles from his head to his face and replied, "Agreed."

"Agreed," Grant echoed, checking with Kinsley.

She nodded.

"Okay," Hal continued. "I'll take the lead. Kinsley, you next, followed by Grant, Canyon, and Lisa. Walsh will be the sweep."

Everyone nodded, lowered their goggles, and secured poles in gloved hands. Having an established lineup was cru-

cial, as was waiting a sufficient amount of time between skiers. Walsh was assigned pickup duty for any "yard sale" mishap ahead of him. Poles, skis, gloves, goggles—skiers could
lose all sorts of items if they took a tumble, and Walsh was
their backup for retrieval. Hal liked to think of the sweep as
the "broom" that would clean up any mess the others left behind.

Hal jabbed his poles into the snow, leaned forward, and,
with a slight hop, took off down the mountain. Icy cold stung
his exposed nose and cheeks as he found his rhythm sailing
through the deep powder, effortlessly linking each turn with
the next. It felt more like silently floating through clouds than
skiing in snow.

Allowing sufficient distance to form between them,
Kinsley launched into action and worked her way to the right
of Hal. Grant waited for his turn, then chose his line and followed. Maintaining position, Walsh scanned the horizon. He
glanced toward the spot where the chopper had dropped them
and, to his surprise, clouds were rolling in—clouds that
hadn't been there thirty minutes ago. A sudden breeze
whipped at his cheeks. Walsh dropped his gaze to the skiers
below him. That was Colorado Rocky Mountain weather for
you—it changed in the blink of an eye.

As the skiers cut deep swaths through the snow, their
bodies bobbing gently down the mountain, they left a spray of
snow cloud in their wake at every turn. It was rhythmic, grace
in motion. Watching them, Walsh felt an itchy sensation. It
wasn't nerves. He didn't get nervous. It wasn't the weather.
These skiers could soar through a blizzard if need be. Moving
his gaze toward Canyon and Lisa, he paused. Maybe they'd
only get two runs in today instead of the four they had
planned.

Canyon sprang into action and, within seconds, was
cruising down the mountain, his pace swift and sure. Walsh
snorted. If he wasn't careful, he'd overtake Grant and Kinsley
before they made it halfway down. *Newbie.* Walsh slid his

gaze toward Lisa. He actually wasn't the newbie around here—that title belonged to Kinsley.

Scooting closer to the edge, Lisa planted her poles and peered down at the others. Adjusting her gear one last time, she waited for Canyon to get well ahead of her before digging in her poles...

"Don't!" Walsh barked.

Lisa stopped mid-motion. Turning to him, her surprise was complete. "Why?"

That's when she saw it.

The mountain broke away.

There was no noise.

Not a sound.

Walsh bolted forward. "Stop—Canyon! There's a slide!"

An entire section of snow-packed surface that had been embedded against jagged rock was no longer. It was sliding downhill. Toward his friends.

Lisa gasped. "*Avalanche*!"

Horror exploded inside Walsh as he watched the block of snow plummet toward Canyon.

Canyon heard the call and looked uphill. His heart caught, then pounded wildly out of control. It would be on him in seconds. A vision of Katharine popped into his brain. His dog, Buck. "No!"

Chapter Two

Kelly Jones was growing impatient. This was nothing more than a play of ego by Roan Phillips—local helicopter-pilot extraordinaire and sole flight instructor licensed to sign her off for search and rescue—and she refused to give in to him. She was more than capable of hovering in the Augusta K2 and they both knew it. The Augusta was Roan's aircraft of choice for mountain rescue and certainly within Kelly's realm of expertise. She hadn't spent the last four years twiddling her thumbs in the Army. No. She'd been piloting the military's number one attack chopper—the Apache, the most lethal piece of equipment the Army owned—and she'd been the youngest female pilot to have earned the right to fly it. Her path had been "high school to flight school"—it was the Army's special initiative to circumvent time and churn out combat-ready pilots.

When Kelly turned eighteen, she signed on with the service, scored in the ninety-ninth percentile on her aptitude tests, proved her supreme physical condition and passed every test they threw at her. After she passed her training with flying colors, they shipped her off to Afghanistan. It had been the happiest day of her life. All she'd ever wanted to do was fly. It was in her blood, flowed through her veins like oxygen. She could hover on command just as easily as she could fly at high speed and shoot things out of the sky. Roan was being difficult. His pride was on the line because he knew she could outperform him and his only out was to make her feel like his inferior.

She wasn't. Not in the pilot seat, she wasn't.

Allowing the helicopter engines to wind down, she chucked the headset, pushed out of the right seat and strode over to Roan. The man was classic all-American sexy in his blue jeans and black leather jacket, short-cropped hair and gold-rimmed aviator sunglasses. From what she'd seen, he was definitely accustomed to the adoring eyes of females. None of them tried to hide it, waltzing through the hangar where Roan worked, batting their eyelashes as they made some silly flirtatious remark. Roan ate it up, smiling with the knowledge that he could have his pick.

Not that Kelly could blame the women. His attractiveness was unmistakable. But Kelly wasn't about to be held captive by his charm. They'd been at these lessons for months now and it was getting ridiculous. "Accept it. We both know you're going to sign me off. Why the delay?"

"Why the rush? Aren't you enjoying my company?"

She couldn't see Roan's dark eyes behind his aviator sunglasses, but she didn't need to—they undoubtedly matched the smirk on his face. "Your company's fine," she replied, refusing to let him know exactly *how* fine. "But I'm ready to get up in the air," she slapped back. "And we both know that I'm capable."

"Great. You're free to fly any time you want."

"But not for SAR." Which was her goal. Kelly had moved to Colorado for a new start after leaving the military and flying for the mountain search and rescue team was the closest thing to excitement she could find. She'd had offers to fly media choppers for news stations and film runs for movie sets, but after flying combat, none of it sounded appealing. She needed a mission, a reason to fly. She needed to make a difference in people's lives, not pass the time to make a buck. Not that money was a bad thing. It just didn't fuel her desire to fly. Urgency, crisis, need... Those were her stimuli.

Roan shook his head. "Not yet."

"You're wrong."

He chuckled. "I might be, but I'm still in charge."

Kelly clenched her jaw. The man was purposely being difficult.

"This job requires a delicate balance between experience and finesse," Roan said and held up his hand, where he brought forefinger and thumb to within an inch of each other. "You're almost there, but not quite."

"I've flown over three hundred combat hours and—"

Roan raised a hand between them. "Yeah, yeah, yeah. And over two thousand total flight hours, top of your class, Chief Warrant Officer, ceiling-breaker, amazing most phenomenal female pilot to ever walk the earth... I've heard the spiel. You're great when commanding an Apache helicopter over enemy territory, but you can't hover on a dime to save your life. And that's what we do here, Kelly. We save lives."

"I can hover fine," she snapped, frustration boiling to the point of choking. What she would say to him if she didn't need his signature on the dotted line... But as lead pilot for the local search and rescue team, it was his approval or nothing.

"Not fine enough for a crew to load up an injured hiker before you fly him to safety," he returned, his tone growing serious. "You're impatient. And worse, you're dangerous, because you think you can do more than you actually can."

Kelly glared at him and almost shoved a finger in his face. "I can out-fly you any day of the week."

"Maybe so. But you can't out-hover me and that's what you're tasked with doing around here. Hovering—as in remaining still for longer than sixty seconds."

Kelly whirled and stormed off.

"See what I mean?" He called after her. "You can't stay still. You can't even *stand* still!"

She stopped and turned. "It's only out of the kindness of my heart that I'm walking away from you right now. I'd hate to see that pretty face of yours split in two by my fist."

Roan laughed. A gut-wrenching, deeply annoying belly laugh as he shouted, "I bet you think you could actually do it!"

Now it was her turn to smirk, and she took a step toward him. "Wanna watch me?"

He shook his head and held up his hands. "No. Please, no. But let me know when you want to try hovering again.

That I can handle," he said and walked past her, headed for the offices of Summit Aviation Services.

Attached to the steel hangar where the helicopters were kept, Summit Aviation Services was the fixed base operator that housed Roan's base of operations for mountain search and rescue. From the outside, the FBO, as it was referred to by pilots, was nothing special—a pale gray steel building boasting the Summit Aviation Services logo in royal blue along with a single glass door for entry. But inside, the FBO was a different story. Housing some of the finest aircraft money could buy—helicopters—specially outfitted for medical rescue and planes shinier than most racecars—it held the most technologically advanced computers on the market and served as home base for a fleet of volunteers dedicated to the mission of search and rescue.

Summit Aviation Services was a place Kelly desperately wanted to belong.

Watching Roan strut off with a noticeable swagger in his step, she spewed a sigh. And he was her ticket in. A man like every other male pilot she knew—cocky, thought he was boss of everyone and everything, and more than a little condescending when it came to dealing with the ladies—he was her only hope. Kelly had worked with her share of pilots in the military and could count the number of men who didn't act the same way on one hand. Maybe two, if she were feeling generous. But Roan?

He was text book. He had skill, attitude, and looks—an aggravating combination, to be sure. Roan could easily fill the pages of a pin-up calendar and she doubted a single woman missed that fact. She hadn't. But if Roan thought he could push her around, he'd better think again. She wanted this and she would have it. Unable to resist a look at his rear, Kelly quickly flicked her glance away. She'd met her share of good-looking pilots, the kind that wanted to bed a woman before they knew her last name, and she knew how to handle them. Roan hadn't made the first pass at her, but he fit the bill. Probably hadn't tried because he was threatened by the possibility of rejection from a woman supremely qualified for his job—*his* job, soon to be *her* job.

Kelly heaved a sigh. If only he weren't so obsessive when it came to his flight instruction. To say she couldn't hover on a dime was ridiculous. Sheer exaggeration. She could fly that bird from zero to sixty and back in a heartbeat, hovering whenever and wherever she wanted in between. Roan's problem was that Kelly didn't react to his whims fast enough—not a required skill in the rescue business, and one she personally rebuked. He was just being difficult and making her work for it. But she was nobody's lackey. Nobody's. On impulse, Kelly took off after him. She'd take him up on that offer to try again and show him once and for all, whim or no whim, that she could handle the Augusta as well as he could—if not better.

Apparently sensing her approach, Roan stepped aside and grabbed the glass door to the hangar office and swung it open. Whisking a hand out in front of her, he said, "Ladies, first."

Kelly stopped in her tracks and faced him directly. "Let's go up again."

He smiled. "Change of heart, have you?"

Change of angle, she mused, but kept that thought to herself. The goal here was to fly search and rescue, and if that meant sucking up to Roan for an hour, then so be it. She could do anything she set her mind to. *Watch out, world—the eagle is airborne.* A fondness flitted through her as she recalled her father's words. He used to tell her that when she became discouraged. After a hard knock, when her confidence was shaken, her dad would remind her that when the times got tough, the "tough" kicked butt. They got the job done and asked for more. It was his idea of a pep talk, one that now brought a smile to her face.

Kelly Jones was a fighter, not a whiner.

Sometimes the advice meant taking a step backward to reach the goal. *Keep your eye on the prize*, he would tell her. That was the key.

When she didn't reply, Roan muttered, "Let's go check the weather."

Kelly walked into the FBO and went straight for the refrigerator. Let Roan check the radar. She was starving. Crossing the spacious lounge, a room decked out with fancy leather furniture and carved wood tables, wall art depicting the Colorado Mountains and wildlife, she reached into a fridge beneath a brown granite counter and pulled out a Styrofoam container of hummus. She grabbed a bag of celery sticks and tossed the door closed. Popping the plastic lid open, she dropped to a seat in an armchair and kicked her feet up onto a matching ottoman. Splitting the bag open, she pulled out a celery stick and dipped.

From his seat behind one of the two wooden desks in the room, Roan arched a brow. "How can you eat that stuff?"

Dragging the trimmed celery stalk through creamy tan hummus, she quipped, "Like this." She crunched down half the stick and chewed noisily. Roan returned a look of disgust and returned to his computer, clicking through screens. Amused by his reaction, Kelly finished one stick and went for another. Surprised by the sharp rumble in her stomach, she wondered, *When did I last eat?*

The answer was instantaneous—yesterday with her father. They had gone to Adele's, a local gourmet restaurant in town, where Kelly had discovered this gem of a snack while enjoying an early dinner with her dad. The fragrant hummus was flecked with roasted red peppers and a touch of garlic and was oh-so-delicious. Kelly closed her eyes and savored the flavor. It was sharp and distinct without overpowering. Definitely worth buying by the case, she thought.

Kelly had brought this container home as leftovers from dinner with her father. He was in town for the week, on his way back home to Tacoma, and had been told that Adele's was the place to go in town. Known for its elegant atmosphere and healthy focus, incorporating all-natural and locally grown organic produce on its menu, her dad had suggested they try it. Not that he cared about a restaurant that catered to vegans, but if it was good, that was his bottom line. A career military man, he'd dedicated his life to the service, where fancy meals were not on the priority list.

Finishing her second stalk of cold stringy celery, she swallowed. It was definitely good, she mused.

Roan frowned. "Looks like a no-go."

Kelly popped up from the couch, hummus and celery in hand, and walked over to him. "What do you mean, a no-go?" Circling the desk, she checked the radar for herself.

"Front's moving in."

"Damn," she muttered under her breath, noting the distinct line of rapidly approaching weather. She glanced outside. Over the distant mountain range, rays of sunshine slanted through the clouds. Flying east of the airport, she hadn't noticed any weather, but according to the line of blue headed their way, the sunshine would soon give way to snow.

"We can go up again on Thursday, but not until the afternoon. My next forty-eight hours are completely booked."

"Thursday?" She stared at him. "Are you kidding me? I can't wait until then."

Roan stood, his dark eyes penetrating as the two became face-to-face. Drifts of his cologne entered her nose, and Kelly's heart skipped a beat. It was a clean, mellow, and entirely masculine scent. One she liked very much. Kelly took a step back, pressing, "You can't fit me in at all? Not even for an hour?"

"I'm booked. And I'm your only choice."

"That sucks."

He laughed. "Way to hurt a guy's feelings."

Her pulse hammered. "You don't have any feelings," she rebuked, and walked back to the lounge area. Being too close to Roan Phillips tangled her thoughts. She wanted to be mad, but being near him was too distracting.

"What? I'm one of the nicest guys around here."

"Save it for the fan club," she muttered in a blasé tone, swiping a healthy chunk of hummus onto a celery stalk and plunking it into her mouth. *Distance, Kelly. Keep your distance.*

"What are you talking about?" he asked, as though genuinely surprised. "I don't have any fan club."

She rolled her eyes and finished chewing. "No. No fan club around here," she lobbed back. "Only a slate of female students battling for your attention—none of whom would know a tail rotor from a tail boom, I might add."

Roan shot back, "You're dreaming."

"Not me, sweetheart." Kelly pointed her celery stick at him. "I'd wager money that your name is scribbled in somebody's diary, locked away in a drawer by her bed. She probably hugs herself to sleep with it." The image of a girl doing exactly that suddenly grated on Kelly.

He laughed but didn't deny it. She shook her head, taking it as tacit concession. Denying it would be silly. The women didn't try to hide their attraction—on the contrary. They practically shoved each other out of the way as they lobbied him for special attention, which men loved. They wanted women to fawn all over them, as opposed to entertaining women as their equals. Kelly crunched down on a celery stick. The behavior was disgusting. Absolutely disgusting.

Roan's cell phone rang. Staring at Kelly, he answered, "Hey, Goose. What's up?"

Kelly flipped her gaze to the ceiling and shook her head. *Goose.* Who has a friend named Goose? Probably some buff ski guy with nothing better to do than shred moguls. There were plenty of them out here. *Hack. Trey. Red.* Their names were as odd as they were. *Goose.* Kelly tossed the last bite of celery into her mouth. *Go figure.*

"When?"

Her heart kicked as she tuned in to Roan's conversation. All humor drained from Roan's eyes as he looked at her. "What?" she asked automatically.

Pulling the phone from his mouth, he said, "There's been an avalanche."

Chapter Three

Hal Richardson winced in pain. The intense throbbing in his leg matched that in his skull and shouted compound fracture. From the feel of it, he judged it to be his femur, the break in possibly more than one place. He grimaced, then clenched his teeth. He needed to get it stabilized—ASAP—but not until he accounted for his crew. Hal scanned the blinding sheet of snow for signs of them, but he saw nothing. Eerily quiet, there was nothing but a flattened mass of white. "Can anyone hear me?" he shouted.

Suddenly, Walsh and Lisa skied into view. Relief flooded him. *Thank God. They missed the avalanche.* Had anyone else?

The two came to a hard-edged stop near him, snow flying from their skis. "Dad, are you okay?" Lisa asked, mild panic in her voice.

"Yes, yes," he replied at once. "But find the others! I don't see them anywhere."

Walsh and Lisa sprang off and skied twenty yards downhill from him. Lisa tossed her poles as she shrieked, "Kinsley!"

Hal's heart stopped. What had she seen? Was Kinsley dead?

Next to Lisa, Walsh kicked out of his skis, dropped to the ground, and pulled the backpack from his back. Grabbing an avalanche shovel, he began to dig furiously. Lisa did likewise and in less than two minutes, they had Kinsley free.

Staggering to her feet, Kinsley's ski clothes were caked with snow. Lifting the goggles from her face, she wiped the snow from her mouth with the help of Lisa then stammered, "Grant! Grant! Where is he?"

The fear in her voice pierced the quiet. Walsh pulled an avalanche beacon from his jacket and held it over the ground, turning in a circle. "Over there." He pointed, and the three of them ran to the spot, their gait robotic and awkward as ski boots crunched over the compacted snow. Kinsley, Hal noted, was limping.

"He's buried!" Kinsley cried out.

Unable to see Grant, Hal wondered if he was completely buried or only partially. Although he'd been tossed about like a rag doll, somehow Hal had managed to avert submersion. Pain shot through his thigh, reminding him of the brutal beating.

"Kinsley!" Lisa exclaimed. "We've got to get him out. Hurry!"

The girls dropped to their knees and began jabbing at the snow in short bursts, Kinsley using gloved hands while Lisa used her shovel.

Walsh remained standing. He glanced up and down, left to right. "Where's Canyon?"

"I don't know!" Kinsley responded. "We've got to get Grant out!"

Walsh bolted. Running to his skis, he slammed his boots into place and crossed the snow in giant cross-country strides with his avalanche beacon held out in front of him. Apparently, there was no sign of Canyon. Hal's gaze darted between Walsh criss-crossing and moving in no particular direction, and the girls. His gut twisted. Everyone was accounted for except Canyon. But Walsh would locate him. They'd found the others; he had to be close. Memories of past accidents pushed into Hal's mind—avalanche victims tumbling thousands of feet below fellow skiers in their group, others buried so deep the beacons were unable to locate them in time. Hal refused to give in to worst-case scenarios. They would find Canyon. They had to.

The alternative was unthinkable.

"Grant!" Kinsley shouted. "Can you hear me?"

Locked under the snow, Grant wouldn't be able to move a muscle. He might not even be conscious, or alive. Under the weight of an avalanche, fresh powder would feel more like cement. Getting hit was like getting plowed over by a freight train. Snow was heavy and had the power to crush. Hal had seen people entangled in trees, plastered against rocks, and, of course, buried under feet of snow. Most didn't suffer. They died doing what they loved. Hal shoved the negative thoughts from his mind. Action. Lisa and Kinsley had to get Grant out and assess his condition before any determination could be made.

Either way, Grant would need help. They all would. Using his collar microphone, Hal contacted the search and rescue base on Peak Five. "SAR, do you copy?"

"Copy. Is that you, Hal?"

"Yes." It was Sean Blair, a man who'd run SAR—search and rescue—for the last six years. "Emergency," Hal stated flatly. "There's been an avalanche. I repeat, *avalanche*. We need our pilot to return for pickup."

"Copy that. We'll call Jack and send him your way."

"Call Summit Aviation. We're gonna need backup helicopter support. I'm down with a broken leg. We've got another skier down, status unknown." Hal didn't want to mention Canyon. Not yet.

"Roger," Sean clipped back. "Will confirm."

"Thanks." Hal dropped his head back onto the snow. Roan Phillips would move heaven and earth to get here as quickly as humanly possible. Canyon was his best friend. Helicopters were his business. If anyone could get up here—and fast—it would be Roan.

Rolling his head, Hal peered over at Kinsley and Lisa. Through the amber hue of his goggles, he watched the snow fly from his daughter's stub of a shovel. Kinsley worked furiously by her side. Suffocation would be imminent if they didn't act quickly...assuming Grant hadn't been killed instantly upon impact. If he was alive but not breathing, they'd have to perform CPR.

Lisa darted a hand down into the hole.

"Does he have a pulse?" Hal asked.

"Thready, but there," Lisa replied.

His daughter was not a medical specialist, but she was trained in basic first aid. She knew what to do when crisis hit and how to keep her cool. Hal had insisted she learn. Knowing her penchant for toad research that took her deep into the mountains for days at a time, he argued that she needed to be as fully and completely trained as any SAR member, including certification as Wilderness First Responder and Outdoor Emergency Care. He'd also made it a point to enroll Lisa in martial arts training. After a rash of rapes sprung up on her college campus, Hal demanded that she know how to handle herself when faced with a physical threat. Recalling the mountain stalker who nearly killed his daughter, Hal suppressed a swell of nerves. Anything could happen when she was alone and out of his sight, and she had to be prepared. He couldn't live with anything less. She was the only family he had.

As heavy emotion seeped into his heart, Hal switched focus. He needed to stay strong and alert. He needed to know his crew was okay. "Any sign of Canyon?"

"None," Walsh replied, followed by an angry, "I don't understand it! I'm not getting any signal!"

But he had to be, Hal thought. The digital equipment they were using was top of the line. They could pick up buried beacon signals up to sixty meters away. And not only did they have distance capability, they could indicate direction as well. Walsh had to be getting something.

Kinsley bent over and shrieked. "Grant! Grant! Can you hear me?"

"Kinsley!" Lisa grabbed her arm. "We can't stop. We've got to get him completely out of the snow."

Yes, Hal silently agreed. Lisa understood the drill. Clear the face, get the snow out of the mouth and off the chest so the man could breathe, then uncover the body. Get him out of his icebox and above ground, where they could warm him.

Kinsley frantically stabbed her hands at the snow around Grant's body.

At least the first hurdle for Grant had been cleared. Pinpointing people beneath the snow was crucial. Time was of the essence. Hal's gaze sought Walsh and his heart squeezed. There was still no sign of Canyon.

The microphone at Hal's collar erupted. "Hal, do you copy?"

"Copy."

"Jack is an hour out," Sean said. "He was low on fuel when he dropped you."

Hal groaned inwardly. An hour out? His gaze flashed to the sky. Clouds were building, steadily creeping over the ridge. That front hadn't been expected to arrive until hours from now. But it would be here soon.

"I called Roan and sent a team his way," Sean went on. "He and the guys should be up within fifteen."

"Thanks. I'll let my guys know."

Watching Walsh continue his methodical search, Hal cursed himself for not insisting they wear inflatables. He'd brought a probe, shovels, beacons, and a collar microphone to radio for help, but the jackets would have popped them above the snow in case of avalanche. As it stood, they had two buried. One found. One missing.

Using his beacon as lead, Walsh angled it in every direction as he moved methodically across the snow, searching for a signal from Canyon's transponder. "Damn it!" he yelled. "Where is he?" Walsh whipped his head toward the group. "Lisa, did you see which way Canyon went before it hit?"

Looking up from Grant, her arms never broke stride as she replied, "No. I was looking at you."

"How long before we get help up here?!"

"Jack's an hour out," Hal told him.

Walsh turned away and charged left, gliding across the surface. He craned his head toward the snow, listening for a beep from Canyon's beacon.

Lisa tossed her shovel and, with Kinsley's assistance, dragged Grant from his cavern in the snow. Slipping a hand to his neck, she hopped onto his body and began compressions. Kinsley looked on, panicked.

Hal had never seen her this way before. Kinsley Fairchild was a pretty cool cucumber. She didn't wither under pressure. She didn't shrink from a challenge—quite the opposite. With her protester background, she instilled fear; she didn't suffer from it. But worrying over Grant's condition had clearly rendered her stricken.

"He's breathing!" Lisa called out excitedly. With a hand to his neck, she announced, "His pulse is steady."

Hal closed his eyes and recited a silent prayer.

"His lips are blue!" Kinsley cried out.

"We've got to keep him warm," Lisa said to Kinsley, glancing at Walsh as she spoke. "Use your gator, your balaclava—anything that you can find to warm him." The neck and face coverings were made of top-quality material. They'd at least help to keep Grant warm.

"Yes, okay," Kinsley replied as she dug into her jacket pockets.

Hal flashed to Walsh. With every passing minute, Canyon's predicament became more dire. The cell phone in Hal's jacket vibrated. Unzipping it, he reached in to an interior pocket and pulled the phone free. When he saw that it was Wade Davis calling, he snapped, "Wade—talk to me."

"Jack just called. Said you and your crew were caught in the avalanche?"

"Yes," Hal confirmed. Cold seeped into his upper chest area and he re-zipped his jacket. Lying on the ground, he was beginning to feel the bite in his toes as well. "The situation is grim. We've got three down. My leg is broken. Grant is breathing, but we've yet to determine the extent of his injuries. We'll need to be airlifted out."

"I'll get Roan on the line."

"Good. Sean said he was going to call him."

"Do you think Canyon can stabilize your leg for transport?"

Hal paused. "Canyon is missing."

"*Missing*?"

"Walsh is searching for him, but he's getting no response."

Wade muttered something unintelligible, followed by, "I'll get Roan in the air, *stat*."

"Roger, that. Sean should have a team heading his way." Hal looked up into the sky. No longer a spray of wisps against the vibrant blue, the clouds were beginning to take form. "They have to move fast. Weather is turning on us."

"I know. Radar shows a front moving in."

"Do whatever you can," Hal said, his gaze darting to Walsh's figure. Like a dog on a scent, the man was working his way across the snow in a grid pattern. He would scour every inch of this area until he found his friend. Hal could only hope that he'd find him alive, though with every passing minute, the prospects were dimming.

"Will do."

Hal ended the call, his breath escaping in heavy thrusts of steam. Seconds felt like hours. Canyon was strong, but no one could survive without air for ten minutes. Hal checked his watch. Almost five had passed since the avalanche hit. His heart pounded suddenly.

Time was working against them.

Chapter Four

Roan ended the call and strode toward the flight desk. His cell phone rang again and he quickly picked up the call. Kelly jumped up from the couch and followed him over to the desk. "Wade, did you hear?"

"Yes," he replied.

Wade Davis was Chief of Police in Silver Creek and a close friend of Roan's. In the event of an avalanche, he'd want to be front-and-center with rescue operations. Goose was a member of SAR and on his way over after getting word of the emergency. "Goose said there weren't any resort skiers involved."

"No, but we have a group of heli-skiers up there—our guys."

"Our guys?" Roan asked. His stomach tightened before he heard their names.

"Hal, Canyon, Walsh, Lisa, Kinsley, and Grant."

Roan felt like he'd been sucker-punched. "You're serious?" Why hadn't Goose told him? Beside him, Kelly stood staring, her weighty brown gaze latched firmly to his. She was waiting for information, but Roan had no words for her. These were his friends.

"Afraid so," Wade continued. "And Canyon's missing."

"Missing?"

"As of two seconds ago, they hadn't located him."

Roan's world stopped moving. Canyon was missing. Missing after an avalanche hit.

Dread slithered deep into Roan's bones. There was no mistaking what that meant. Heartbeats thwacked hard in his chest. "But everyone else has been accounted for?"

"Yes. Hal's injured pretty badly. He thinks he might have a broken leg. Walsh and Lisa are fine. They went last and weren't hit. They're still assessing the damage to Grant. Sounds like he's going to need medical assistance, the extent of which I don't know yet. Hal's calling me back in five."

Roan clicked into action. "Goose is on his way over with a crew."

"Good. How's Kelly? Did you sign her off today?"

"No, I, uh—" Roan slid a glance toward her, then gave her his shoulder. Kelly's father was good friends with Wade Davis, and Wade wanted her signed off. But it was Roan's call, his decision to send her up or not. "She's not ready. She's almost there, but she needs to master a few more techniques."

"If she can fly," Wade demanded, "sign her off. We need her help."

"What? Why?" Kelly moved in front of Roan and drilled him with a questioning glare. He turned away and said briskly, "I can get another pilot in here within the hour."

"We don't have the time. Weather is moving in and we don't have a second to waste. Radar looks like it could get pretty bad, pretty quick. Kelly is there with you. She's our best option."

"What about Jack?" Roan was personal friends with the pilot who had flown the group up that morning. He should be closer than anyone.

"Jack was low on fuel and won't be able to turn his bird around for at least half an hour."

Roan stilled.

"Has she mastered these 'techniques' you're talking about well enough for an emergency situation?" Wade asked.

Roan clenched the phone to his ear. Wade's impatience was palpable. Canyon was missing. Hal's leg was broken. Grant was in bad shape. They'd definitely need two birds in the air if they were going to get everyone off the mountain before the storm hit. Wade knew the debate Roan and Kelly were having and couldn't care less. His friends were in danger.

Ambivalence zipped through Roan's gut as he replied, "Yes."

"Call me when you're in the air," Wade said, then rattled off the GPS coordinates Hal had given him.

"Copy that," Roan said.

"What's going on?" Kelly demanded. "Are we going up?"

The eagerness in her gaze unsettled him. The bulldog was pulling at her leash, ready to be let loose, whether or not her master agreed. Stuffing his reservations to the corner of his mind, Roan challenged, "You can fly in a snowstorm, right?"

Kelly glanced outside. The sky was overcast, but far from snowing. "With my eyes closed."

Roan stared at her. The brown pits of her eyes within the chiseled features of her flushed skin shouted strength. There was nothing easy or light about Kelly Jones. Every step she took, every word she spoke, was done with an intensity that could make a cobra rethink an attack strike. Roan had no doubt that Kelly believed she could fly search and rescue. The question was: Did *he*? "Kelly, this is serious. I need to know you're ready, that you can handle this."

Muscles jumped in her rattlesnake jaw as she stated unequivocally, "I can handle it, Roan."

A million doubts dashed through his gut, but he had no choice. "Let's go." He slapped a hand on the flight desk counter and told the guy standing behind it, "We're taking the Euro up. Tell the crew to get it ready, *stat*."

"Ten-four." The man picked up the phone and dialed.

Roan hurried for the door and pushed through, Kelly hot on his heels. "Where we going?" she asked.

"East of Peak Four. SAR team is on their way now and we need to get up as fast as we can." He stopped suddenly and turned on her. Emotion swirled like a tornado as he fought a tidal surge of misgiving. "These people are my friends. You're going up because I have no other options. Do you understand that?"

"Yes, sir."

Roan pointed a finger at her and clipped, "You better bring your A-game."

"I always do."

"You do what I tell you to do and not a single thing otherwise."

Kelly pulled back, and Roan could see a flare of temper rise in her heated gaze. *Bring it*. He didn't care. Making the stakes clear came first. All she had to do was give him a reason and he'd ground her. On the spot. Nerves fired through him as the stakes sank in. With the number of injuries they were talking, it would be tough enough as it stood. If the weather fell apart, things would be ten times harder. "For the record, you're not ready for rescue."

"I think I am," she shot back.

"Not in my book, and it's my book that counts. I'll take the Augusta. You take the AStar. You'll pick up the skiers that are mobile and ferry them down. I'll handle the others."

"Fine."

Roan turned and jogged toward the red chopper, leaving Kelly to do the same. She'd be flying the AStar, an aircraft that would easily accommodate the passengers he couldn't. Hal's leg was broken. Grant was in need of medical attention. Canyon was missing. Roan's heart pounded—they had to get in the air, *now*!

By the time the SAR team arrived by truck, an F150 covered in the muddy grime of Colorado winter driving, the snow was beginning to fall. It served up a mess November through May and every vehicle looked the same—brown, dingy, and totally covered in dirt. Goose didn't bother to wash his vehicle until spring. Not that Roan could blame him. It was a waste of time. *Time*—something they didn't have a lot of at the moment.

Sitting right seat in the Augusta K2, Roan waved them in—one flight medic and one flight nurse plus Goose Wilcox, all similarly dressed in red jackets and black pants. Each carried a backpack and wore heavy winter boots. Not that Roan needed to signal them at all, but it gave him something to do. Goose and his team were the best of the best. They knew the drill and could perform it in their sleep. Briefly, Roan wondered if Goose knew who they were searching for, but dismissed the thought at once. The man would do his job the same way no matter who was on that mountain.

Goose was standard fare around the Colorado Mountains, with his easy disposition, ready grin, and a stamina that would make any triathlete envious. Like most members on the SAR team, he was physically fit, knew his stuff, and would do whatever it took to get the job done. He was good, as were the other two. All were experienced members of SAR, and all were men Roan had worked with on numerous occasions. Roan felt good about taking them up. If there was anyone he wanted by his side, it was this crew. There was only one weak link in this chain. Roan glanced across the tarmac. Kelly sat in the AStar as they warmed up engines, awaiting Goose's arrival. She was the wild card, but Roan had no choice in her participation. Circumstances dictated that she be included. Period.

"I'll take the crew with me." Speaking via the comms, the intercom system used between helicopters, he added, "You follow."

"Ten-four," she replied.

Roan could see Kelly through the windshield of the AStar. She had her headset on, wore a pair of aviator sunglasses identical to his, and looked every bit the part of pilot-in-command. Both had grabbed winter jackets for the ride up. Hers was an insulated black parka. His was red—the color of business, matching his SAR team's jackets. They were an established team. Kelly was not a member. She was the rookie.

Roan's pulse quickened. Not that he didn't think she was competent—he did. But more than competent, she was good—highly skilled from her military experience flying the Apache. Kelly flew choppers like the birds were an extension of her mind. She was a natural. She lived and breathed heli-copters. Actually, she reminded him of himself; she was all in, all the time. But this wasn't a war zone, and her full-throttle attitude concerned him. Mountain rescue was unpre-dictable, even more so with weather rolling in. He flicked a glance upward and took note of the light breeze kicking about the flurry of snow. It was a warning of what was to come. Blizzards could drop like bombs out of nowhere. Forecast said light snow and the sky delivered a punch that stopped you cold. This was unfamiliar terrain for Kelly. Not only would they be flying in snow, but they'd be flying in and around the mountains. Kelly had only been in Silver Creek a few short months, not nearly enough time to learn the twists and turns of these peaks. One wrong move and—*bam*—you hit a wall of rock and it's "game over." Impatience filed through Roan as the SAR team ran toward his chopper. En-gines hot, all he needed was for his crew to jump in, and then he could lift off.

Goose Wilcox jumped in the front seat. Without a word, he donned his headset and adjusted his mic. "Hey, Roan."

"Hey."

The two exchanged a glance, sharing the unspoken words both were feeling. Roan couldn't see Goose's eyes be-hind his jet-black Oakley's, but he didn't have to. His somber expression said it all. This mission was personal. These vic-tims were friends.

Goose secured his seatbelt and glanced over his shoulder as the others climbed on board behind him, then gave Roan a thumbs-up. "Let's get this bird in the air."

Roan's sentiments exactly. He said, "Kelly, copy."

"Copy."

"We're going up. You ready?"

"Ten-four."

Roan rolled the throttle of the K2 forward. Featuring four-blade construction and a powerful Allison turboshaft, this chopper could deliver a smooth ride at speeds up to one hundred and forty knots, demonstrating stellar performance at higher altitudes. It was a superior aircraft and one Roan trust-ed to do the delicate job required for medical transport. En-gines whirred loudly as the blades picked up in velocity, lift-ing the chopper neatly from the ground. Especially equipped with rescue gear, Roan had everything he needed for today's flight.

"Delta three-eight to base. Do you copy?"

"Copy that," came the static reply from Wade Davis. "You en route?"

"Affirmative. Any word on Canyon?"

"Nothing. I haven't heard from Hal yet, so let's count no news as good news."

Roan's gut clenched. He'd rather hear it confirmed; *Canyon found. Condition stable.* "Roger," he replied evenly. "Destination fifteen, twenty minutes."

"Copy."

Roan rolled hard left as he skirted over the village of Silver Creek. Streets below were crowded with tourists while the gondolas and chair lifts carried more up the mountain. A light snowfall peppered rooftops already fat with snow, some with almost twelve inches. To the casual eye, the snow cover looked harmless, like a frothy meringue spread over candy-topped roofs in a child's winter-wonderland toy village. But Roan knew there was nothing fun about snow encapsulating a roof. He'd seen more than a few collapsed under the sheer weight of it.

Drawing his mind back to business, Roan synced his thoughts with the constant whir of the engines. His senses were sharp. He was primed for the unexpected. Whatever they found, Roan would deal with it.

Goose scanned the horizon and flashed him a tense look, silently voicing what Roan already knew. Those gray clouds shrouding the peaks spelled trouble, the snow flurry over town a mere hint of what lay ahead. Not what either of them wanted to see. Mountain rescue was hard enough without the complication of weather. But, like a true professional, Goose stuck to the basics. "What are we looking at up there?"

"Two men down, possible third," Roan replied. "One leg fracture with the others' conditions unknown at this point. Six passengers total."

Goose nodded and Roan could feel his apprehension. The two men had flown together countless times, on countless rescue missions, but this time nerves were on edge. Hal Richardson and Canyon Laredo were SAR family. This rescue hit the team where it counted. Home.

Quickly gaining altitude, Roan hugged the mountainous terrain as he swept up and over snowfields and stands of twiggy aspen laid bare against wind-scoured mountain ridges. There were blocks of evergreen forest, a patchwork of dead spots, victims of the pine beetle that had devastated the trees over recent years. Scientists had worked diligently to shore up tree health, stressed from years of recent drought, enabling the trees to withstand the pine beetle's voracious appetite, thereby allowing the two to co-exist in harmony. Unfortunately, the damage had been severe and remained visible even today. Roan hated to see the carnage, but understood it was nature at work—much like the wildfires that ripped through the mountains, wreaking havoc for humans and animals alike. It was nature's process for cleansing the landscape, ultimately safeguarding the ecosystem for the animals that lived here.

Born and raised in Colorado, Roan loved this land. Skies were bluer over the Rockies than anywhere else in the country. Dry air was partly responsible, but the higher elevations also contained less atmosphere—air, humidity, dust, particulates—a factor that reduced the white hue that could soften a blue sky. Stretching as far as the eye could see, Colorado skies were usually unblemished by clouds or haze, giving the state a reputation for gorgeous sunny days. The brilliant sky held a special allure for a pilot, calling to his need to soar untethered. When Roan wasn't flying, he enjoyed hiking through the mountains, studying the geological formations that created the stunning beauty around him. His mother often claimed that if Roan hadn't become a pilot, he would have become a geologist. Sinking into his seat as he ascended sharply, he thought, no way he could settle for "ground" work. His heart was in the air.

"Kelly, stay close and wait for my instructions when we arrive at destination."

"Ten-four."

Keeping tabs on her, Roan noted that she followed close behind, keeping precise timing with his aircraft. He still had his reservations about her, but knowing that he needed her on this mission, he had to let them go. In the military, she'd been trained at levels exceeding most civilian pilots. She had the skill. She could handle the job.

Roan would have been military-trained had his parents not lost a brother, a son, and a nephew to the cause. When Roan put in his application, they insisted he re-think his desire to join the service when he graduated high school. *Please. We can't lose you, too.*

He understood the plea. He missed his brother every day, but serving in the Air Force would have been an honor. It would have meant serving a cause greater than himself. But staring into the eyes of his mother, there was no way Roan could sign on the dotted line. Not in good faith. Not knowing it would break her heart.

All he really wanted to do was fly. And he could fly at home.

Snowflakes pelted the windshield—windscreen, as he thought of it—as he mentally ran through his mission. Hal would need to be stabilized and airlifted to the hospital ASAP. Possibly Grant, Canyon. Roan wasn't giving any power to a negative outcome. Canyon would be found. He might be a little banged up, but Canyon would be found. He had to be.

Until then, Walsh and Lisa could ride back with Kelly. Kinsley would probably want to stay with Grant. Depending on what they found on the ground, Kelly could take one of his crew back with her, if needed. Riding heavy was not advisable. They'd have to distribute passengers between the two choppers, first according to need and then to weight considerations.

Rotor blades reverberated through him. Math didn't leave room for error. Weight either worked with angles of lift and speed, or it didn't. They'd make do, even if it meant leaving an SAR member on the ground. It wasn't anything they couldn't handle.

Speaking of ground, Roan didn't like what he was seeing as he scoured the landscape. The tree line was pulling back giving way to terrain layered with snow-covered rocks. The angle of slope was steep. Higher up, mountainous snow drifts appeared more like windblown sand dunes. On a sunny day, the snow would glisten, a sea of shimmering pearlescent beauty. But with the clouds taking over, the ground appeared cold and barren. Frigid.

How in the heck was he going to land? Roan checked his GPS. According to Hal, Jack dropped the group just past Peak Four, commonly referred to by the locals as Baxter Peak. It was named after a famous Colorado climber who fell to his death almost twenty years ago. It was steep—treacherous—especially in winter. It also packed some of the best powder-skiing around.

"Wish I was skiing in this crap instead of flying through it," Goose remarked.

"I hear ya," Roan replied. The higher they flew, the more snowfall they encountered. Visibility was quickly worsening. "It's ugly."

"Kelly, copy?"

"Copy."

"Our destination is over the next face, bottom of the slide."

"Copy that."

"I'll assess conditions when we're overhead and instruct from there."

"Ten-four."

Over the comms, her voice sounded far away, an echo against the roar of engines. He didn't like it. Not when he needed reassurance that she was checked in and engaged.

Goose turned and gave a hand signal to the group in the back. Working as Roan's right-hand man, he would handle the crew while Roan focused on flying. He'd also act as his communication liaison on the ground. And Kelly?

Roan bit back a rise of angst. She was the unknown in the equation.

Chapter Five

Why weren't they picking up Canyon's signal? Walsh looked to Lisa. Now that Grant was confirmed to be breathing, she had joined him in the hunt for Canyon, leaving Kinsley alone to see to Grant's needs. The man was lapsing in and out of unconscious, but he was breathing. It was more than Walsh could say for Canyon. "Are you getting anything?" he yelled to Lisa.

From across the expanse of snow, the area littered with footprints and ski gear tossed about as though from an Oklahoma twister, she shook her head. Casting his gaze uphill, Walsh grunted. The area had been wiped clean by the avalanche. The slide leveled everything in its path, including their deeply-carved tracks. It was doubtful Canyon was there. He turned and scanned the fall line. "We've got to keep looking," he said and waved her over. "Head farther to your right. I'll clear the search area from here to the cliff and then we'll regroup."

Together they'd been able to double the search zone. But if they continued to come up empty, it wouldn't matter if they tripled the size. It would be too late. Canyon would be dead.

Walsh didn't like to think about it, but he was a realist. Not that it meant he would give up—he wouldn't. Couldn't. It had only been sheer instinct that saved him and Lisa from getting caught up in the avalanche, a sixth sense that had warned something was wrong. One split second saved their lives, allowing them to ski down over the avalanche of snow and dig their friends out quickly. Canyon might not have been so lucky, though Walsh wasn't pronouncing anyone lost until he had a cold dead body to prove it.

Tension curdled in his gut. It was amazing that they were only dealing with one potential death and not several.

Hal had managed to evade complete burial. Kinsley had been partially submerged, but easy to spot with her dark hair against the white sheet of snow. They located Grant fairly quickly, but not Canyon. Somehow he remained undetectable. Anger rose hot in his chest. It didn't make sense. Canyon had to be here somewhere! He couldn't have simply vanished.

Tucking the search beacon under his arm, Walsh pulled out his cell phone, yanked the glove from his hand, and checked his avalanche app. Canyon used the same app, had the same brand of phone. If he was down there and physically able, he'd have it activated. It was a GPS locator meant for these exact conditions and would reveal Canyon's position to within feet.

Staring at the device, Walsh struggled to stay calm. The signal was zilch.

Icy flakes of snow battered the bare skin of his cheeks and hand, but Walsh ignored the biting cold, searching the horizon for ski tracks. Had his buddy taken a turn? Had he escaped the slide altogether and made it farther down?

Walsh saw no tell-tale snake trails in the snow. There was no evidence that Canyon had skied down. No text, no phone call. If Canyon were alive, he would have made contact via radio or Walsh's cell phone. Staring at his phone, Walsh registered the blank screen. No contact.

None. Skiing over to the cliff's edge, Walsh cut a hard-edged stop at the precipice. Heat built under his three layers of thermal wear as his hand grew numb. Shoving the phone back into his pocket, he replaced his glove. Calculations automatically fired through his brain as he peered over the edge. Walsh estimated the distance down to be about a hundred feet, maybe less. Canyon could have jumped it, but there would be tracks in the snow, evidence of his landing. Granted it was snowing, but not enough to conceal the mark a hundred-foot landing would have left. Walsh moved his gaze to a line of trees, weaving his attention in and out of a sparse group of evergreen trunks, branches heavy with snow. Canyon couldn't have disappeared. It wasn't possible.

But he saw nothing—nothing but a narrow chute of untouched snow lined by rocks and trees that forked downward. Walsh pushed off and skied back toward the group. It was time to expand the search. He was heading downhill. If he was wrong and Canyon wasn't there, the climb back up would be brutal. But if Canyon had gone ahead and taken a tumble, he could be seriously injured and in desperate need of medical attention. And he was his friend's first line of defense, his only hope at this point. "I'm going down, Lisa."

"What? Wait—do you see him?"

"No. But I'm not getting anything up here." He patted his coat and said, "Call me when help arrives."

She nodded and Walsh couldn't mistake the distress in her eyes. Beneath her tinted goggles, Lisa's gaze was soaked in worry. The landscape below was dicey. It was one thing to ski the terrain with your momentum beneath you. It was another to slowly thread your way down in search of a downed skier. Joining Walsh at this point would only put her at risk and hinder rescue operations. There was nothing more she could do for Canyon. If he was alive, Walsh was right—he was probably somewhere below. They'd scanned every inch of this area. No sense wasting time repeating the effort. Besides, there were people in need of help right in front of her.

Lisa blew Walsh a kiss then watched him zig-zag downhill in short S-turns as he negotiated a slim passage between stone-faced mountain and pristine snow. *Canyon, where are you?*

Discharging the angst from her mind, she skied back over to Kinsley and Grant. Laid out on the ground, helmet on, black goggles raised onto the front of his helmet, Grant didn't move. He looked completely lifeless, actually. Kinsley sat huddled over him, her face cheek-to-cheek with his as she wrapped her arms over his body.

"How is he?" Lisa asked, skiing to a slow stop next to them. If he was conscious, she didn't want to startle him.

Kinsley raised her head. "He's coming around. He opened his eyes, knew who I was."

"That's a good sign," Lisa said. "Is he in any pain?"

"That's what I've been asking him, but he's drifting off and won't really say."

"Keep him warm and still. Help should be here any time." Lisa glanced upward and frowned. Snowfall was increasing, the sky turning a leaden white-gray. How much snow they would get was anyone's guess, but it was the wind that bothered her most. Roan was a good pilot, but his helicopter couldn't circumvent aerodynamics. Nerves skittered through her belly. Nor should he be forced to chance it. It wasn't Roan's fault they had chosen to heli-ski and ended up in the path of an avalanche. "How about you?" Lisa asked, noticing a redness swelling on Kinsley's cheek. She kicked herself for not thinking about her friend. "Are you okay?"

"I'm fine."

There was no hesitation in her voice, no concern over her own well-being. Kinsley was laser-focused on Grant. Lisa quelled a growing concern and replied, "I'm going to check on my dad."

Kinsley nodded and placed her gloved hands to Grant's cheeks.

Lisa skied over to her dad. The bruises on his face were significantly more pronounced than Kinsley's, especially against his fair complexion. She winced inwardly. The scrape on his chin was particularly nasty and had to hurt. "How's the leg?"

He chuckled. "Getting a sufficient amount of ice to keep the swelling down, courtesy of Mother Nature."

Lisa smirked. Leave it to her dad to find the positive. "Well, that's one ray of good news, huh?"

Hal's gaze flickered with sadness as it darted past her. "No sign of Canyon?"

"Not yet. Walsh is heading down to search for him. He thinks he might have skied farther down."

"It's possible," Hal said. "I didn't see him pass me, but it's possible he skied ahead and I missed him. He's a pretty fast skier."

"Yes," Lisa agreed, willing it to be true. "Everything happened so fast. One minute you guys were skiing down the mountain, the next there was nothing but snow."

"They hit quick. Hundred miles an hour and a few seconds are all it takes."

"And so powerful." Lisa's gaze moved to the swath of snow. An entire section of mountain had shifted position. To think she and Walsh could have been caught up, too...

Lisa swallowed back a rise of nerves and said, "I'm amazed any of us survived."

Hal grimaced.

Noting her father's pain, she unclicked her boots from her skis and stepped clear of them. "You and I need to get that leg stabilized for transport."

"Yes," he said weakly. "I was thinking we could use my safety harness and skis to create a splint."

"Good idea." Lisa dropped to her knees and helped her dad remove the safety harness he wore.

"Careful," he said, stopping her hands mid-motion. "I bruised my shoulder pretty badly."

Lines formed across his forehead, the skin around his eyes white and delicate compared to the windburn that had formed beneath his goggles. Every ski season, her dad sported the same raccoon expression, the tell-tale sign of a snow skier. Her pulse fluttered. But it wasn't every season he nearly died. "Do you think you broke anything else?"

"I hope not," he replied. "As it is, this leg injury is going to put me down for some time." Slowly unlocking his carabiners, he allowed Lisa to gently pull the harness from his body. "I need to call Adele."

"Do you think you should? I mean, don't you think she'll worry?"

"She'd want to know and I don't want her to hear it from someone else before she hears it from me. She'll worry either way."

Lisa nodded. Adele Simms ran on the anxious side. A New York City girl, her emotions were wound tighter than a golf ball. She had definitely learned to relax some in the time that Lisa had known her, but she still grew tense when things went wrong, especially when it concerned someone she cared about. Adele was a little neurotic that way, and wouldn't rest until she saw the whites of Hal's eyes at the bottom of the mountain.

The snow began to fall harder as Lisa worked with her father to form a stiff support for his leg. Using the straps of his harness, they secured his leg against one of his skis, wrapping it to a snug fit. The configuration was crude—the wide powder ski much too long for their needs—but effective. Her dad couldn't bend his leg even if he wanted to, though it didn't appear to prevent the injury from hurting, not if his labored breathing was any indication. "Do you need anything?" she asked him.

"No. I'll be fine until help arrives." His gaze slid sideways. "Make sure Grant is okay."

"Will do." Lisa popped up, her ski boots pounding hard over the snow as she trudged back to Grant and Kinsley. Snowflakes covered her pink jacket, blended seamlessly with her white pants and boots. Lisa flicked a glance around the area. This section of mountain provided only a narrow band of landing strip for Roan's helicopter. Everything uphill was too steep and downhill was too crowded. But if the snow continued to fall, he might not be able to see well enough to set down. He might have to call off the rescue and let them fend for themselves.

Lisa hoped not. If Grant or her father stayed up here much longer, neither one would have good outcomes. Pain, weakness, frostbite—the problems were endless! And then there was Canyon. She didn't even want to think about his condition.

Expelling a sigh, she pushed the angst from her mind. Walsh would take care of Canyon. Helicopters and landings were Roan's department. She needed to focus on the things she could control—like helping her friends. Plodding over to Kinsley, Lisa's toes were growing cold in her cumbersome boots, her ankles sore. Ski boots weren't meant for walking. They were tight and stiff and meant to keep a skier grounded to their skis. The inflexibility was beginning to hurt but it beat the alternative. Her feet would freeze without the thick construction housing them. Nearing, she asked, "How's Grant?"

Sitting by Grant's side, Kinsley snuggled close to his body, sharing her body heat with him as best she could. "Hanging in there."

Grant's eyes fluttered. A strip of black fleece lay over his forehead—Kinsley's full-face head cover, otherwise known as a balaclava—but the accumulation of snow was hard to prevent. Lisa didn't like to see his normally tanned skin tinged red, his lips dry and cracked, covered by a pasty film of lip balm, but it wasn't unexpected considering the circumstances. Lisa kneeled and reflexively her hand went to his face. His skin felt cool to the touch. Maybe they should replace his goggles, she thought, and place the fleece over his nose and cheeks. It would give him more protection than Kinsley's gloves.

Kinsley removed her hand from his cheek and Lisa saw the small white paper sack in the palm of her black glove. *Hand warmers*. Maybe those were a better idea. His ski clothes should provide enough warmth for his body, but with the snow falling, it would be a constant battle to keep him warm. Lisa wished she had packed an emergency thermal blanket in her backpack, but with all the other safety gear, there hadn't been the room. Keeping warm hadn't been a priority, not with the technical skiwear they had. Now, it proved their top priority.

"He says he's okay," Kinsley continued. "He's breathing, doesn't seem to have had a heart attack. I'm trying to warm him up, for all the good it's doing."

Lisa nodded. "Using your hand warmers is a good idea."

Kinsley laughed. "For once, I'm glad my fingers get ridiculously cold in my gloves! These little packets are coming in pretty handy at the moment."

"She's a smart one..." Grant spoke up.

Drawn to the faint utterance, Lisa thought it made him sound weak and frail. And while she didn't think the hand warmers would make a dent in Grant's overall body temperature, if using them made Kinsley feel better, then the effort was worth it. Staying calm and collected in the face of crisis was half the battle.

"You gave us a pretty big scare, Mr. Powell," Lisa scolded lightheartedly. "How are you feeling?"

Grant nodded. "Alive."

"Are you able to move everything?"

"We haven't tried yet," Kinsley remarked bluntly.

The apprehension in her friend's eyes was raw and spoke volumes. They hadn't tried because they didn't want bad news. Swallowing over a rise of nerves, Lisa counseled, "Might be best to wait for the medics."

Kinsley returned a grateful smile. "Yes. I thought he should rest." But her relief was short-lived. "Any sign of Canyon?"

"Not yet." Tears pricked Lisa's eyes as she envisioned Walsh desperately searching for his friend. The day had started out so well. Everyone had been so happy, mapping out the day before they took the first run. Canyon had been ribbing Walsh, who quickly returned fire, but now...now...Canyon might be—

Lisa couldn't bring herself to complete the thought. Canyon had to be okay. He had to be somewhere farther down the mountain. He was a skilled skier, an experienced SAR volunteer. He was healthy and fit. If anyone could escape injury, it would be Canyon. Walsh would find him. He had to. If he didn't, Lisa wasn't sure how Walsh would deal with it. Walsh had few friends, Canyon being one of his first. If anything happened to him and Walsh was within reach to be able to do something about it, he'd be crushed. For a long time. If losing his fellow Marines in the heat of battle had left a mark on him, losing Canyon during a backcountry ski trip would cut deep. But Lisa knew one thing for sure. Walsh wouldn't leave this mountain without Canyon. He was a Marine first, second, and third.

Marines didn't leave anyone behind.

Feeling a crack in her walled emotions, Lisa's heart ached. It was tough to lose people you cared about, the ones you couldn't save. She knew firsthand the pain of loss. Her mother had passed when Lisa was only twelve. Ovarian cancer. It had been a cruel blow and one neither she nor her father could prevent. Lisa's eyes shuttered as she suddenly recalled how they had scattered her ashes here on the mountain. Lisa's gaze darted about. This very mountain. Her mom had loved it up here. She was a *granola*, her dad used to say, same as Lisa. The term of endearment washed through Lisa with an unexpected ferocity. It was her dad's way of calling her a naturalist, a nature-lover. It was one of the things he loved most about her.

Moving her focus to her father, Lisa thought of the pain, the loss. Whether it was a mother taken too soon, the brothers in combat that couldn't be saved, or the search and rescue missions that proved unsuccessful, the hardest part was failure. Doing everything you could and still coming up short. Whether it was on the battlefield of war, in the wake of an avalanche, or in everyday life, a person couldn't dwell on what they *could* have done, or that they didn't try hard enough, work smart enough, act fast enough. Sometimes fate stepped in and swiped the matter from your hands.

Lisa pulled her gaze back to Grant. She knew the odds. No matter how well-trained the rescuer, fatalities happened. The chance of surviving an avalanche was about eighty-six percent, depending on a number of factors including an ability to remain near the surface. Then there was the terrain, the size of the avalanche, the time until rescue, and "luck." There was always the "luck" factor—or lack thereof. Lisa had missed being caught up in the avalanche because of Walsh's warning.

Grant and Canyon hadn't been so lucky.

"How are *you* doing?" Lisa asked Kinsley, realizing at once that she had seen her limping earlier. She dropped her gaze to Kinsley's leg. "Is your ankle all right?"

She nodded. "It hurts, but I think it's only twisted."

"Are you sure it's not broken? That avalanche hit pretty hard, tossing you a good twenty, fifty yards."

"I wouldn't be able to walk if it were broken."

"Not necessarily," Lisa corrected. "The rush of adrenaline can temporarily erase pain. You might have been able to walk on it because you were caught up in the moment. Doesn't mean there isn't an injury."

Goggles pulled up onto her helmet, Kinsley blinked, her long thick black lashes seeming harsh against the pale white of her skin. She glanced down at her leg and reached a hand toward her ankle. "I guess it could be. Now that you mention it, it is throbbing something fierce."

"Stay put when the guys arrive," Lisa ordered. "We'll get them to help you to the helicopter so you don't put any weight on it."

"Probably a good idea. Besides a visit to the doctor, I'm going to hit the spa and get a massage. I've got some serious kinks in my muscles!"

Lisa smiled, overtaken by the brief respite of humor. It made her long for normalcy—the boring "nothing happening" kind of normalcy. "I think a massage and hot bath should be on the agenda for all of us."

"And a glass of wine," Kinsley added. "A nice, full-bodied Cabernet to warm the blood."

"Hot chocolate for me," Lisa replied, her pleasure fading. Odd how "normalcy" was the unappreciated luxury that compelled a person to seek the thrill of heli-skiing, placing their life in jeopardy and then coming up short.

Chapter Six

Kelly glanced out her window as she shadowed Roan formation-style over the mountainous terrain. Her headset was situated snugly against her ears, the hollow static emitted by the radio muting most of the engine noise. Conditions were deteriorating and her nerves were taut. Ready. She was plugged in, the mission objective clear. They had people on the ground—some injured, one missing—who needed safe transport out. Getting in wouldn't be easy, the snowfall intensifying with every hundred feet of elevation, but it was doable. Maintaining an eye on the flashing red taillight of Roan's chopper, Kelly held steady to his left side a safe distance behind. It brought back memories from her combat days when she and her fellow pilots would fly in tandem over enemy territory. Each had the other's back. Each understood the target. There was power in numbers.

Roan had outlined the drill in abbreviated terms. They would fly up the mountain where he would drop his team while she maintained a holding pattern. Roan couldn't get any more specific. Conditions on the ground would dictate where they went from there. Six people were in question. Four men, two women. They'd been overtaken by an avalanche. They were experienced. They were friends, three of the men volunteers for summit SAR. Didn't take a rocket scientist to understand that this operation was personal for Roan. And while this group was experienced and knew what they were doing, even the best of the best could find themselves in hard times. It had happened to Guy Flannigan.

Memories competed with her focus as she thought back to the man. One of the most unbelievable pilots Kelly had ever met—smart, experienced, and fearless—Guy had gone down. Forget that he'd never met a challenge he couldn't conquer, never met a battle he couldn't win. He'd gone down. It happened when they were in the thick of it, receiving shoulder-to-air missile fire and "low-profile" gunfire. Nothing they couldn't handle. Then a sand storm swept in and flipped the balance of power. It became "advantage, bad guy" and Kelly and Guy were ordered to bail.

But Guy didn't bail. It wasn't in his DNA. Ditching Guy wasn't in hers. Kelly stayed in the hot zone and flew on instinct. She knew the landscape like the back of her hand. She worked from her mind's eye and visually sketched the battlefield as her gunner hammered the ground with hellfire missiles, yelling, *Abort! We've got to abort!*

Kelly wasn't going anywhere without Guy whose voice she could hear crackling over the radio as if it were happening all over again. *Hostile fire! I'm taking hostile fire!*

Kill those bastards! Kelly had shouted to her gunner.

What the hell do you think I'm doing?

Everything happened so fast. Grounded in her seat, Kelly commanded the chopper through the cloud of sand, granules penetrating the cockpit. She could almost taste it in her mouth as the memories filed through her—repugnant, filthy desert sand infiltrating her mouth and nostrils. But she pressed forward, the sound of gunfire ripping through the aircraft. Shouts blasted through her headphones. Moments later, she heard the explosion. Guy's chopper went down.

Shaking the awful scene from her mind, Kelly refocused on the snowy conditions around her. Altimeter indicated they were nearing twelve thousand feet. Snow pelted harder, faster. Tightening the grip on the lever between her legs, she pushed back into her seat. *Relax*, she cautioned herself. *You're not in Afghanistan anymore. You're in Colorado.*

Static spit from her headphones as Roan's voice burst into her ears. "Kelly, copy."

"Copy," she responded, using the same even and controlled tone as Roan.

"Keep me in sight. We'll be over the target in less than two."

"Copy." Anticipation flushed through her midsection. Narrowing her gaze on his taillight—the anti-collision beacon meant to prevent pilots from flying up one another's butt— she prepared for duty. It was time for action. Roan didn't think she could hover on command, but she could hover on command and stay hovering, despite the fact that there would be no need in this rescue. With Roan handling the heavy lifting, so to speak, she was ancillary at best, ferrying passengers from the top to the bottom, which she could do with her eyes closed.

Up ahead, Roan's helicopter swung right, then swept straight up. Kelly did likewise, her stomach pitching with each motion. She could see Roan easily through the snow, though the cloud ceiling was closing in. Beneath her a spattering of snow-covered trees blended in with mountain, their numbers and size diminishing as they climbed higher. They were cruising pretty fast, which was fine by her, but light was turning flat. Looking out her chopper, she oriented herself to the conditions. Visibility was turning to crap.

"Location is over the next ridge," Roan informed her.

"Copy."

"Delta three-eight to base," she heard Roan clip over the radio. "Do you copy?"

"Copy, base," Wade replied.

"Status on the ground?"

"Canyon's still missing, Roan."

"No sign of him?" Roan asked.

"Not yet," Wade returned. "Walsh headed downhill from the group in search of him. You'll need to grab him separate from the others."

Kelly could get him. She'd let Roan handle the medical rescue angle while she went down and plucked up Walsh. She liked Walsh. Fellow military, he was a Marine through and through, and a top-notch guy by her standards. She liked Lisa, too. They'd met during a recent Christmas party held at Summit Aviation's hangar. The SAR team was celebrating, and Roan had invited her to hang around and join them. She agreed. Not like she had anything else going on. Her dad still lived in Tacoma and she hadn't planned on heading home for the holidays. The memories of her mother stained every wall of her childhood home, the house too dreary to be cheery, a place Kelly wanted nothing to do with. She couldn't understand why her dad hung on to it. If it were up to her, she would have sold it the day after her mother walked out on them. The woman was weak. Visions of the petite blonde crowded Kelly's thoughts and she shook them off. The woman might be weak, but the memories were strong.

Thinking back to the Christmas party, she recalled how she and Walsh hit it off right from the start. Lisa did most of the talking—until Walsh learned that Kelly was ex-military. A man of few words, he had suddenly opened up—if one could call it that—and began asking her where she served and when, and with what unit. The conversation had been easy from there on out until she took exception to Walsh's assumption regarding Roan. Apparently Walsh thought the two had a "thing" going on—which they didn't. Kelly had no idea why Walsh believed otherwise. Even Canyon seemed to think they had something going on. Truth was, Roan had never made the first pass at her. She probably would have refused him, considering that he was her instructor and held the keys to her flying future with SAR, but he never attempted. Not once. Had Roan acted as though the two of them had a romantic relationship?

Some guys did. They pretended to be driving it home with a woman when, in fact, they couldn't get it into first gear. She couldn't imagine Roan talking trash, but she couldn't rule it out, either. Where else would they have gotten the idea?

"Heading in," Roan announced, severing her thoughts. His chopper banked hard right and disappeared from sight.

"Copy that," she said, pushing her stick forward. The higher they flew, the worse the visibility, causing her to lose sight of him. No problem. Once over the ridge, she'd stay high. Dropping airspeed, she looked out her side window then forward—

Kelly cursed. *What the*—?

She jerked back the controls, nearly slamming into a snow-covered ridge. Her stomach lurched as the aircraft swung up and pitched hard right.

The mountain had come out of nowhere.

"Kelly!" Roan shouted.

Heart pounding, adrenaline flushed her limbs. "Copy," she uttered shakily, more automatic than intentional. She searched for sight of him, but saw nothing. Then remembered he had banked right. She looked through the windshield. He should be directly ahead of her.

"What the hell happened?"

What the hell happened? *I nearly hit the side of the mountain, that's what happened*! she wanted to shout. *Where the heck was he*? Kelly strained for a glimpse of him. But she saw nothing.

"You're too fast—you're coming down at me!"

What? Instinct manned the controls, pulling the chopper up and away. Craning her neck to see outside her side window, she dipped the nose of the chopper and spotted him at once—she was practically on top of him! Swinging the tail around sharply, she dived right, dodging him in another near miss.

"Are you insane?!" he barked, his voice cracking loudly in her headset.

Circling back, Kelly expelled her breath. Heart pounding, she thought, *No, but I feel better now that I can see you*. "Where are we landing?" she asked matter-of-factly.

"You nearly crashed into me!"

Yeah, yeah, she muttered silently. *But I didn't*. "Flat light snuck up on me," she said, her calm tone a stark contrast to the thrashing of her pulse. That had been closer than even *she* wanted to admit, but she'd be damned if she was going to let Roan know. He'd never let her hear the end of it. "I don't see any skiers."

"Apparently you can't see mountains or choppers, either!"

Kelly gritted her teeth. Roan was losing his cool. *Stuff happens*, she wanted to chuck back. *Enough already! It's finished. Over and done.* They had a job to do and it was time they do it. "I repeat," she stated. "Where are we going?"

"*We're* not going anywhere," he told her. "You hang back while I go in and assess conditions."

The radio crackled and Wade's voice broke in, "Problem?"

"No problem," Roan answered.

There was no way Wade could have missed the anger in Roan's voice. Kelly gulped. Or her part in causing it.

"Arriving vicinity," Roan continued. "Currently in search of skiers."

"Let me know when you have a visual."

"Roger that," Roan replied.

Kelly maintained her visual on Roan, casting the occasional glance out her window to scan the ground. Conditions had definitely deteriorated. At this elevation, the snow was hammering them, Roan's blades making matters worse as they churned the snow into a tornado-swirl. There weren't a lot of trees up here as far as she could see, save for a thin line over a nearby ridge. The terrain was steep. How did Roan think he was going to land? Or did he?

"I've got a visual," Roan declared, and suddenly his chopper kicked into motion, dropping in a wide spiral.

What was he talking about? Kelly scanned the ground. She didn't see anyone. But holding steady above him, she assumed he had a better line of sight. He was probably analyzing ground conditions before setting down. Her job was to do as she was told. Hold tight and hover overhead.

"Roan," Wade said.

"Copy?"

"I just got a call from Walsh. He's requesting an SAR team for assistance with his ground search."

"Roger that."

"They're over at Peak Five. How much time are we talking to get them?"

"Twenty minutes, roundtrip."

Kelly mentally calculated the trip they were discussing. She had a vague idea of where Peak Five was located, but in these conditions, factoring in a margin for error—wind, snow, visibility—anything could throw her off course and delay her flight time. Blades pumped above her. Roan was hovering beneath her. What was he doing? Why wasn't he responding?

With near whiteout conditions, Kelly grew anxious for direction. "Roan, what am I doing? You want me to head over to Peak Five?"

"Give me a minute," he replied.

"Ten-four." Kelly didn't care for his crusty-edged tone but chalked it up to tension. This rescue was harder on Roan than it was on her. He was not only dealing with crap conditions, but also the stressful fact that one of his friends was still unaccounted for. And Kelly knew as well as anyone; it was the not knowing that killed you.

Especially when it came to the important people in your life, like the female pilot she'd met while training at Ft. Rucker. The woman had a laser-sharp mind and guts the size of Texas. Kelly liked her from day one. The two had spent some time together outside the base, talking shop and sharing bits and pieces of their past. Not long after she'd been shipped overseas for duty, her patrol unit was ambushed and she went missing. They finally found her body a week later, left in a heap on the side of the road a few miles outside their base. She'd been unceremoniously dumped out in the open so the American soldiers wouldn't miss her. Then there was Guy, a man who should have seen his thirtieth birthday, but didn't.

Old feelings bubbled to the surface and Kelly tamped them back. Both had been too young to die. Both had been senseless incidents, situations sparked by the heat of war. Butterflies swarmed and she tensed. There was no use in reliving the past. There was nothing she or anyone else could do to change it. It was over and done. History. The drum of rotor blades reverberated through her skull. Not everyone made it out of combat. Not everyone survived. That was the mantra. *We won't all make it out of here alive.* Soldiers understood the risk. Each and every day they went out, they faced it. *This could be the day I die.*

It wasn't the mindset the brass wanted to see in its men and women who wore the uniform, but Kelly knew it was the reality. She had been no different. Every day could be her last. It was simply a matter of time.

Kelly didn't like being yelled at. She wasn't some novice pilot who had to be warned the sky was blue, the clouds were high...she was an Apache combat pilot. She flew circles around civilian pilots and one near miss didn't mean squat. If Roan knew how many "near misses" they'd had in Afghanistan, he'd wet his pants. It happened. Skilled pilots worked around the mishaps and continued with the mission. It was called being a professional. It was known as understanding the risk.

Mixed feelings rumbled through her as she gleaned the outline of his chopper in the mess of white. But that was just it; civilian pilots and military pilots worked different terrain. Combat was an entirely different environment. Unfortunately, schooling Roan with a crash course on the subject would be impossible. Unable to suppress her impatience, she mumbled, "What's going on? Am I going or not?"

Chapter Seven

The sound of incoming helicopters ripped over the mountain, echoing through the canyons like music to Hal's ears. *Roan Phillips. The man of the hour has arrived.*

"They're here!" Kinsley exclaimed, more frantic than elated. "I can hear the helicopters!"

Thumping rotor blades were unmistakable, Hal thought. You felt the pound in your chest before you could see them. Looking up through the slant of snowfall, Hal searched the sky for sight of Roan. Clouds and ground combined in one big whitewash of landscape. The temperature had dropped. Wind had picked up. The snow continued its assault, pricking his face with an icy burn. He frowned. Conditions were souring. There was no way to sugarcoat it.

But Hal took heart. If anyone could pilot through this mess, it would be Roan.

Kinsley jumped up and began waving at the helicopter.

"Stay clear of the chopper!" Hal shouted. "He might not be able to see you!"

Roan swooped overhead and, immediately circled back, the echo of engines sweeping across the ground. His rotor blades seemed to move in slow motion. It was an optical illusion, Hal mused, the blades spinning at speeds faster than the human brain could process. Hal skimmed the terrain. At the moment, Roan was probably getting a head count before he attempted to land. *Where* he'd land was another question; while the avalanche-packed snow was pretty solid and should prove no issue for his skids, the angle of slope bothered Hal. It was too steep for a heli-pad.

Suddenly a second helicopter appeared overhead, moving quickly toward Roan—too quickly. Hal's heart caught. Oh my God—were they going to collide?

"Get down! They're going to crash!"

Hal barely registered Kinsley's shrill voice as the second chopper dropped away and disappeared from sight. He could still hear it, but struggled to comprehend what had just happened and watched in disbelief as Roan tried to set down. Hovering in place, the downwash from his blades stirred up a blizzard of snow. Lisa covered her exposed cheeks with gloved hands and hunkered down. Kinsley hunched over Grant. Worried that his friend hadn't moved, Hal had to trust Lisa's assurance that Grant was alive and "fairly" well. Less than encouraging words, but better than what he'd just witnessed above.

Snow whipped at Hal's face as he watched Roan lower the bird. Pulling his goggles over his eyes, Hal was mildly concerned about the other aircraft. He could hear the faint sound of rotor blades, but that was it. *Must be too high to see*, he mused, and focused on the comfort of Roan's presence.

Lisa popped up from the ground and ran toward Hal.

"Where's he going?" Kinsley yelled.

Engine noise lessened as Roan lifted up and away from the ground. Hal's heart fell, his attention split between his daughter and Roan. *Careful*, he wanted to warn her, but Lisa knew how to behave around helicopters. Not that it mattered. Roan was abandoning his effort. He couldn't do it. He couldn't land. Which meant they'd have to run the line. Hal closed his eyes and dropped his head back onto the snow as Lisa latched onto him. Running a line from the helicopter to air lift him out was no easy feat—not in good weather, and especially not in this mess. But emergencies were emergencies. He and Lisa shared a sober gaze. If Roan decided to chance it at all.

It was a big "if."

As the helicopter descended again, Hal's spirits lifted. *Please, let this work.*

The whine of high-pitched turbine engine intensified as Roan lowered his bird about thirty yards away. It was shaky, the aircraft hovering at an awkward angle, pitching toward the mountain. Hal feared Roan would ditch the effort again. Didn't take a helicopter pilot to understand that there was no way he could land. Suddenly, Hal spotted the familiar red jacket of his SAR team. A man jumped from the helicopter, landing in a squat on the ground about ten feet below. A stretcher dropped from the underbelly of the chopper and the man caught it. Two others jumped out and the team split its attention between Hal and Lisa, Kinsley and Grant. Roan lifted off the ground, whipping the air into a frenzy of snowflakes.

Running through the spray of snow, stretcher in hand, the man yelled, "Hal!"

Pleasure exploded in Hal's chest. "Goose!"

The man was solid, devoid of fat, and fit enough that running across the snow carrying a spine board didn't put a dent in his energy level. He wasn't the least bit out of breath and instead looked like he could lap the chopper a few more times.

Goose scrambled over the snow and dropped to a knee, slapping the stretcher onto the snow-packed ground beside Hal. "How's the leg?" he asked, shouting over the rising roar of engines.

"Useless," Hal grumbled good-humoredly. "But better now that you're here."

Lisa slapped him on the back. "Hey, Goose!"

"Hey, girl! You responsible for this beautiful piece of artwork?" he asked, gesturing toward the makeshift splint as he slipped a black pack from his back.

Lisa grinned. "We survivalists do the best we can, you know!"

"And a mighty fine best you do," Goose complimented. Wasting no time in retrieving his supplies, he ripped open an orange packet and pulled out a silver reflective warming blanket. Lisa took one end and together she and Goose wrapped it over Hal's body.

"What's the status of the other two?" he asked. "Everyone mobile?"

Lisa shook her head. "Uh-uh. Kinsley hurt her ankle and Grant is out of it."

"Okay, we'll work it out." Goose shoved up from the ground and jogged over to Grant and Kinsley, where he exchanged words with his team.

"I've never been more glad to see that man in my life," Hal said, watching his fellow SAR members with a swell of satisfaction.

"Me, either," Lisa agreed. "Now let's get you worked up and ready for transport."

"You'll get no complaints from me."

Across the snow, one red-jacketed figure huddled over Grant while another tended to Kinsley. Now that help had arrived, they would be okay. Except for one.

Goose jogged back to Hal and Lisa, puffs of breath billowing in the air as he asked, "Any word on Canyon?"

"Not yet," Hal responded. "Walsh is looking for him farther downhill. He believes he skied ahead and may be waiting below."

"Sounds like Canyon," Goose quipped, then grabbed straps and carabiners from his pack. With Lisa's help, Goose slipped Hal's body onto the board, then onto the transport bag. Unraveling the mess of straps, the two secured him in place and pulled the straps snug. "That slide came out of nowhere," Goose said.

"Tell me about it."

"Avalanche forecast didn't indicate we had any issues today."

"Could have been skier-triggered," Hal suggested. Or any number of things. It was par for the course when dealing in avalanches. They were unpredictable. One minute conditions looked good, the next you had a slide on your hands.

Lisa pulled out her cell phone. Pushing a key, she slipped the phone inside her helmet. Flat, cold metal pressed against her ear.

Walsh answered on the second ring. "Did I hear a chopper?"

"Yes. Roan's here," she told him. "Goose is with Dad. Any luck on finding Canyon?"

"Negative," he replied. "Tell Goose I need SAR up here, *stat*."

"Walsh needs another SAR team up here," she told Goose. "Do you think Roan can get one?"

Goose looked up into the sky. "No. But that wildcat up there can."

Lisa followed his gaze.

"It's Kelly Jones. She nearly dive-bombed a cliff a couple of minutes ago." Goose shook his head. "That chick is crazy."

"Crazy good," Lisa uttered without thinking.

"Crazy-*crazy*," Goose corrected.

"I was wondering what happened..." Hal reflected aloud. "I thought they were going to have a mid-air collision."

"It was close."

"Poor visibility?"

"Who knows," Goose replied. "But yeah, Roan is calling SAR now. I guess he'll send Kelly over to pick up the team."

"How soon?" Lisa asked, her gaze zeroing in on the second helicopter in the sky. Not a hundred feet above Roan's, it was now hovering in a tight circle above his aircraft.

Goose adjusted his mic and clipped, "Roan, how soon before we get that SAR team over here?"

No response. Seconds passed. Snowflakes continued their batter, filling spaces between goggles and helmets, accumulating on shoulders.

Lisa waited as Walsh asked, "How soon?"

"Goose is calling," she told him.

Lisa peered at Goose, who continued to work on her father. Why wasn't Roan responding? Was something wrong?

"What's going on?" Walsh demanded, his voice grating in her ear. "Can we get a team up here or not?"

"Goose?" Lisa questioned.

"Roan," he said into his radio. "Can she go, or not?"

"I'll send her," Roan replied suddenly. "How long before you get Hal ready?"

"Give me ten."

"Roger."

Hovering above the action, Roan felt trapped. Swamped by emotion, bound by time, he didn't want to send Kelly—but he had no choice. Literally. Walsh needed an extra team to search for Canyon. At this point, it was unlikely that Jack could make the flight back up. The weather was deteriorating to the point of hazardous. Roan's gaze fell. They had people on the ground that needed transport out. A team was needed to continue the search, but losing a chopper to weather to bring a team up here to save a man they had no way of knowing was alive or dead pushed the limits of reason.

But this was Canyon they were talking about. Roan stared down at the ground. Red-jacketed figures were split between skiers in a cyclone of snowfall, yet they worked oblivious to the conditions. Every member of this team would risk their own life to save Canyon's, no questions asked. They would stay through the night and search the mountain for days until they found him. This team would be relentless. All volunteers, they would willingly brave the storm to save their friend.

Roan held his aircraft steady, maintaining visual contact with his ground crew as they packaged their cargo. "Kelly, do you copy?"

"Copy."

"We need an SAR team from Peak Five."

"Peak Five? Roger."

Did she even know where that was? He could tell by her voice that she had no clue. *Dammit*. If his hands weren't tied to the controls, he'd slam a fist against something. She had no clue, and there wasn't a thing he could do about it. She was his only option. Gnashing his teeth, Roan said, "Peak Five is due west, about a five-minute flight time. Once you get near, you can't miss it, even in this crap."

"Roger."

"I'll call over and have them ready. You'll have to set down near the top of the gondola and they'll come to you."

"Copy that."

"And don't take any chances," he growled into his mic. "There are a lot of people over there at this hour and we don't need any accidents."

"Roan, I *got* this."

Somehow, her assurances weren't very reassuring. "Stay high and land tight."

"Very funny."

"I'm not trying to be funny. You don't know the outlay of these mountains well enough to navigate between them— especially in this weather—so act like it and stay high."

"Ten-four."

Chapter Eight

Katharine Wainwright stood in the office of Wainwright Ranch, her eyes glued to the snowy mountain ridge. She couldn't see the peaks. Cloaked in gray, they were shrouded, as though a blizzard had descended upon them. Which was crazy. It had been clear as spring water this morning when Canyon left! Maybe a stray cloud here and there, a wispy line of soft white, but mostly clear and crisp—a beautiful day for skiing. Katharine shuddered and wrapped her arms around her body. She didn't like the idea of him being up there. Not with an avalanche. Not with a search underway. *Missing.* Heartbeats fluttered in her chest. *What did that mean? Had Canyon tumbled down the mountain? Was he buried alive?*

If anything happened to Canyon—

Katharine couldn't imagine it. The two had only been dating since last summer, when the financial failings of her mother's charity ranch impelled Katharine to fly to Colorado, but had since grown closer than she believed two people could become. Wainwright Ranch was a working ranch that acted as a summer camp for terminally-ill children, and a dream come true for Katharine's mother. After losing a child of her own to leukemia, Eleanor Wainwright wanted to create a place where kids could feel normal—powerful—by working and achieving and doing as much as any other child their age. By treating them with the same expectations she would any other rancher, Eleanor instilled a sense of pride in the children, a belief that anything was possible.

But a year after her mother's death, the ranch had gone nearly bankrupt. At first, Katharine believed it had been a matter of poor management. As an investment banker at Wainwright, Emerson—her father's firm in New York— Katharine assumed the problems were something she could fix quickly and then return to her life in the city. She had been wrong. Digging into the numbers uncovered the fact that Frank Dillard, a longtime family friend and confidant of her mother's, had been embezzling from the ranch. He'd even gone so far as to kidnap Katharine in an attempt to get away with his scheme. If it hadn't been for Canyon, Frank might have gotten away with it—but Canyon and his friends saved the day and with his guidance, Katharine reorganized the finances putting the ranch back on track. Because of Canyon, she had also decided to stay on and run the ranch—with Canyon.

But now he was missing. Hal had mentioned that Grant and Kinsley were accounted for—injured but okay. Walsh and Lisa had missed the slide entirely, and Canyon had skied down right before them. Katharine's mind worked through the possibilities. No one had heard from him. He wasn't answering his cell phone and wasn't calling.

It was possible he had no signal. It was also possible he had escaped harm, she reminded herself. Thank goodness Adele was on her way over. There were too many scenarios, too many what-ifs for Katharine to digest. After Adele had called with the news, she had insisted on driving over, declaring that the two of them needed to be at the base when their men came home. Katharine couldn't agree more. She needed to see Canyon for herself when he made it down, but she was in no condition to drive. By her side, Cody whimpered and pushed his nose against her leg. Reflexively, her hand sought the comfort of his soft fur—fluffy, baby-soft fur coating his neck and shoulders. Katharine massaged his ear, the cartilage bending easily beneath her touch. Her yellow Lab knew. Animal instinct. He could sense when things weren't right. "It's going to be okay, baby. He's going to be okay."

Canyon's instincts were good, too. He knew those mountains as well as anyone, understood his way around the rocks and trees and could navigate his way in the dark. And crisis didn't shake him. As a member of the SAR team, he dealt with these situations all the time. Usually he worked the other end of the crisis, but he knew how to handle himself either way. He was strong. He was a survivor.

"Katharine."

She turned at the sound of the familiar voice. Tears sprang to Katharine's eyes and she felt her grit dissolve quickly. "Adele. Have you heard anything?"

"No, nothing. I called Wade. He said Roan was up on the mountain. They're going to airlift Hal to the hospital." Adele's enormous dark eyes were lined in burgundy and set against ivory skin and prominent cheekbones, and they mirrored the fear and concern swimming through Katharine's heart. A quiet person, Adele was one of Katharine's closest friends. She knew her inside and out. She understood what Katharine was going through and was here to provide support.

It was an intimacy Katharine desperately needed during this time of uncertainty. "You need to be there, too," Katharine said and grabbed her purse from the desk. "We need to go."

Adele met Katharine halfway and stopped her in her tracks, enveloping her in a fierce hug. "He's going to be okay," she whispered. "You know that, right?"

Gripped within the indomitable strength of her petite friend, Katharine nodded, unable to summon words. She tried, but she hadn't yet managed to entirely convince herself. There was always that smidgen of doubt, a dark hole siphoning her hope like an evil force mocking her courage. *Canyon is dead. Gone. You're engaging in wishful thinking.* Pressing her eyes closed, Katharine scolded herself. She couldn't fall apart. She had to keep it together. She had to be strong for Canyon. Fighting back an onslaught of tears, she squeezed and released. "He's going to be okay."

"My car is parked out front," Adele said. "We'll take Cody."

"Yes. I'll tell Amanda that we're going." *In case anyone calls*, Katharine mused. In case anyone had answers regarding Canyon's whereabouts. *In case.*

Katharine capped the lid on any more negative thoughts and hurried out of her office. She couldn't think that way. She couldn't dwell in worst-case scenarios. She just couldn't.

Stopping at Amanda's desk, Katharine cleared her voice and announced, "I'm going into town. If anyone calls, please call my cell phone right away."

Heavily lined dark eyes rounded and Amanda Bell nodded. "Call when you hear something, will you?"

"Of course."

Normally upbeat and more than a tad flirtatious, Amanda was grave now, her expression somber. As Wainwright Ranch's secretary for the last four years, Amanda had known Canyon longer than Katharine had, same as the rest of the Wainwright staff. He was a fixture around here, an integral part of the ranch and the kids' lives. If anything happened to Canyon, the ranch staff would be devastated. The children—

Katharine's heart thwacked and she swallowed hard. "I'll call the minute I know something."

"Thank you," Amanda mouthed.

Katharine plucked her coat from a hook by the door and walked wordlessly to the white Mercedes SUV. Haphazardly parked just beyond the wooden gate lining the rear of the administrative building, the car's engine was running. Katharine cautiously made her way down the stone path, mindful of icy patches. While the ranch usually didn't receive as much snow as the village of Silver Creek and the mountains above, several inches had accumulated and, coupled with frigid temperatures, was enough to freeze a thin sheet of ice over the ground.

Adele opened a back door of her vehicle for Cody, who hopped in easily. Katharine took her seat up front and gazed out through the windshield. Snowflakes were beginning to fall. Melting instantly as they hit the dark brown roofs and oiled wood fence posts, they were the first sign that the storm front was pushing its way through. Within the hour, the flurries would become heavier, and who knew how much accumulation this system would bring—an inch? A foot?

Katharine pulled the black parka snug around her shoulders. She had dressed casually in jeans and boots, and her white button-down provided little protection against the weather. But she hadn't been expecting to be outdoors. Today had been scheduled as an office day; with Canyon out skiing, her plan had been to catch up on paperwork. As Adele's car leapt into drive, Katharine burrowed into the hard leather seat. Her gaze sought the peaks in the distance and a jittery panic skittered into her stomach. Heavy snowfall would hamper rescue efforts. She could recall more than one story where a team had to call off a search due to weather—rescues gone wrong, or at least not as successful as the team would have preferred. It was the reality of dating an SAR member. She'd been treated to countless stories, each one more harrowing than the last—a fact that suddenly felt like a drawback. Knowledge wasn't always a good thing.

At the moment, it felt more like a curse.

As Adele sped over the gravelly driveway, Katharine glanced across the deserted ranch property. Home to dozens of children over the summer, it was a ghost town off season. Horses were corralled, staff was limited. The spirited sound of laughter was nowhere to be found. Other than Amanda, there was hardly anyone on property, no one to inform about Canyon's situation. Not that she had anything to tell, but for some reason Katharine yearned for the consolation of numbers. It meant she wasn't alone. And truth be known, it wasn't only her world that would be turned upside down should harm befall Canyon. Numerous lives would be affected for the worse.

Katharine's gaze rose to the sky. *Was Roan up there? Would he be able to fly in these conditions?*

Blizzards grounded aircraft. There would be no way around it. If skiers got caught in a remote section of the mountain, there was nothing Roan could do but wait out the weather. Ground teams traveling on snowmobiles could be dispatched, but they were also limited in their capacity to help, usually reserved for tourist rescues in normal skiing zones. There was no way they could navigate the steep terrain that heli-skiers preferred. The allure was its remoteness.

Eyes glazing over as she continued to stare out the passenger window, Katharine forced herself to be calm. She might not know much about aviation, helicopter or otherwise, but she did know Roan. The man was an incredible pilot. She'd witnessed his ability firsthand when he prevented Frank Dillard from kidnapping her. Roan had commanded his helicopter like the ace pilot he was, swooping in to save the day—literally—and preventing her plane from taking off by flying head-on toward Wainwright's company jet. Watching the entire scene unfold from her seat inside the aircraft, she thought they were going to collide for sure, but they hadn't. Roan's courageous tactic worked, convincing Wainwright's panicked pilot to abort takeoff.

Now Roan was tasked with saving his friends. Katharine's heart squeezed. She couldn't imagine the pressure Roan must be under. It was one thing to save complete strangers—there was objectivity, dispassionate professionalism. But saving your *friends*?

Sinking into her seat, Katharine brushed the thought away and tried to focus on the road. She couldn't take on the stress of everyone else. She had enough of her own to deal with.

Adele reached her hand for Katharine's. "How are you holding up?"

"Terribly. I'm thinking of everything that can possibly go wrong which is absolutely the worst thing to do! I know better, yet I can't seem to stop myself."

"This is tough business, Katharine. Don't be too hard on yourself. You're allowed to worry."

"But I'm worried about everything—Roan being able to fly, Canyon being okay, the ranch moving forward if something happened to..." Katharine's throat closed. She was obsessing, and she had to stop!

Cody pushed his nose into the back of her shoulder and her hand reflexively went to him. His textured snout and prickly whiskers sought her palm and burrowed in. The connection was comforting.

"It's normal," Adele counseled. "You're a smart woman and you can't simply shut down your mind. We just have to redirect our energy, right? Isn't that what you used to tell me?"

Katharine looked to Adele and suppressed a rise of guilt. Yes. Talk about challenges—Adele had faced many in her life, including breast cancer, divorce, and a cross-country move as she sold her business. Through it all, Katharine had urged her friend to redirect her energy away from the things that weren't serving her and focus on those that would. Katharine frowned. How could she have been so insensitive? "I'm sorry."

"Don't be. It was good advice. You're the reason I got out of New York and moved to Colorado. You said I needed to ditch the city stress for a fresh start and a simple life. You were right. I'm wildly happy and fairly successful. Now let's focus on you. We need to redirect your energy toward what you can do and away from what isn't serving you."

"Yes," Katharine replied, recalling words spoken many years ago. "You're right. I'm wasting valuable energy. Action. I need an action item—something to redirect my thoughts." Glancing out the windshield, she asked, "Where are we going?"

"I was going to drop you at police headquarters. Wade said you could wait there with him and receive first word as to Canyon's whereabouts."

"Yes, that sounds fine. And what about you? Are you headed for the hospital?"

Adele's black brow puckered. "Do you mind?"

"Of course not! You need to be there for Hal the second he lands."

The lines around Adele's eyes softened. Together with the black curls of hair poking free from her white wool ski hat, her expression held an entirely warm and feminine appeal. "Thank you. I'd like to be."

Adele dropped Katharine at the police station. A modest
two-story building from the outside, it was warm and elegant
on the inside, with leather and bronze furniture, indirect light-
ing and gorgeous artwork. Scribbling her name and purpose
on a sheet of paper at the front window, Katharine asked a
woman behind the glass partition, "Is the dog okay?" Most
places in Silver Creek were dog-friendly, but Katharine always preferred to ask, rather than assume.

"Yes, of course," the receptionist replied pleasantly.
"Chief Davis is expecting you. Do you know the way?"

"I do, thank you."

Unfortunately, Katharine had been to Chief Davis' office
on more than one occasion due to Frank's embezzling of
funds from Wainwright Ranch. Frank had nearly bankrupted
the charity in the worst sort of betrayal and if it hadn't been
for Wade and his officers, he might have gotten away with it.
But the men and women of this office were talented and professional, and Katharine was forever grateful to them.

Walking down the spacious corridor of dark wood floors
and amber-toned walls, Katharine couldn't deny that thoughts
of Frank's betrayal still hurt. He had been her mother's closest confidant, a family friend for more years than she could
remember. To know that he was capable of turning on her
family—her mother's life's work—had been a crushing blow.
But ironically, his betrayal was the reason Katharine was living in Silver Creek full-time and loving a certain Canyon Laredo. Tears loomed she brushed them away. This was not the
time to break down. She had to be strong. For Canyon's sake.
For her *own* sake.

The door marked "Chief of Police" at the end of the hall
was open and Katharine walked up, pausing briefly. Inside,
Wade Davis was pacing the floor in front of his desk. Filled
with expensive wood furniture, regional artwork, and the latest in technology—boasting three computer screens—the office was everything she expected from a police department
that served an upscale ski resort. No luxury had been spared

to keep the tourists and locals safe and secure, and one man was in charge. Dressed in a navy blue suit—almost black— Wade had an imposing stature underscored by his height and solid build. His dark brown hair was thick and trimmed short, his brunette brow and mustache full against a face deeply lined. They were the lines of age and wisdom that lent him an air of the competence that comes from experience. Katharine found him handsome, though every bit as tough as any New York police officer she had come into contact with during her years living in the city.

Wade walked over to her at once, and she noticed he was wearing a pair of sleek, black snake skin boots. He might appear New-York-City tough, but this man was Colorado cowboy through and through. "Hello, Katharine."

"Hello, Chief Davis."

His gaze was grave and his voice deep as he gently set his hands to her arms. "I'm sorry to have to see you under these circumstances."

"Me, too," she replied, and biting back a fresh rush of tears. Nerves tore her insides.

"Roan is on the mountain. They're loading up Hal as we speak."

"And Canyon?"

"Walsh is looking for him. He feels Canyon might have skied farther down to avoid the avalanche."

Hope bloomed in her chest. "He thinks he made it down without getting hit?"

"It's a possibility. Kelly Jones is working with Roan and went to get another SAR team from the resort. She'll drop them with Walsh and remain on standby to transport everyone out." Wade paused, and his gaze felt every bit as heavy as her heart. "They'll find him, Katharine. One way or another, they'll find him."

One way or another. It was the "another" part that she feared most.

Chapter Nine

Pressing her foot levers, Kelly worked the stick-lever between her legs in sync with the lever at her side as she slowly lifted the AStar. Swinging the tail around, she checked her compass headings and headed west. *Peak Five is due west. Five minute flight time. You can't miss it. Even in this crap.*

Roan was right about the *crap* part. The skies were littered with snow, reducing her visibility to zero. Well, almost zero. She could make out the mountains well enough to avoid them, but in doing so, had to reduce her speed considerably. Another near miss would only send her chances of being officially signed off down the drain. And while this weather was the stuff of blizzards, flying through crappy weather was what she'd been trained to do. Advised not to do, but trained to do in the event she found herself in a "situation."

And this was what she'd call a situation. Kelly fine-tuned her senses to the job at hand. Pulsating rotor blades reverberated in her chest. Dials and mini-screens glowed from her instrument panel and she continually scanned for variances, discrepancies—anything that could pose a problem. With the loss of visual clues outside, she had to rely on her instruments. Numbers didn't lie. They told you when you were losing altitude. When you couldn't see it with your eyes, or feel it in your stomach, they told you when you were losing power, when you were losing your ability to lift—perhaps when you needed it most. Instruments gave you air speed, altitude, enabled you to calculate your power margin and avoid dropping out of the sky.

Kelly understood it all. Flying almost every day of her life since the age of sixteen, she lived and breathed it all and loved it. Every second of it. There was something about the freedom of unlimited sky that appealed to her. Infinity was the limit—literally—which meant there was no limit, no one and nothing to keep her down.

Watch out world—the eagle is airborne. Her father's words floated into her mind and made her laugh. He'd always believed in her. Come sun or rain, he never lost faith in her ability to "bring it home" in the air. And she did. With skill and precision and a professionalism that made him proud, Kelly had mastered the necessary skills and excelled in doing so, earning her easy access to military flight school. Her father had been Army. She'd been Army. Both flew helicopters in the service—the Apache, the Army's primary attack helicopter—and both had been decorated for it. Kelly had actually learned to fly planes first, from her grandfather, but when her father discovered how much she loved it, he introduced her to helicopters and she had never looked back. This was her life.

Glimpsing the shadowy outline of the gondola station in the distance, Kelly quickly cut her airspeed. Roan said the SAR team would meet her once she touched down. Hopefully, they had warned the gondola staff she was coming. Making a low pass, she swept the area with a wide turn and scanned the ground for hazards. Located within the gondola building was a restaurant and patio. Outside, picnic tables were piled with snow, but no people. Between the gondola and a nearby chair lift, the space had been cleared of skiers. Looking oddly deserted, only the racks of skis, poles, and snowboards were any indication that the place wasn't closed. Then she noted that people were skiing downhill from higher elevations and being funneled around and behind the gondola building, a safe distance from her makeshift landing pad. Good. It meant they had received Roan's call and the team would be waiting.

Shooting for dead center between the chair lift and gondola building, Kelly estimated that the snow should be packed and fairly easy to negotiate. There were no steep angles to worry about, only the deluge from the rotor blades as she lowered the chopper, picking up snow and recirculating it in a swirl, forming her own mini-blizzard. *Nothing these guys shouldn't be used to by now*, she mused.

Setting the helicopter down, Kelly watched for incoming crew. As if on cue, three red-coated figures filed out of a small hut situated near the main building and ran toward her, followed by a dog. She gaped at the shaggy-furred black Labrador Retriever decked out in a fitted vest strapped around its midsection. A *dog*? Roan hadn't said anything about a dog!

Kelly groaned inwardly. But what did she expect? People in Colorado treated their dogs as if they were fellow human beings. Why wouldn't they include a dog on the SAR team?

Of course, she knew its purpose. Using their superior power of smell, avalanche dogs were trained to pick up the scent of humans buried under the snow. It was an ungodly task, but someone had to do it. Or *some animal*. Kelly hoped that didn't turn out to be the case with Canyon. She didn't know the guy very well, but Roan did, and had a lot of good things to say about him. Kelly hated to think she'd be transporting his dead body down the mountain, but if that's what was required, that's what she'd do.

A guy entered the chopper and took left seat. "Hey, nice to meet you!"

"Likewise," she replied.

Without being told, the good-looking blue-eyed blond pulled the headset on and keyed up his voice-activated mic. "I'm Sean."

"Hey, Sean. I'm Kelly."

Dressed in identical jackets to the others, he cast a glance over his shoulder and checked on his crew in back. The man, woman and dog climbed aboard. When the rear door slammed to a close, Sean gave her a thumbs-up. *Ready for liftoff.*

Kelly glanced around, ensuring the area was clear for takeoff and lifted the bird from the ground, quickly banking hard left as she headed back. "Delta three-eight, copy?"

"Copy."

"I've got SAR on board and heading your way. You have a destination for me, yet?"

"Will secure," he replied.

Kelly waited. There was no telling what Roan was in the middle of at the moment. He could be loading the first patient, maybe the second. He might be in flight, though she doubted it. There was no way he could have already loaded his cargo in the short time she'd been gone, but he was likely finishing now.

"Pretty messy out there," Sean said, his voice sounding as though it was traveling through a hollow tube.

"Pretty much," she agreed. Not one for casual conversation while she was flying, Kelly dropped her gaze to the landscape below, a changing mass of gray and white. Especially when it was messy outside. She needed to focus. Careful to adjust her line of vision as far ahead into the distance as possible, she piloted more by feel than procedure as she worked to recall the line of mountainous ridges she had traveled over to retrieve the team. She planned to simply reverse the order in her mind and double back over the same route. *Keep it simple—keep it safe*.

The man beside her fidgeted with his gloves then tightened the cords on his jacket. The ride must feel pretty cold to him, but dressed in the best thermal gear money could buy, she felt fine. Warm, even. Her cheeks were slightly cold from being exposed briefly by open doors, but she barely noticed. Her energy was channeled from brain to stick to chopper. She was one with the aircraft.

Roan's robotic voice erupted in her ear. "Kelly, copy?"

"Copy."

Roan rattled off a series of numbers and Kelly repeated them aloud to memorize, noting that Sean entered them into his phone. "Find a landing spot as near as you can," Roan directed. "Walsh will find you from there."

"Ten-four."

Kelly wanted to ask as to Canyon's status, but figured the less conversation the better. She didn't care to be interrupted with useless chit-chat when she was in the middle of a mission and had a hunch that Roan would feel the same. They were alike that way, sharing a single-minded focus when it came to doing their job. It was one of the things she admired most about him—Roan wasn't military, but he could've been. He had the skillset, the temperament, and certainly the ego for the job. She wondered why he had never signed on when he would have been an easy fit. But some guys weren't interested in giving back to their country, in serving a cause greater than themselves. She didn't fault him for it. She chalked it up to the eighty-twenty rule: eighty percent of the work was carried out by twenty percent of the people. Human nature. The way of the world, and nothing she could change. Why bother trying?

Settling into the drone of the engine, Kelly glanced between her GPS and the terrain. She was getting close, and searched for signs of Roan. Snow blew sideways, blurring the lines between air and ground. A red chopper shouldn't be that hard to spot, but she saw nothing. Beside her, Sean was looking out the window. "Do you see anything?" she asked him.

"Nothing."

"Roger," she said, slightly confused. From her calculations, she should be damn near over top of him.

"Kelly," Roan said over the radio. "Copy?"

"Copy."

"Keep your eyes out for Jack. He's the chopper pilot who dropped Hal's group and is headed our way."

Instantly diverting her attention to scan the skies around them, she wondered why he was headed back up in this mess but only replied, "Roger that." Exchanging a glance with Sean, she asked, "Do you have a visual?"

"Not yet," Roan replied.

Suddenly, a dark mass was barreling toward her. Instinctively, Kelly dodged right, heart beating wildly in her chest. *What the—*

She jerked her gaze out the window. She swore she saw the strobe light of another chopper—

"Chopper down!" Sean yelled, pointing out his window.

"Chopper down?" Kelly hardly registered what he'd said when a wall of mountain came crashing at her. *Oh my God*! She yanked the stick back to the left, her hands working controls automatically. The helicopter swung up, rotor blades nearly clipping the mountain, and she felt the bird lose lift. Rotor blades churned overhead—*thump, thump, thump*.

"Kelly!" Roan's voice yelled over the radio. "What the hell are you doing?"

Her stomach hit the ceiling. *Crap.*

Chapter Ten

"Kelly, talk to me!" Roan shouted. "What the hell is going on?"

Radio silence.

"Kelly!" Heart racing, Roan yelled, "Jack! Do you copy?"

But Roan didn't expect an answer from Jack. He'd seen Jack's chopper tumble out of the sky. Like a toy helicopter, rotors turning in slow motion, it had fallen at a grotesque angle in a vertical plummet to the ground. Roan couldn't see it, but he could imagine the twisted, mangled mass of metal rolling downhill. Toward Walsh.

Walsh.

Roan's heart skipped a beat. Had Walsh seen Jack's chopper go down? Had Kelly gone down, too?

Time froze. With a hoist line dangling from his chopper, Roan fought to hold steady in the wind while his crew secured Hal to the line. He couldn't do a thing to help—not Walsh, not Jack, not Kelly—no one. Roan couldn't do a thing to help any of them.

Kelly's scream echoed in his skull. *Had she crashed?*

Last he saw, her chopper was headed straight up. Not good. But it was a whiteout. Roan could barely make out Grant and the SAR team attending to him, let alone other helicopters in the sky. Below him, Hal was bundled up like a mummy in the distinct orange bag used for transport. They were almost finished preparing him for lift into the helicopter. Because Roan couldn't land, they had to use the line. There was no way he could set down for any length of time—not reliably so, not without the chance of inadvertently chopping a blade into the mountainside. Or a person, for that matter. It was too dicey. Too unpredictable.

Goose radioed to Roan. "Package is clean!"

"Package is clean," Roan repeated. "Affirmative." Which meant Hal was secured and ready for lift. With one eye glued to the happenings on the ground, Roan tamped back his concern and concentrated on the lift. "Delta three-eight to base, patient is loaded and ready for transport."

"Ten four," Wade replied. "Silver Creek Medical Center is on standby."

"Wade, we have a situation. We have a chopper down. I repeat: we have a chopper down."

"Where?"

"Not exactly certain," Roan said, his gut twisting. "Directly west of my location, but I have no visual. I've still got nine on the ground. I need secondary transport."

"Okay," Wade replied, his voice thick with concern. "Have Kelly ferry the second group down."

"I can't," Roan replied quickly. "We've lost radio contact."

"Lost contact?"

Roan was at a loss. For the first time in his career as a pilot, he was at a complete and utter loss. "I think Kelly went down," he said, "but I have no confirmation." He waited through the pause. It was not the news Wade wanted to hear, and not the news he wanted to deliver.

"Report status of rescue efforts," Wade said.

"Hal's coming on board. Grant is being secured as we speak." The remaining crew was busily tying him in a similar bag, Grant's body covered by a silver warming blanket while his friends huddled near.

"Canyon?"

"Nothing yet."

"Copy."

Wade heaved a sigh and tried to avoid making eye contact with Katharine Wainwright—a tough proposition when the woman stood three feet away from him and had heard every word.

Tears filled her eyes. Color drained from her face. Wordlessly, she dropped to a leather chair. Her dog went quickly to her side.

Wade winced. On so many levels, he felt her pain. Canyon was his friend. Kelly was the daughter of Bill Jones', a good friend, and a man who happened to be in town visiting. *Kelly went down.* God help him if he had to make *that* phone call to Bill. Staring at Katharine, Wade had a horrible sinking feeling. There was no way he could order another chopper in the air. There was no way another SAR team could get to them in time. He only had Roan.

And Roan was in the middle of a rescue.

Wade expelled a ragged sigh. These were the days he hated. Most days on the job, he loved, but there were days he could do without, days when accidents turned tragic, days when lives were lost. Moving his gaze to the windows, he raised it higher, to the mountains. Jagged peaks were no longer visible as the soft flurry increased with the advancing storm. Soon the village would be a winter wonderland of white. On a good day, he could see almost the entire resort ski terrain as though mapped out for his personal pleasure. But, like an eagle on its perch, Wade watched and waited until he was needed, when crisis struck or criminal mischief broke out. It was a satisfying life. As Chief of Police, his position afforded him a nice office, a hefty amount of prestige around town, and excellent job security—all of which he'd trade for the opportunity to start this day over. Wade closed his eyes. This was not supposed to be how it ended.

After several moments, Wade keyed up his mic. "ETA to hospital helipad?"

"Estimate twenty minutes, maybe sooner."

Wade did the math. Twenty minutes plus unload time meant thirty. Add a return trip—*if* he could send Roan back up for a return trip—and they were looking at another hour. Wade slid his glance upward. How many casualties would they ultimately be facing as time squeezed them in?

But Wade had to send someone up. He had no choice. He had too many people who needed transport down. He might need an SAR team to travel by foot. Stealing a glance toward Katharine, he settled his weary gaze on her. This was a rough mix. A tough call—one that was going to be tough on all of them.

Static erupted over the radio. "Roan, do you copy?"

His heart leapt at the sound of Kelly's voice. "Kelly—yes, I copy! What's going on? Where are you?"

"A chopper went down."

"Who?"

"He went down—I can't see him!" she shrieked.

Roan felt an uneasiness at the shrill tone. Something was off.

"They shot him!"

Fingers of fear curled around his heart. She wasn't making sense. "Kelly, who went down? Where are you?"

"I don't know..." she stammered.

Then it hit him. Jack was in the vicinity. If Kelly hadn't gone down, that meant Jack had.

"I don't know," Kelly repeated. "He's down."

Roan heard the unsteadiness now, loud and clear. She wasn't listening to him. She was jabbering, talking nonsense. The significance sunk in. Kelly was losing it. "Kelly, who's onboard?" At her pause, he repeated his question quickly. "Who's onboard with you? The SAR team?" he prompted.

No response.

Dammit! Roan fought for calm as he began to lift his helicopter higher from the ground, the flight nurse dangling from the line below, secured to Hal's transport bag by a web of straps and carabiners. In minutes he'd be on board. Roan checked his fuel gauge and estimated he could make the return trip. It would be close, but he could do it. He could drop Hal and get back up here for the others.

"I have to go back for him," Kelly said, her voice eerily trancelike. "The sand, it's too dense. I can't see him!"

"Kelly, listen to me," Roan said, injecting his voice with a calm he didn't feel. "You're in Colorado. You're flying an SAR team on a rescue mission. Can you drop the team? Are you close?" he asked, working to keep his tone as measured and even as possible. Kelly was obviously having some kind of flashback, sounding as though she thought she was back in Afghanistan—somewhere over there—when he needed her *here*. Physically *and* mentally. If she couldn't do it, if she lost it, Kelly could kill everyone on board that helicopter.

Chapter Eleven

Kelly's mind was reeling. Staring out into a sea of white, she tried to make sense of it. *This doesn't feel right. Something is wrong.* Guy Flannigan was dead. He and his co-pilot had been killed when their chopper went down. *We've got to abort! We've got to abort!*

Kelly ejected the voices from her head. Guy was dead! He'd been shot down by hostile fire! But the voices persisted. *We can't leave him! We've gotta go back!*

But there was nothing to go back for. She'd seen it for herself.

Kelly tried to shake the muddled images from her brain. This wasn't happening. It wasn't right. But she saw the chopper. She had nearly crashed into it. A sick feeling overwhelmed her. It had gone down. *Hard.* Her heart lurched. *Was he dead?*

"We've gotta go back! We've gotta go back!"

Suddenly, Kelly realized it was Sean's voice she heard. Heart pounding, she glanced askance. She was flying over the mountains of Colorado. Blizzard conditions. She couldn't see. No visibility. This man was yelling at her. "We can't!"

She'd lost all visual clues. She couldn't go back even if she wanted to—she didn't even know where "back" was! Kelly stiffened. Her hands froze on the controls. She'd lost all fluidity, all ease of thought and motion.

"We've got a chopper down!" Sean shouted into his mic. "We've got to go back!"

Panic skirted up her spine. There were people on the ground who needed her. She was flying a SAR team.

"Turn around!"

She stole a glance at him. *I can't—don't you get it?*

I don't know where I am. I can't think. Kelly stared out her windshield. Fear wound through her, but it was the smell of panic that unsettled her most—a mix of fear, sweat and uncertainty. Time was closing in on her. Her mind was in upheaval. Guy was gone. Dead. Heartbeats fluttered in her chest. Tears pricked her eyes. He was never coming back to her. Ever.

Tightening her grip on the controls, Kelly flew mindlessly. Through the snowy sky, through a tangle of emotion—memories, doubt, guilt, and regret—she flew. Kelly lost all peripheral vision, all sense of time and space. Her body was filled with the drone of turbine, the constant whir of engines as she operated on auto-pilot. Guy was dead. The love of her life, the only man who'd ever felt her equal, was gone. She couldn't even retrieve his remains.

Because the enemy had torched them.

Anger ripped through her. Images peppered her vision. Guy's face popped into her mind's eye—his sunny smile, the deep dimple that punctured one side of his face, the strong line of his jaw, his defined brow—the one she used to trace with her fingertips and kiss on moonless nights. He was a brilliant aviator, a gorgeous man and the kindest, gentlest soul she had ever met.

And he was never coming home. All thought ceased. Kelly choked back tears. Guy Flannigan was never coming home. Because he was dead.

Kelly loosened her grip on the controls. Her mind unwound. Her heart spilled open.

"We've got to turn around," the man next to her said urgently as he reached for her. "We've gotta go back."

No longer screaming at her, his voice was calm. Cool. Collected. Kelly checked her instruments. She had altitude. Airspeed was good. Moving her gaze up and over the instrument panel, she was met by a whitewash of sky ahead. The dark helicopter wasn't coming at her anymore. It had gone down.

The realization slit like a knife. A chopper was down.

She whipped a glance out her window. *Which direction was she flying?*

Dropping her gaze to the compass, she noted they were heading east. *East*. How far had she flown? How far past her drop spot had she gone?

Kelly had no way of knowing. With no landmarks to work from, it was like flying through a bowl of milk. She glanced to her side. *Did this guy know?*

Sean stared at her with hard blue eyes, eyes that felt like they could see right through her.

Kelly was lost. He knew it. She knew it.

"Are you okay?" he asked.

Kelly looked at him. No. She wasn't okay. None of this was okay.

"Bravo six-niner, do you copy?"

Kelly's mind blanked momentarily at the numbers being recited over the radio. Sean gave a subtle nudge with his gaze. *He's talking to you.* Recognizing the voice, she realized at once that yes, *she* was bravo six-niner and she sputtered, "Bravo six-niner, copy."

"Report status," Roan said.

Kelly looked out her window. She had no idea. "I'm headed east."

"Are you coming back?"

Coming back. Her heart wrenched. *I am, I am—but Guy...*

No. He wasn't coming back. He was never coming back.

"Repeat, are you coming back?"

"Yes," she replied shakily, plugging back into the situation, the voice skewering her through her headset. She had to stop. *Get a grip.* This wasn't Afghanistan. It was the mountains of Colorado.

"Are you okay?"

The caginess of Roan's voice said it all. He knew she'd lost it. She'd lost it in front of him—in front of the entire team on board her helicopter. *They all knew...*

Shame buckled her confidence. "I'm fine," Kelly lied, dodging Sean's hard stare. She wasn't fine. Everyone knew she wasn't fine—the Army staff therapist, her superiors, her father—everyone. They had claimed she wasn't grieving properly. Said she wasn't taking the time to mourn the loss of her fellow soldier, enabling her to continue the mission. If she didn't grieve, she'd never heal.

Seriously? How did one heal a gaping hole in their chest? Her soul had been ripped from her body and tossed into the flames of war. You didn't *grieve* a loss like hers. You lived with it, dealt with it—that's what a soldier did. That's what she did.

"I need to know if you can continue with the rescue."

Drawn to the steady sound of Roan's voice, Kelly wrenched her attention back to him. She was back in the cockpit of the AStar. She was flying search and rescue. She had a duty to perform. "Yes, of course. I can continue."

"Kelly...you don't have to do this."

Roan's guttural soft whisper cut her in two. *Yes*, she did. She did have to do this, more than anything else in the world. Tears burned in her eyes. If Sean looked at her, he'd plainly see, her sunglasses providing no protection from his stare— his impenetrable, unforgiving stare. But Roan. He was giving her an out. He was giving her a pass, a ticket to return to base.

It was an out she couldn't take. Not now, not like this. "I do," she said, before her throat closed. This was about her, about Guy. She couldn't turn back in failure. *Not again*.

"Then you need to turn around."

"I know, I know," Kelly replied. As if ensnared in a spider's web, she tried to untangle her mind from the threads of her past. She had to focus. Her mind had to be clear. But there was nothing clear about this weather. "I'm coming back, but I don't know where I am."

"Sean can help you."

Kelly darted a glance at him. Sean was looking at her, the icy blue of his eyes questioning. He wasn't convinced. He doubted her. The scent of dog trickled into her nostrils. She could only imagine what was running through everyone's minds. The guy in the back was oblivious to the conversation, but not the logistics. He would have felt the near miss, seen the chopper go down. At this point, the SAR team probably questioned their odds of getting home alive.

Kelly firmed her resolve. She couldn't let it get to her. She couldn't give up and return to base. She'd come on this mission to save lives and that's what she was going to do. She had the GPS coordinates for the downed skiers, same as Sean. Mentally refiguring her whereabouts, her hands moved the controls, altering her course back toward the original heading. Sean watched but said nothing.

"I'm transporting Hal down," Roan said, "but I'll be back up."

"Roan—you can't!" she blurted, surprised by her own outburst. Darting a glance to her side, she saw her shock mirrored in Sean's gaze. "You can't come back—you have zero visibility."

"I'll be back," he said flatly. "Your job is to drop the team so they can help with the search."

For Canyon. The missing skier. "What about the others? Did you get them?"

"I'll be back," he repeated.

What was he thinking? Nerves skittered through her pulse. Roan couldn't land in this mess any better than she could. Worse, now he felt like he had to take the risk and come back for the others because she had disgraced herself. She had fallen apart before their very eyes and no one believed her capable. Not that she could blame them. Had she been sitting in Sean's seat, she would have yanked the controls away and taken over command of the aircraft!

Drilling into her instruments, Kelly couldn't escape a sense of looming disaster. The SAR members on board had lost confidence in their pilot. Their lives were in her hands and they'd lost confidence, but no one uttered a word. What could they say? *Hey, don't crash? Hey, get us down immediately?*

It was a joke. A very bad joke. They were the helpless ones in the situation. Kelly was in control. She was in charge of the aircraft and all lives aboard. Normally, it was a position she lived for, one she'd been groomed for. But staring at a sheet of nasty white swirling snow, she couldn't blame them for fearing the worst. She hadn't given them reason to think otherwise.

Watch out world, the eagle is airborne.

The words pulled at her. The drum of rotor blades vibrated in her chest. She could do this. *Kelly Jones is a fighter, not a whiner. That's right*, she reaffirmed silently. She was an Apache combat pilot, a skilled aviator. She'd been in worse predicaments than this—

Instantly, visions of Guy's chopper going down erupted in her mind but she pushed them away. No. *Yes,* that was a bad day—a tough day and one she'd survived—but there had been others. She'd flown a ton of missions and survived them all. *Remember*, she told herself, resisting the urge to think of Guy. *Remember who you are, what you can do. Don't let this situation best you.*

Tightening her hold on the controls, Kelly repeated her silent mantra. *You can do this. You've done it before and you can do it again.* Sharpening her gaze on the instruments, she oriented herself to the situation at hand.

"We're nearing the zone," Sean said.

Yes. Her mind registered the fact as he said it. They would be there within minutes.

Glancing out the side window, she saw dark patches against the white of snow. *They must be clumps of evergreen or boulders, neither of which bode well for landing*. Which was her next task. She had to get this bird on the ground—a ground she couldn't altogether see. She couldn't see the ski-ers. She couldn't see Roan. She could barely define separate mountains from sky.

Sean leaned forward and to the side, also scouring the ground below.

"Do you see anything?"

"Negative."

But they were on the coordinates. Had Roan been estimating? Were they off, and if so, by how much? Kelly circled the area, scouting for a place to land—a tough proposition considering she couldn't see a hundred feet ahead of her, let alone below her. The snow should be fairly packed, but how steep? And if she landed too far from the skiers, could they physically get to the helicopter? What were the conditions on the ground?

There were too many variables. Kelly glanced over her shoulder to the man in the back, then to Sean. That's where the SAR team came in. It was their job to rescue the skier and get him on board. Only one problem. They first had to find their victim—make that two victims; Canyon and the downed chopper.

"Drop us!"

Kelly flinched, startled by the sharp bite of Sean's voice.

"Drop us—now! There!" he shouted, pointing out his side of the aircraft. "I see the chopper!"

The downed chopper?

Kelly swung the helicopter hard right and instantly glimpsed a dark mass of black on the ground. Her heart missed a beat. There was no denying what that was. The outline was unmistakable. Memories of another downed chopper shoved in, but she shoved them back. This wasn't Guy. This wasn't a combat zone.

This was Colorado. "I see it," Kelly said calmly.

"What's going on?" Roan asked.

"We have visual on the downed chopper," she replied without thinking and pushed her controls forward. "I'm going in."

"Kelly, wait—" he said.

There was no waiting. There was no else but her. Decisions needed to be made and they needed to be made quickly. Years of training suddenly took over and Kelly dropped the AStar in a swirl toward the ground.

Chapter Twelve

"Kelly, do you copy?"

She didn't respond. With every foot of altitude, Roan's stomach twisted tighter and tighter. He had to get Hal down, then get himself back up to rescue the rest of the crew. He couldn't trust her. Not by the sound of her voice. She was losing it. Recalling the hollow sound, he corrected himself— make that *lost* it.

Roan stared out into the mess of weather, the unforgiving terrain. The system was ruthless. At this point, he could only hope that Kelly wouldn't crash, killing all on board the AStar.

"What's going on up there?" Wade demanded.

"I thought Kelly went down," Roan replied.

"Is she okay?"

"I think so," he returned, confused by the fact that Wade didn't seem to understand the extent of the situation. *Had he not heard?*

It was possible, Roan mused. It was known as a communication shadow, and it sometimes happened when pilots flew in and around the mountains. Sometimes signals from peak to base dropped. Sometimes radio transmission could be intermittent. If Wade had heard, he would have said something. Roan pushed the thoughts from his mind. He steadied his hands on the controls, shifting his focus to getting Hal Richardson off this mountain. The doctor was stable, but clearly in pain. But he'd be okay. The flight nurse would see to his condition until they made the handoff at the hospital. It was Roan's job to get them there.

Lifting just above the mountains, Roan chose his line of travel. He'd head straight down the ridge, bank west, and fly the remaining distance over town. Watching his instruments, he noted the winds had picked up. It would slow his rate of descent—a snail's pace as it was—but there wasn't a thing he could do about it. Weather was volatile. Unpredictable. All he could do was react accordingly.

Unpredictable. Roan couldn't get the sound of Kelly's voice out of his head. It had been so unlike her. Normally she was a bull. Rock-solid. She was cocky, confident. On top of her game. What he'd heard coming at him over the radio was anything but. It sounded like a panic attack, like she was reliving a bad day in combat. *Did she have PTSD?*

Roan was familiar with the post-traumatic stress disorder of combat veterans. His uncle had become a horrible alcoholic because of it, refusing help from the service, from his family, opting for relief from the bottle instead. Over the years, he revealed little about the events that had caused the stress, and Roan's mother never asked. She simply loved. She loved her brother until the day he died, never once forsaking him because he'd come home from faraway places angry and bitter. He wasn't the same man who had gone to war, but she never gave up on him.

A deep ache swam through Roan's heart. His mother was amazing. She was strong and sensitive, but the battle with her brother had been difficult, a private hell Roan had once witnessed late at night. He found her sitting alone in the dark. She'd been crying. Said she didn't want to disturb anyone, but couldn't get the tears to stop as she imagined what her brother had gone through, what he had endured. She said it almost felt like she was imagining the trauma, visualizing the horrors and then reliving them herself.

It made Roan hate the enemy. Scars had been cut deep into his family, emotional in nature, exacting physical consequences. His uncle drank himself to death. His mother was worrying herself to death. Watching it all unfold before his eyes made Roan burn to carry on the fight...if only it wouldn't take a toll on his mother.

At the sudden pound in his chest, Roan took a deep breath. *Breathe*, he reminded himself. *Fly. You don't need to*

*be flying over a foreign land to serve. This is where you be-
long. This is where you help. The man in this helicopter needs
you.* Like so many who had come before him, Hal needed
Roan's experience and expertise—it meant the difference
between life and death.

Steadying his breathing, Roan methodically swooped
down and turned, cruising over the first rooftops, brown and
heavy with snow, as he flew his bird at very low altitude.
These were some of Silver Creek's most expensive homes
located midway up the mountain and boasting ski-in, ski-out
luxury for those who could afford it. The real estate was
pricey and while he had to admit they were beautiful, owning
a fancy house wasn't an indulgence he desired. He preferred
the freedom of flying overhead. Flying gave him pleasure;
flying with the SAR gave him purpose.

He saved lives.

"Patient status?"

"Stable," the flight nurse replied.

Goose and his medic had stayed back with the others, in-
sistent on securing their safety in case of unexpected circumstances. They already had one downed chopper. Kelly could
make it two, and if the storm worsened, it would prevent
Roan's return. He closed his eyes and mouthed a silent prayer. *Let them be okay. Let everyone be okay and ease this
storm. Give Kelly the guidance she needs. Shield those on the
ground from the battery of wind and snow.*

But despite his best efforts to the contrary, Roan
couldn't shake visions of Kelly losing control. The repercussions of her failure couldn't be ignored. Not professionally,
not personally.

Static erupted over the radio jarring his thoughts.

"We have you in sight."

"Copy that," Roan replied and shifted his attention back
to where it needed to be: the hospital and his patient's
transport. He could see the hospital's rooftop helipad, where a
crew of about a half-dozen people hung near the stairwell
exit. It was their usual drill, one he'd worked a hundred times

before. At least the weather wasn't an issue here. Down in the village of Silver Creek, snowfall was more of an angry flurry than the relentless blizzard he'd just flew out of. It was a fairly normal phenomenon in high country and, at the moment, a fact for which Roan was grateful.

In the muted gray cabin of his chopper, he detected a rustle of activity behind him. The flight nurse was preparing to unload the patient. Roan had no idea what condition Hal was in at the moment. He only knew that the man had been stabilized but, was in severe pain and in need of emergency surgery. Roan's current objective was about to be complete. What came next wouldn't come easy. Not if he knew Wade Davis, it wouldn't.

Roan hovered over the helipad with a steady hand and a focused eye, the men and women below him bracing against the whip of rotor blades while he lowered his aircraft. Landing was a process that couldn't be rushed, though every fiber in Roan's being was firing in a hot frenzy. He didn't have time for slow and steady, not when he had Kelly flying wild in the mountains, his friends stuck on the ground, and Canyon still missing. Roan needed to be up there.

Touching skids to the ground in a soft thud, he held steady while the flight nurse went into action. He had to unhook Hal from the spine board and transfer him to the awaiting gurney but he couldn't do it alone. The team on the ground rushed toward the aircraft, ducking as they neared. Assisting the onboard nurse, they unwrapped Hal from the board and carry bag and transferred him to the gurney.

Can you speed it up? Roan wanted to shout, knowing an outburst would be useless. There was no hurrying the process. This group was experienced; they knew how to make the transfer, detach the patient from the helicopter rescue equipment, assess his condition, immobilize his leg. It was a process that took time. Time *nobody* wanted extended. In fact, if anyone wanted that patient unhooked and wheeling away on a gurney as quickly as possible, it was the hospital crew. Dr.

Hal Richardson was one of their own. This was his base of operations, his team of co-workers. Hal might be a valued member of SAR, but he was a physician first, volunteer rescuer second.

Roan swung his gaze up the mountain and buried it in the plume of gray and white clouds. There was too much for one helicopter rescue team to handle. Especially with a pilot who might be mentally compromised. Kelly needed help. They all needed his help, but he couldn't make a move until he delivered his cargo safe and sound.

Once the staff had Hal secured, they would transport him to the operating room, where one of his orthopedic associates would perform a procedure to repair the damage to his leg. Roan inwardly cringed. From what he understood, it was bad—an injury Hal wouldn't walk away from for quite some time. It was a reality that wouldn't sit well with Hal, but the man had assumed the risks willingly. *No guts, no glory. Thrills can kill.* Every skier up there understood what they were getting into—the potential of what they were facing—and they went for it anyway. Roan knew firsthand that the thrill of untouched powder was worth it. Most times it proved an incredible experience. Other times, not so much.

At least Hal was alive. It was more than he could say for some of the skiers they'd come across in their roles with SAR. Roan's stomach tensed. Buried alive, crushed like ragdolls against trees and boulders, others lost for days due to the extreme conditions. Ski accidents could be a brutal way to go. Roan's thoughts immediately went to Canyon. Had they heard from him?

Roan had received no further contact from Kelly and her crew. He could only hope it was because they were in the middle of a rescue operation but staying in communication was critical. Especially between pilots. Speaking of communication, it was time to touch base with Wade and let him know what was going on. A flurry of nerves skirted through his pulse. Wade wasn't going to like his decision, but Roan had no other choice. Steeling his resolve, he said, "Delta three-eight to base, do you copy?"

"Copy, base," Wade replied.

"Patient is being transferred to hospital. Heading up to recover the remaining skiers."

"Don't take the chance, Roan. Kelly said she has it covered. At this point, it's too dicey for you to head back up."

Roan's heart stopped. Wade didn't know about Kelly. She had lost it. *They shot him. He's down.* She'd lost touch with reality and Roan couldn't be certain that the break wasn't complete. It sounded like she thought she was still in combat. Could Sean talk sense into her and get her under control?

They had a downed chopper. A real one. Doubt pushed in and Roan fought a wave of panic. Kelly couldn't handle it alone. There were too many variables. These people were his friends. The conditions were treacherous. Wade was right. No one should be flying up there but these were extreme circumstances. And no one knew how to navigate them better than Roan. Friends or not, there was no way he was chancing fate to an unstable pilot.

A rock formed in the pit of his stomach as he considered his next words. Telling Wade about the incident with Kelly would ground her. There was no way she could be signed off without a complete psychological evaluation and that, in and of itself, could possibly end her aviation career. Every pilot understood the drill. Any hint of mental instability on a pilot's medical record could mean losing the license to fly. Whether it was a bad breakup with a girlfriend, a solitary panic attack, or full-blown PTSD, a mark was a mark—and in this game, you only got one strike.

You're out.

"Wade," Roan began. "Kelly can't do it alone. There are too many passengers that need to be ferried down and I'm already in the air."

"I can't send you up there, Roan. You know the danger of this weather better than I do. It'll rip your bird to pieces."

"I can't leave them up there, Wade." Roan paused and let it sink in. Them. Lisa. Walsh. Canyon. They were Wade's friends, too. "I can do this. The weather is flyable. The Augusta can handle it."

"I can't authorize it."

"I'm volunteering."

"In SAR's chopper!"

Roan heard the implication. He was risking an aircraft he didn't own—a very expensive aircraft at that. Frustration welled. But the alternative was unacceptable. He couldn't abandon his friends! Gritting his teeth, he said, "I can do it, Wade. You've gotta trust me on this one. I can do it." He *had* to do it. There was no way he was leaving them up there.

"I'll take responsibility for the aircraft," Katharine said urgently.

Shocked to find Katharine at his shoulder, Wade's heart pinched at the desperation in her golden brown eyes. *She shouldn't be here listening to the blow-by-blow. There's no telling what she might overhear.* "Katharine..."

"Please," she implored. "Canyon trusts Roan. If anything happens to the helicopter in the process, I'll replace it. Brand new, better than before."

Wade had no doubt that Katharine had the money to do so. The cost of a brand spanking new Augusta K2 wouldn't put a dent in the Wainwright fortune. If the mishap with her company jet caused by one Roan Phillips didn't prove it, nothing would. Katharine hadn't blinked at the cost of repairs for the Gulfstream, the damage caused during the process of saving her life, and she wouldn't blink now. This time, it was to save Canyon's.

Wade hesitated. Still... Just because she could afford it, didn't mean that he should condone it. It was too dangerous. They already had one chopper down on his watch. He didn't need a second.

Katharine placed a hand on his shoulder and whispered, "I'm begging you. Please. If Roan wants to go up, *let* him."

Cody whimpered.

The dog's cry drew a haggard sigh from Wade. "Okay." There was no way he could argue with her. He could only hope he didn't regret the decision later. Keying his mic, he said, "Go ahead, Roan. But be careful."

"Roger that," Roan replied.

Chapter Thirteen

Kelly blocked out everything but the outline of the downed helicopter. Switching her line of vision from instrument panel to her target drop, she gauged distance and angle and tried to determine her best descent path for landing. But with the snow whipping sideways and steam fogging her windows, nothing looked good. Nothing!

How could she possibly land in this mess? She looked to Sean. He was as intent as she, his gaze moving between her and the landscape outside. It seemed he was thinking the same thing. *Where do we put down*?

Maybe they could jump. The thought was as instantaneous as it was crazy. Kelly kicked herself. They couldn't jump—it was too risky. But as she talked herself out of it, she realized it might be the only way. She flicked her glance sideways. "I might not be able to land."

"Get us as close as you can."

Her insides zipped closed. Sean understood. This wasn't his first leap off a cliff. He understood the stakes and was willing to risk them. Behind them, the dog whimpered, more eager cry than whine. Seemed everyone was ready for the challenge at hand. But was she?

The eagle is airborne. Kelly swallowed hard. The eagle was airborne, all right, and coming in for a hot landing. "I need all eyes on the ground," she commanded. "I'm circling around. I might be able to squeeze in to the right of the aircraft."

Sean turned, following the spot she indicated.

It looked clear enough, with no huge obstacles or dark colorations indicating rock or tree.

Finding comfort in the constant whir of engine, Kelly relaxed her grip, took a deep breath, and slowly maneuvered above the wrecked chopper. The blades of her AStar picked up snow and swirled it around in a frenzy competing with the storm, but it wasn't enough to hide the sickening display below. Kelly's insides cringed. The black helicopter was a crumpled mass of steel, its tail broken clear from the fuselage, the rotor blades half buried in snow. She could barely make out the white identification numbers painted on its side. Scanning the immediate vicinity, she saw no sign of the pilot or co-pilot. Which wasn't good. It most likely meant they were trapped inside the aircraft and would require extraction. She wondered briefly as to their condition, but training kicked in and warned her that that was not her problem. Getting the rescue team to the chopper was her one and only goal.

Continually scanning the area around the helicopter on the off chance the pilot might have escaped and now would pose a hazard for her landing, she didn't see any signs of movement and continued with the painstaking descent. No mistakes. She could make no mistakes.

The door of the cabin slid open, allowing a brisk wind to lash her cheeks. Were they crazy? They couldn't jump from here! "Give me a minute," she said quickly. "I'm going to try to land."

Sean raised a hand to his cohorts in the back, signaling them to hold up.

Wait.

Let's see if this woman can get the job done.

Kelly grounded her jaw and brushed the imagined insult from her mind. She could do this. She was trained to do this. This is what she lived for. Well, maybe not a snow-covered mountaintop rescue, but flying through the thick of it, going where others feared to tread—that's who she was. Kelly Jones was a combat pilot, a woman who feared nothing.

Using the constant whir of engines to settle her mind, she steadied her hand, sharpened her senses, and lowered the bird. Snow swirled into the aircraft from the downwash. She wished the crew would close the door, but at this point it was irrelevant. They'd be opening it within seconds, anyway.

"You don't have to land," Sean told her. "We can take it from here."

They were fifteen feet above the ground. There was no way that dog could jump fifteen feet into the snow without injuring itself. "No, give me a second. I'll get you closer, though I might not be able to set down completely."

Now that she was this close, she realized the area was steeper than she first thought. Fighting against the chopper-induced whiteout, she couldn't be certain of the depth or density of the snow. If she landed and it was too soft it would spell disaster. She'd have to take it slow, foot by foot, and needed all eyes on the ground. "Keep watch for any objects."

"Roger," Sean replied.

Keeping a safe distance from the crashed helicopter, Kelly fought a gust of wind. It swept the aircraft upward as she tried to negotiate downward. Gritting her teeth, she pushed forward, downward, as the aircraft swung from side to side. The first skid made shaky contact and she gave Sean the thumbs-up. "Now's your chance!" she told him.

Sean yanked the headset from his head and hooked it to the cockpit ceiling its spiral cord dangling as he pushed out the door. The team in back did followed suit, jumping out after him. Kelly concentrated on the feel of her skid against the mountain. It was her one point of stability. It was also her greatest weakness, should the wind thrust her into the mountain. A black figure caught her attention as the team cleared the aircraft. Huh?

A gust of wind pitched the helicopter suddenly and her stomach lurched. "Crap!" She pulled back. It was the dog. Heart pounding, she thought she might have hit him. But glancing out her window, she counted three members of the SAR team steadily moving from the aircraft. She gulped. *Make that four*. The dog counted as a member of the team. More importantly, none had been sliced by the dip of her rotor blades. Kelly calmed her breathing. Heartbeats refused to settle, but she maintained a steady grip on the controls. Staring out the windshield, she debated what to do next.

This wasn't good. There was no way she could hold position very long without risking being blown off-kilter and into the mountain. Should she lift off? Should she hover above?

She flipped her gaze upward. Not in this mess. The ceiling was low and flat, the snow hammering at her. Kelly decided she was safer with at least some point of stability and that stability was her visual connection to the ground. Manning the aircraft, she had no contact with the men as they disappeared into the snowstorm. All she knew was that they were headed toward the chopper. Would they find a dead body? Men in need of medical help?

Alone with her thoughts, Kelly couldn't stem the flow of emotion. Guy Flannigan had probably been killed upon impact. She'd seen his chopper go down. It had hit hard, slammed into the ground. It was the kind of crash you didn't walk away from. But that didn't mean she had given up hope. She'd wanted to go back. She'd wanted to kill every sonofabitch within sight who had fired upon Guy's chopper, but her orders had been clear: return to base. There were too many of them and not enough of her.

A shiver raced up her spine. Sinking into her seat, she was covered in winter gear—gloves, helmet—the works. But her exposed nose and cheeks had been pricked by the freezing temps from the open cabin doors, and her seat felt cold. Ice-cold.

She hated the cold. Why was she here again?

She and Guy used to talk about retiring to a little coastal town in Southern California where life would be nothing but blue skies, sunny days, and easy living. They'd paid their dues working for the Army and would look forward to teaching civilians how to fly. Guy joked it would be as easy as pie. Kelly's heart wrenched; those days would never come to pass. Guy had paid the ultimate sacrifice and his easy days were now called "eternity" while hers... Hers were called—

Kelly staved off a rush of tears. Hers promised nothing but turbulence. Unable to brush the moisture from her eyes, she tried to rid herself of it with a shake of her head. *Focus, dammit! Forget about the past. This is your future. Saving lives, getting the job done. This is your new mission. Get these skiers off the mountain and down to safety. Serve others.* Like her father said, it would restore her sense of purpose.

She had agreed, and it was his suggestion that had steered her journey to Silver Creek. But working SAR could never do the one thing she needed it to do. Nothing could erase the memory of the one life she couldn't save. That was a mission she had failed and would have to live with forever.

"Bravo six-niner, do you copy?"

The crackle of static in her ear pierced her to the core. "Copy."

"I'm en route. Can you update me on your status?"

Kelly's heart squeezed. Which status was Roan referring to—her mental and emotional state of being, or her operational status? Deciding to opt for the easier response she replied, "We are making contact with the downed chopper. Crew is on the ground and in the middle of search and rescue operations."

"You're on the ground?"

Finding his skepticism humorous, she said, "Sort of. I'm holding one skid to the ground. It's pretty gusty up here, but we're managing."

Roan paused. "Weather getting worse?"

"Wouldn't say worse." Analyzing the situation on the fly, she said, "But if I had to call it, I'd say we might be swimming in soup for some time."

"Soup. That about sums it up," he agreed. "Any word on the pilot's condition?"

"Zero."

"Okay. I'll make contact with the others and keep you posted."

"Ten-four."

"And Kelly—" Roan stopped short but she could hear his next words before he spoke them. "Are you okay?"

Her first instinct was to lie. *I'm fine. Stupendous.* But Roan had done nothing to warrant a cursory brush-off. He was her team member, her partner in this disastrous rescue mission and she owed him the truth. Besides, he sounded sincere, his voice soft and genuine. A lump formed in her throat. It was the least she could do. "I've had better days."

"Are you sure?"

"I'm sure." Kelly fought a rise of doubt and expelled, "I've got this, Roan. We've got this."

"I'll update you in five."

Roan coasted over the issue without another word. "Roger that," she replied, overcome with a sea of emotion. Gratitude. Roan was a good guy. A bit cocky, a bit too good-looking for his own good, but he was decent. The women loved him and the men respected him. It wasn't a fatal combination. What *was* fatal was Kelly's come-apart in the sky. There was no hiding it. Not from Roan and certainly not from Sean. But Roan was the man in charge. If he wanted to make trouble for her, he could. Easily.

Would he? The question struck like a bolt of lightning. Would he turn her in for the episode? There was no way he could comprehend the depth and breadth of her emotions. Didn't have to. He knew what he'd heard. She had confused time and location. Sean saw it. Roan heard it. Fear peppered her chest. Her career was in his hands. Would he scrap her lessons and send her packing to the nearest psychiatrist?

Kelly didn't want to think about it—the repercussions not only with her license, but with her father...

Her life would be over. Plain and simple. If Roan turned her in and she lost her right to fly, her life would be over. Or might as well be, anyway.

Chapter Fourteen

Roan felt a rising tide of mixed emotions. Kelly sounded fine. She sounded in control. *Was she really holding skid to mountain in this mess?*

That was pretty ballsy stuff, even for him. Exhaling a tight sigh, he counted it as a positive—for the moment. PTSD was unpredictable. Things could change with a hair-trigger pull. One snag in the operation and Kelly could spiral right back to where she'd been—wherever that was—and Roan would be dealing with one colossal crisis.

"Delta three-eight to base, copy?"

"Copy base," Wade replied. "How's it going up there?"

"Kelly has affirmative contact with the downed chopper. Team's on the ground but no word on pilot status yet."

"Where are you?"

"I'm heading for the skiers, ETA four minutes. Any word from them?"

"Lisa and her group are holding tight with the medic. Goose went down to Walsh's location."

"Copy that. Any word from Walsh?"

"Negative."

Roan wasn't surprised. Walsh was used to working solo. He could move faster and stealthier than most men and was trained in medical rescue. He didn't really need Goose on his heel, but he wouldn't turn him away. An extra set of eyes on the ground would be welcome. "I'll set down and get the skiers loaded. Advise Walsh I'm en route."

"Will do."

"Five minutes before we hit destination," Roan alerted his flight nurse.

The man returned a thumbs-up.

Roan inhaled deeply. Five long minutes before he would know anything new.

His thoughts went to Kelly. He could only imagine what she must have gone through to cause such a breakdown. Had she lost someone close? Had she had a close call of her own? The triggers for PTSD were too numerous to count and custom-tailored to the individual involved. What spurned nightmares in one person didn't faze the next. What one couldn't bear to think about, another could tolerate with ease. Kelly seemed so competent and secure, so totally in control. It had to have been something bad to unravel her so completely. Concern pulled at him. Not that he faulted Kelly for her reaction—he only wanted to know more about its cause.

Sweeping his aircraft up over ridge after ridge, Roan relied on instinct and rote memory as he handled the controls. Commanding the helicopter through a sea of white, Roan felt like the storm was letting up. At least he was beginning to see the outlines of the mountains before he was practically upon them. Glancing at his navigation screen, he mentally mapped out the course he would take. Coming in from the west, he'd swoop over the area for a visual before deciding on a spot to land. If he *could* land. While the storm might feel as if it were easing its grip, that didn't mean it actually was. It could be wishful thinking. There was no denying that he was pushing the limits of his aircraft. Setting the bird down would be tough.

I'm holding one skid to the mountain.

Roan suppressed a swell of admiration. Kelly was a damn good pilot. For all the grief she'd given him, she knew her stuff when it came to flying. Like him, flying was an extension of her. It was part of who she was. He could tell when he watched her fly. She was fluid, natural. There were no jerky movements, no long hesitations. Even her near miss earlier had been followed by a clean, swift recovery. He'd given her a hard time about hovering in place, but that had more to do with her attitude than her ability. Flying was in her DNA. Thinking back to the sound of her voice—the distress, the momentary confusion—he imagined that losing her license to fly would probably kill her.

"I've got a visual on the skiers."

The flight nurse's voice brought Roan back into focus. "Where?"

"Down there, eight o'clock."

Roan dipped left and brought the skiers into view on his right. Sure enough, he could see Lisa's pink helmet and waving arm. A tightly wound sigh of relief escaped him. *Okay*. They had his chopper in sight. Counting bodies, he had four, plus Walsh, Goose, and Canyon not currently on scene. Despite receiving no word on Canyon's whereabouts, Roan wasn't counting him out. He'd be cargo, one way or another.

Cocking his head backward, he said, "I'm going to attempt a landing uphill of them. Keep your eyes peeled for any actives."

"Roger," the nurse replied.

"Actives" was Roan's term for people on the move. Not like anyone in this immediate area didn't know how to behave around a helicopter, but it was always better not to take chances.

Rotor blades whirring rhythmically above him, he moved in concert with the steady beat and worked his chopper downward. He wasn't worried about the quality of the ground snow. It would be hard-packed from the avalanche and solid as a rock. Not that he'd be getting out, but it mattered for his flight nurse. Struggling against a burst of wind, the aircraft rocked back and forth before touching down.

As the nurse unbuckled from his seat, Roan told him, "Tell Lisa to come here, then get the others loaded ASAP."

The flight nurse nodded and hopped out. Running crouched until he cleared the blade span, he continued full-height toward the skiers.

Roan counted the seconds as he watched the man exchange words with Lisa. She looked toward the helicopter, then to her friends, and gave what appeared to be a final few words of instruction to the flight nurse. Turning, she jogged toward Roan, her slender body traveling over the snow-packed terrain with more ease than the flight nurse had displayed. Ducking as she neared, she opened the door and popped into the seat next to him, quickly yanking the door closed. Her boots hit the ground with a noticeable thud. Without being told to, she removed her helmet and donned the headset. Bright-eyed and pink-cheeked, Lisa's smile was filled with enthusiasm. "Hey, Roan!"

"Hey, Lisa."

"Thanks for coming back for us. I don't know if Grant could have waited out the storm. Not in his condition."

"No problem. We'll have them on board in minutes. What about Walsh? Have you heard from him?"

As if this were the first time the subject had been mentioned, she pulled her cell phone from an interior pocket and stared at it. "No." The light extinguished from her eyes as she explained, "Last we spoke was twenty minutes ago. He and Goose were triangulating a search for Canyon. I'll try him again now."

Roan bit back the litany of questions pouring through his brain. Did Walsh have anything to go on? Did he have a Plan B? Did he intend to stay on the mountain until he found Canyon, dead or alive? It would be true to form. *No man left behind.* How many times had Roan heard that sentiment uttered from the man's lips? A Marine didn't leave his brothers on the battlefield and to Walsh, all of life was a battlefield.

He wouldn't be alone if he stayed. Goose would stay with him. The guy made a hobby out of summit climbing—including the big one, Mount Everest. Running marathons for fun, the guy was as fit as a triathlete. If anyone could hang strong with Walsh, it would be Goose.

Urgency gnawed at Roan as he waited for Lisa to get through. "No response?"

"He's not answering," she said grimly.

"Do you have reception?"

She looked at her phone screen and nodded. "Two bars."

At this altitude, two bars proved sketchy at best, but they couldn't give up. "Can you try again?"

Lisa did so, then slipped the slim phone inside her headset. The two waited.

Roan stared at Lisa. *C'mon, Walsh. Answer your phone!*

"Is it going to voice mail?"

"No," she replied, seemingly as surprised as Roan that Walsh wasn't picking up. "It's still ringing. Oh, wait—voicemail picked up."

"Try again," Roan clipped. "Please." He didn't want to be rude to Lisa, but they had to get through. He wasn't leaving here without knowing what was going on with Canyon.

Lisa dialed and this time, Walsh answered on the first ring. "Hello?"

"Walsh! What happened? I've been trying to call you."

"The damn phone slipped out of my pocket!" he barked.

Roan released a jagged breath. He could hear Walsh shouting through Lisa's headset. Thank God his failure to answer hadn't been due to anything more serious.

"Have you found Canyon?"

"No. Nothing. No beacon signal, no tracks, no response to voice calls."

Lisa slumped. "Oh, no." Her gaze dashed to Roan. "I'm in the helicopter with Roan."

"Good. You guys airborne?"

"No, not without you and Goose!"

"Go. Get the others down. I'm not leaving without Canyon."

Which Lisa knew full well, Roan mused. It was only the desperation of a woman in love undercutting her clear thinking.

"What do you want me to tell Roan?" she asked.

"Tell him status unchanged. Goose and I are covering as much ground as we can. We'll stay in contact with Wade."

Lisa turned to relay the information but Roan raised a hand. "I can hear every word he's saying," he said, and tapped a finger to the side of his helmet.

"Now what?" she uttered.

"We get you and the others loaded and go from there." Roan didn't want to leave Walsh up here anymore than Lisa did, but his decisions had to be rooted in more than personal concern. He had an aircraft to worry about. Make that two. Realizing he hadn't thought once about Kelly in the last five minutes, he quickly patched in. "Bravo six-niner, copy?"

"Copy."

"I've landed and am in process of picking up the stranded skiers. Walsh and Goose are off location searching for Canyon. What do you have, over?"

"Team is pulling pilot from crash site. Far as I can tell, it looks like he's alive, but I can't determine the extent of his condition. Will report back as soon as crew pulls him aboard."

"Roger." Roan breathed easier. Kelly sounded a lot better. Curt, professional, on top of her game. He felt better about the prospect of her ferrying the patient down. "Okay. Take him to the hospital. I'll let the staff know to expect you. Radio me when you're en route with ETA."

"Ten-four, over and out."

"Ten-four."

Roan couldn't shake the unsettling feeling in his gut. He was glad she seemed okay, but he couldn't let her episode go unaddressed. It would be wrong. Unethical. Maybe if she never wanted to step foot in a helicopter again, he could let it go, but he doubted that would be the case. And if his instincts were on target, he knew she'd be quite happy to sweep it into a dark closet and pretend it had never happened. No words, no worries. But he couldn't. On many levels, he couldn't allow the breakdown to pass unquestioned. He respected her too much.

Roan swallowed. On too many levels.

Chapter Fifteen

Kelly watched as Sean and his crew worked on the pilot while the black Labrador sat idle. They had pulled the man from the wreckage, laid him on the ground, and taken his vitals. Currently they had him covered with a blanket and were moving him to a transport bag, the orange of which was easy to see from her vantage point. Once they got him on board, they'd need to get them to the hospital.

A feat she was in charge of managing. Outside her windows, the storm didn't appear to be letting up. Not that she could tell for sure—not with her rotor blades churning up snow the way they were. At least she could take comfort in her co-pilot, of sorts. Sean seemed like a competent guy. Cool, level-headed, he lived this weather every year. He'd have a better idea of what they were facing. Not that it mattered. Storm or no storm, she was the one flying down to the village, not him.

In unison, the two men lifted the injured pilot from the ground and headed toward her as the woman led the way. The dog jumped to a stand and shook his body, sending snow in all directions before darting out ahead of them. Kelly grimaced at the amount of snow still clinging to the dog's body. Its fur was covered, which meant the interior of her aircraft would soon be covered as well—a mess she'd be responsible for cleaning. She rolled her eyes to the cabin ceiling. One more reason she didn't own a pet. They were messy and time-consuming.

Tightening her hold of the controls, she prepared for takeoff as the SAR team neared.

The dog bolted. Kelly's heart leapt. *What the*—

Bounding through the snow as though summoned by a whistle, the animal took off running. What the heck? Did these people not see what had just happened? She followed its track until she lost sight of it. Where did that dog think it was going?

The back door slid open and a torrent of frigid air whipped through the cabin, chilling Kelly's cheeks on contact. "Your dog ran off!" she shouted, angry they didn't have it on a leash. "Did you see where it went?"

Sean acknowledged her with a brisk nod but remained focused on getting the comatose-looking pilot inside as quickly as possible.

Kelly bit back a slew of commentary. Not like there was anything they could do about it at the moment—they were kinda of busy with a guy who wasn't looking good. He had a gash on his forehead, matting his dark hair against abnormally pale skin, and his lips were dry and bluish. Kelly's gaze swung back through the main windshield in search of the animal. The dog was gone. There was no sight of him. Nothing but snow and gray and mountain.

Dammit—this wasn't cool! Twisting in her seat, she checked the progress of the SAR team.

Strapping the injured pilot in, Sean yelled to her, "I'm going back for the dog!"

Before she could say a word, he disappeared and slammed the chopper door closed.

Kelly wanted to scream. She wanted to scream at the top of her lungs, "How are you going to find a dog in this mess? It's ludicrous!"

Weren't those dogs supposed to be well-trained? They weren't supposed to dash off after squirrels or who-knows-what! And what if Sean couldn't find him and the dog lost its way? A series of disturbing consequences tumbled through her brain and Kelly quickly shoved them aside. No. They couldn't lose the dog. The skiers and pilots chose to be up here—they assumed the risk—but the dog?

It wasn't the dog's choice to be up here! Scowling at the medics going about their business in the back, Kelly thought,

Seriously—can this day get any worse? She peered out her windshield. *Doubt it.*

"What's our ETA to the hospital?"

Startled by the voice in her ear over the comms, she turned. The medic had removed his snow gear and placed a headset over his head. Staring at her, his eyes were brown, the surrounding skin pale with the customary raccoon-eyed look of a skier who spent too much time on the mountain in goggles and sunshine. The look was quite dramatic against his deeply-tanned skin. "I don't know. It's weather dependent but I'd give it twenty, twenty-five once we're airborne." But with a missing dog? It was anyone's guess. Kelly glanced outside and her stomach clenched. "Can we come back for the dog?"

"No, worries," the medic replied. "Sean will get him. Rugby belongs to him."

"Rugby? Is that the dog's name?"

"Yes, ma'am. Rugby the Great."

Glad for the menial chit-chat to unwind her tension, she took a deep breath and asked, "How did he get that name?"

The guy laughed. "Because he's the biggest and the best!"

"Uh, I'd say that's up for debate," his counterpart objected. The woman's ocean-green eyes danced with amusement amidst her fair skin and pert features. "Buck might have something to say about that."

"Buck?" Kelly asked.

"She means Canyon's dog," the other replied. "Buck is a pretty big boy and has been working search and rescue for about as long as Rugby. There's kind of a running contest between the two."

A contest? Between rescue dogs? Kelly had no idea such things existed, but it made sense. Men made a contest of most things. Why *not* their dogs' performance on the SAR team?

Talk of Canyon saddened her. He was the missing skier, the one Roan had still made no mention of finding, a fact she was sure he would have shared with the team on board her helicopter if he had news to report. She didn't know Canyon personally, only knew that he was an integral part of SAR. "How's the patient?" she asked, abruptly changing subjects. "Is he going to make it?"

"We think so," the gal answered. "His vitals are weak, but steady, and he responded in pain when we moved him."

Kelly pulled back. "And that's a good sign?"

"It means he's conscious and semi-alert. We think he might have some broken bones, but we have no way of assessing any internal injuries until we get him to the hospital."

And that's where you come in—we hope. They were unspoken words, but Kelly couldn't imagine the two weren't thinking them. They'd been onboard for her meltdown. They had heard the crazy talk spewing from her lips. *They shot him. I have to go back for him. The sand, it's too dense. I can't see him.* Kelly remembered her lunacy verbatim. Did they?

She turned a shoulder to the crew and settled into her seat, forward-facing. The vibration of engines reverberated through her hand, up her arm. She looked at her instruments, out the window. Kelly didn't want to look at them anymore. Or wonder what they must think of her. She shuddered. Could they ever work with her again? Would they revolt if they knew she was the pilot in command on future operations?

Kelly looked out her window, overcome by a wave of depression. If she messed this mission up, where would she go? What would she do? Would she ever be able to fly again?

She didn't kid herself. There was no way Roan could let this pass. He had to report her.

Or did he? A burst of hope exploded in her gut. He was a nice guy. Maybe he'd understand. Maybe he'd hear her out and give her the benefit of the doubt. He understood the rules were too strict regarding the mental health of pilots. He knew there were gray areas in a pilot's life. There were gray areas in everyone's life. He could see she was capable of handling herself. She'd come this far, hadn't she? She'd even ease up on his refusal to sign her off. *Take all the time you need,* she'd tell him. *I'll prove to you that I'm fit to fly.*

Tuning in to the pulsations of the aircraft, Kelly sank lower into her seat. One hand on the lever between her legs, one hand on the control by her side, she hunkered down. Roan held all the power on this one. It was his to wield as he saw fit.

"Bravo six-niner, do you copy?"

Kelly jumped at the crackle of Roan's voice in her headset. "Bravo six-niner," she snapped.

"What's your status?"

"I have patient onboard but we've lost the dog. Sean went to go look for it."

"You lost Rugby?"

Why did Roan make it sound like it was her personal failure? "The dog bolted when they were carrying the patient to the helicopter," she told him. "It wasn't like there was anything I could do about it!"

"What more can go wrong?"

Panic rose sharply at his question. She wanted to ask if he was referring to Canyon, but didn't dare. "Did something else happen?"

"It was a rhetorical question."

Flushed with relief, she felt stupid.

"I've landed and the crew is getting the skiers onboard," he went on. "Walsh and Goose are going to stay behind and search for Canyon."

"You're going to *leave* them?"

"I have no choice. Walsh is adamant and Goose is with him. Besides, at this point we have more cargo than space between us. Someone's going to have to stay behind."

"But Roan, there's no telling when this storm is going to let up!"

"Agreed, but Walsh has made his decision. I'm not going to change his mind."

It was a sentiment Kelly understood. Walsh wasn't just a heli-skier—he was a Marine. *No man left behind.* He'd hike down with Canyon on his back if the situation warranted. It was the way he'd been trained. It was who he was. Kelly had met a lot of Marines, and they were all the same.

They were men she admired. "Okay." Switching gears, she said, "The medics say Sean should find the dog pretty easily. I'll radio when I'm en route to the hospital."

"Copy."

Movement out her window caught Kelly's eye. "What the—?"

"What's going on?" Roan asked.

"I don't know," she mumbled into her mic, her gaze following the slow-moving figure as it trudged through the snow. "Is that Sean?" Kelly turned, asking her crew. "Do you see him?" She looked for signs of the dog but saw nothing.

But it couldn't be Sean. This guy wasn't wearing a red jacket. His was black. He was in all black, actually. Kelly squinted. At least it looked like black. Maybe it was red? *Oh, no!* A horrible thought struck and her heart caught. Had there been a co-pilot they had missed onboard the downed chopper?

"What's going on, Kelly?" Roan demanded.

Detecting a suspicion in his voice, like he was worried she was losing it again, Kelly stated firmly, "We've got an individual walking toward the aircraft. I can't make out who it is—could be Sean, could be someone else."

"With the dog?"

"Wait a minute—make that two."

"Two what?"

"Two people." Another black-clad figure lunged through the milky white. "And a dog," Kelly added. There was no mistaking the identity of the animal. She turned backward and asked over the comms, "Guys, what's going on out there?"

The two medics peered out the window.

"Looks like Sean and Rugby and..."

"Did we miss a co-pilot somewhere?"

"I didn't see one," the guy said, sharing a stunned glance with the woman. "But could be he escaped from the aircraft after it went down."

"Roan?" Kelly asked, her eyes glued to the figures moving toward her. "Did our heli-skiing chopper pilot have a co-pilot?"

"Jack? No, he flies solo. Why?"

"Because we've got two men headed toward our chopper."

"Two?"

"Two," she confirmed.

"Call me as soon as they reach you."

"Ten-four."

Chapter Sixteen

At least Roan didn't *think* Jack had had a co-pilot. He turned and asked, "Lisa, did Jack have a co-pilot on board with him today?"

She shook her head. "Nope. Just Jack. Why?"

"Because Kelly's reporting that she found another person at the crash site."

Lisa's eyes rounded. "Another person? Do you think it could be Canyon?"

Roan's heart thwacked against his ribs as Lisa said the name aloud. That had been his thought exactly. "I don't know," he replied, his voice suddenly shaky. "I doubt there were any other skiers up there, but it's possible. What do you think?"

"Ask her!" Lisa exclaimed, punching her gloved hands together.

"Kelly," Roan said. "Have they reached you, yet?"

"Negative. Give me about two minutes."

Two minutes.

Two minutes. Two minutes seemed like an eternity at the moment!

The back door to Roan's aircraft slung open and his crew slid Grant Powell inside. Climbing in behind him, one of the guys reached a hand for Kinsley Fairchild, who scrambled to the opposite side of the interior. "Am I ever glad to see you!" she exhaled in a rush of breath, her voice muted but audible over the sound of engines. "I thought I was going to die of hypothermia!"

Roan nodded, but his thoughts were divided between loading his passengers and the mysterious stranger approaching Kelly's chopper.

Kinsley took position near Grant's head. Sliding her goggles up and over her helmet, she brought gloves to her face and blew. Her nose was bright pink, a matching pair with Lisa's, and her dark brown eyes were vibrant and alert. Long brown hair fell in strands around her face as she steered clear of the crew securing Grant for the flight.

Lisa remained silent by Roan's side, the two of them sharing a weighty gaze. Seconds passed like hours. When was Kelly going to make contact?

"Whew—it's cold enough out there to make a polar bear move to Florida!" Kinsley exclaimed.

Lisa smiled at her comment, but Roan could feel that her thoughts were not here with her friend, but rather with Kelly and her crew. Roan was tempted to call Kelly and ask about the individual in question, but decided to wait. She'd call him.

Roan's radio erupted with Wade's voice. "Was that Kelly I heard?"

"Roger that," Roan replied. Guess some of her signal *was* getting through.

"Do you think they found Canyon?" he asked.

It was the million-dollar question. "Don't know. Kelly found somebody extra up there."

"Okay. Let me know as soon as you hear. I'm not trusting her signal. Damn unreliable is what it is."

"Will do," Roan replied, thinking how lucky Kelly was that Wade hadn't heard a word of her breakdown a while back. Eventually he would hear of it, but not now. Not yet.

Katharine clung to Wade's side and peered up at him with a hopeful, tawny gaze. "Do you think it's Canyon?"

"It could be, but I don't want you to get your hopes up."

"But who else could it be? You said the heli-skiing pilot didn't have a co-pilot."

"No, but he could have picked up a passenger while he was refueling." Wade knew that was unlikely, but possible.

"Wade, *please*." She pulled at his arm. "You told me this helicopter went down near the avalanche site, so it could be Canyon, if he somehow managed to walk over there."

"That's a big '*if.*'"

"But it's possible."

Wade hated to get her hopes up, but yes, it was possible. Even made sense. But it could be a stray hiker drawn to the downed helicopter and the chance for a free ride out of the hazardous conditions. People had freedom to travel high country. There was no telling who was camped out up there at any given time. Take McIntyre Walsh. He'd been up there for almost a year, surprising Lisa with his unexpected presence—luckily for her. A murderer had also been spending time in the wilderness and had been stalking unsuspecting female hikers. It was later discovered that he'd been responsible for six murders—six—across the state of Colorado, and all the while, he'd been taking refuge in the mountains above Silver Creek. Hell—this stranger of Kelly's could be anyone!

But Katharine wanted it to be Canyon. Wade didn't blame her. He wanted the same. Except that he was prepared for disappointment. Katharine was not.

Kelly gaped in disbelief as she glimpsed another figure outside. *Make that three men*, she mused. One had been lagging behind as the first two neared the chopper. The back door slid open and Rugby leapt in with an assist from Sean, who then stepped aside, allowing the stranger to poke his body inside. He was covered in snow from head to toe, his ski jacket collar pulled up to his goggles and helmet so that she couldn't make him out. He looked at the injured pilot, the onboard medics and then to Kelly. He removed his goggles, and the greenest eyes she'd ever seen penetrated her to the bone. *McIntyre Walsh.*

Breath escaped her. She'd met the man on more than one occasion, but coming face-to-face with those eyes was heartstopping. It felt as though he were cutting straight through her with his gaze.

"We need equipment," Walsh said loudly over the roar of engines.

Equipment? *What for*? Kelly wanted to ask, but Walsh was already pointing to a backpack in the rear cabin. "Is this packed for an overnighter?" he shouted to the medics.

The female nodded.

Walsh dragged the bulky pack toward him then slid it onto his back. "You have any supplies in here that you need?"

"No. We can live with what we have in this one." She tapped a hand to an identical backpack that was sitting by her side.

Walsh buckled the waist strap around his body. "Goose and I aren't leaving without Canyon."

Sean pulled a headset dangling from the cabin ceiling by a spiral cord and spoke into it. "Walsh and Goose are going to resume the search. I'm going to stay back with them."

"What? But what are you going to do if you find Canyon? Roan and I might not be able to make it back up here."

"We'll do whatever needs to be done, but at least now we'll better the odds of finding him." Sean glanced toward the rear of the chopper. "I'm taking Rugby with me."

Kelly had forgotten about the dog.

"Are you okay to make it down without me? You want Goose to fly down with you?"

"What?" *No—why would I need that*? she wanted to ask, realizing at once what he was insinuating. Sean didn't trust her to fly without an extra pair of eyes. "No. Are *you* okay staying up here knowing we might not be able to come back for you?"

"It's how SAR operates. We can't fit everyone on this chopper anyway."

She paused. *Good point. But still...*

Kelly glanced back at Walsh, who'd already replaced his helmet.

Sean moved to the rear of the aircraft and made a hand gesture toward the dog. Rugby popped up and stepped gingerly along the body of the injured pilot as he made his way to his master. Sean grabbed a bottle of water from his bag and stuffed it into the front of his jacket. He spoke to one of the flight nurses. The man rose from his seated position and eased out the back.

When the nurse circled around the men and hopped into the seat next to Kelly, she couldn't stave off a flash of resentment. Clearly, Sean had instructed the man to join her up front—to keep an eye on her. But she wasn't about to argue. Picking a fight with either of these two was at the bottom of her to-do list. She needed their silence.

Sean waved to the crew and moved away from the aircraft with Walsh and Goose, their bodies crouched as they waded through deep snow until they cleared the blade-spread. Rugby leapt outside and ran to catch up with them, leaping through the swath of trail.

They made quite a group, Kelly thought, three men and a dog heading off into the wilderness. Her next thought was Roan's reaction. He wasn't going to like this. She could hear it in his voice—he'd been expecting Canyon. "Delta three-eight, copy?"

"Copy. What do you have?"

"It was Walsh."

"Walsh?" Roan's shock sounded complete. "What's he doing near you?"

"He needed supplies. Seems he saw us land and headed over to get a backpack. It appears they're planning on settling in for the duration."

"Ten-four," Roan said, his voice laced with disappointment. "Base, did you copy?"

"Base, copied."

Wade cursed under his breath. He didn't want to look at Katharine, but he couldn't avoid her. She stood squarely by his side. Stunned. Immobile. Tears filled her eyes, rolled down her cheeks. Her lips began to quiver as she unraveled Wade's professionally-imposed calm. "Katharine, don't," he said, taking her into his arms. She fell against him lifelessly. Wordlessly. "It doesn't mean anything," he continued. "No news is good news, remember? Canyon's a strong guy. He's handled worse. He's going to surprise you and your cell phone will ring any minute with the good news. You only have to hold the faith."

Wade hated that he was lying to her, but he couldn't stand to see her in such pain. Odds were against Canyon on this one. Avalanches were unforgiving. They hit and they hit hard taking most everything in their path with them. For good. Wade couldn't count the number of avalanche victims' families he'd had to deal with over the years. The newspaper stories, the television interviews. He hated every last one. But avalanches were a fact of life out here. They had snow slides in the winter and rock slides in the summer. Colorado was a beautiful state, but it could be deadly. Like an Oklahoma twister, a California quake, or a Florida lightning strike, natural disasters struck hard and they struck quick, taking lives in the process.

Canyon understood the risk. They all did. Wade hugged Katharine to him. All that could be done now was to support each other through the aftermath.

Chapter Seventeen

"Bravo six-niner, heading down to the hospital," Kelly announced over the radio. With one last glance outside, she double-checked that the vicinity was clear before she made a slow and steady lift off. The high-pitched whir of engine gathered intensity as it wound up for flight.

"Copy," Roan said. "I'm right behind you. Have Sean guide you in west of town. I'll come in slightly east of you and land first. There's enough room on the pad for both of us, but it'll be tight, so be careful."

"Uh, Sean and the dog stayed back with Walsh," Kelly replied, annoyed by the tone Roan had taken with her. Forget that she had accomplished the mission, was bringing in the injured pilot, same as Roan was doing with his patient—he didn't trust her to fly without supervision. *Have Sean guide you in, west of town.* She didn't need any guiding. She knew where the town was, where the hospital was located, and could handle it without issue. But Roan was in command of the rescue operation, giving her no choice but to listen. More importantly, she reminded herself, she wanted to stay on his good side. He could end her career by going public with the incident from earlier.

Brushing the issue aside, she had to focus full-throttle on the task at hand. Fortunately, flying down over the mountains without hitting anything would be a much easier proposition than flying up had been. On the way down, pilots had easier collision-avoidance maneuvers at their disposal. The reverse track limited those options. If a mountain ridge appeared out of nowhere, a helicopter couldn't ascend fast enough without losing lift and tumbling out of the sky. One need only ask the injured heli-skiing pilot how well *that* worked. It didn't. The laws of aerodynamics ruled. It could have just as easily been her on the ground as him instead of him. Keeping a chopper in the air was a delicate balancing act between several forces working against one another. Unlike planes, helicopters didn't glide very well. They crashed.

Shaking the negative stream of thought from her mind, Kelly settled in and allowed instinct to take over, sweeping over the higher elevation ridges as she banked gently down the mountain. Resisting the urge to look over her shoulder, she hoped the guy pulled through. It had been pretty heroic of him to chance a flight back up the mountain in this mess and he deserved respect for it. Flying could be a tough job. It demanded one hundred percent from a pilot.

But it was a job she loved. Flying was who she was. It was part of her. Saving her bird from dive-bombing straight into the ground came from pure instinct. She could feel when things were running smoothly, and she could feel when they weren't. Flying was second nature to her. It gave her pleasure, satisfaction. More, it fed her soul. It was who she was. Kelly Jones; combat pilot, rescue pilot, plain 'ole general aviation pilot. She loved every minute in the air.

"I see Roan," the nurse said, pointing ahead of them.

"Yes. I have a visual," she confirmed, spotting him through the snowfall. The flashing red strobe light from his tail caught her attention and she adjusted her flight path accordingly. Checking the compass reading, Kelly veered slightly west and maintained a healthy distance between the two aircraft. She would give Roan no reason to complain about her performance. No more reason than she already had, anyway.

Fear slinked in as she was reminded of her "episode." She couldn't explain it, why she had lost her sense of time, why place escaped her. Had her disorientation been caused by conditions? Flying through a whiteout could do that to a pilot. It could sneak up on you, erasing all visual clues until you were completely disoriented and didn't know which way was up or down—until it was too late. It was a circumstance she'd been trained to handle, but that didn't mean it didn't unsettle the mind. It did. Pilots lost their lives because of it. In this instance, Kelly hadn't lost her life. She'd only lost her mind.

Roan blocked out the conversation between Kinsley and the flight nurse and focused on getting his crew to the hospital safely. He didn't blame her for being rattled over Grant's condition, but there wasn't much more they could do for him until they reached Silver Creek Medical Center. Unfortunately, it sounded as though the man's status was deteriorating. From what Lisa had said, Grant had been buried under the snow and had lost consciousness. They'd been able to resuscitate him, but coming back from the brink was tough on a body. Especially an older body with a history of cardiac issues.

Clenching his jaw, Roan knew he couldn't think about it. His job was to fly them to medical help and that's what he was going to do. Where he went from there posed the bigger problem. He had to talk to Kelly about what had happened to her, but he also had to get back up the mountain for Walsh and Goose—a trip which Roan couldn't allow Kelly to join. She had to be grounded, plain and simple. She had to be grounded until they could discuss her situation further. The risk to others was too great.

After what he'd witnessed at the top, Roan couldn't trust her.

And it tore him in two. Whether he wanted to admit it or not, he'd been looking forward to working with her. She was a good pilot. No, make that an excellent pilot—one he'd been looking forward to spending more time with...and for more than just professional reasons.

Wildcat. Roan chuckled at the nickname. Walsh had called it the first time they met. *Congratulations, Roan. You've got a wildcat on your hands.*

He couldn't disagree. Muscular and feisty, Kelly was quick on her feet, both on the ground and in the air—and today's near miss proved it. She had recovered from a dicey situation. Jack was an experienced pilot with almost twenty years under his belt and he hadn't managed to recover, but Kelly had. Imagining her face as she shouted at him over the radio, Roan could almost see the sparks flying from her brown eyes...eyes that drew him in every time he peered into them. When he wasn't looking at her body, that is. She was built like a powerhouse and flaunted her figure with hip-hugging blue jeans and snug-fitting tank tops. Winter time covered her up a bit, but not in his memory. Nothing could conceal that body of hers that hovered in his mind's eye. Walsh had definitely nailed it; Kelly was a wildcat, but now that wildcat was running rabid.

Crazy. All humor evaporated from Roan's thoughts and a sharp sadness pulled at him. *Why? What had caused it?*

In the recesses of his mind, the answer scared him.

"Are you going back up for Walsh?" Lisa asked, piercing the veil of Roan's thoughts.

"I am."

She nodded, but he could see this was difficult for her. Lisa was normally a pretty tough nut, but her demeanor was showing signs of strain. Her mouth was set in an unyielding line and her body sat rigid in the seat. Gone was her easy, relaxed style, replaced with a constant worry. The fact that Walsh had opted for a backpack in order to stay for the duration seemed to unsettle her. And not because she was afraid Walsh couldn't handle the conditions. He could. They both knew he could. Roan suspected it had more to do with Canyon. If Walsh couldn't save Canyon, it would crush him. The two had become very close over recent years and Walsh didn't have many people he counted as friends. In fact, other than Lisa, he had two—Canyon and Roan. That was it. But that was all Walsh needed.

Roan flipped his gaze between Lisa and the terrain ahead. *Except for her*. Walsh needed Lisa in his life more than he needed anything else.

Adele paced the floor outside the operating room. Ridding herself of nervous energy had to be done on the move—

moving spent some of the energy bottled up inside of her. Staring at the floor didn't help, but it gave her mind a focal point other than the doors marked "Surgery."

Hal Richardson meant everything to her. The love of her life, he was her confidant, her support. He was as much a part of her life as the restaurant. He epitomized everything that was good about Colorado and her move here. He was going to be fine. She constantly reminded herself that he was okay—he wasn't going to die. He wasn't going to lose a limb. He was simply going to lose his mind battling rehab after *another* leg injury. Adele shook her head. If she could keep him off that mountain, his problems would be solved. But keeping him off that mountain would mean cutting him off at the knees. He lived to ski—for pleasure, for rescue, for thrill. A future without snow-skiing would be a future not worth living for him, the way he saw it. Like it or not, that was the man she'd chosen. Love him or not, she was a worrier.

At the vibration in her pocket, Adele stopped suddenly. She reached for her phone and saw that it was Katharine. She answered at once. "Hello?"

"Adele."

"Katharine, any word on Canyon?"

"No. Walsh and another man are staying up on the mountain. Roan and his partner are flying Grant and the heli-skiing pilot to the hospital as we speak."

Adele groaned. This was not good. First an avalanche, then a helicopter crash. There were too many injuries, too many near-death experiences to suffer in one day! Shaking the swarm of negativity from her mind, she asked, "Are you coming here?"

"No. I'm going to stay put with Wade. I just wanted to let you know that Lisa is on her way."

"Good. Hal was asking about her before he went in." And if he wasn't under heavy anesthesia at the moment, she'd try to get word to him, but at this point it would have to be enough that Adele and Lisa were together. "Thanks for calling me."

"You're welcome."

Adele felt a pang of guilt, disturbed by the utter desolation in Katharine's voice. She should be there for her friend. She was going through hell and Adele was her closest friend in town, but Adele couldn't pull herself away from Hal's side. Not until she knew he'd made it through surgery. There was always a risk when general anesthesia was used. Feeling a pressure push in her chest, she had to let it go. It stunk when the two closest people in your life were suffering hardship at the same time. It stunk that Adele couldn't be there for both of them. But she was only one woman. Tightening her grip on the phone, she said, "Katharine, Canyon has been through worse. If anyone can handle this, he can."

"That's what they say..." Katharine murmured in reply.

"It's true," Adele asserted. "I remember once when Canyon fell off a cliff during a rescue operation."

"What?"

Adele seized upon Katharine's alarm. It sounded like it could be the shot of adrenaline she needed in order to keep her spirits up. "Yes," she continued. "It was during ski season and they were rescuing a guy who had ventured off the back bowls and was found hanging from a narrow ledge. Canyon went down for him, lost his step, and fell."

"Oh, good heavens! Was he hurt?"

"A few cracked ribs and a dislocated shoulder, but nothing he hadn't experienced getting tossed off the backside of a bull!" Adele quipped, relaying the story the same way Canyon had relayed it to her. "He had to wait out the rescue of the skier first, before the guys could come back for him, and in the meantime a blizzard whipped in and blanketed the ridge with snow."

"Why did he never tell me this story?"

"I don't know. He probably doesn't consider it a big deal. It's the way Canyon thinks, Katharine, and I'm telling you—he will pull through this."

After a short pause, Katharine replied wistfully, "I wish I shared your conviction."

"Then do. Own it. If you want a life with Canyon Lare-do, you have to accept the man as he is—the good, the bad, and the amazing." Adele smiled into her cell phone, pleased by her brainstorm of calm. "He really is amazing, Katharine, and he will surprise you, you watch and see."

"Thanks for the pep talk, Adele. I needed it."

"Any time."

"How's Hal? Any word on his condition?"

"He'll be fine," she reassured Katharine as much as her-self. "Ornery that he'll be confined to crutches again, but he'll get over it. He'll have to if he wants to ski again, right?"

"I imagine that will be the first item on his agenda."

Pleasure washed through Adele as she detected the first trace of stress slipping from Katharine's voice. "You know it will be. Like you, I have to accept the many ways my man is built—even if it grounds out my last nerve." Flicking a glance toward the operating room doors, she tried to laugh. *Which it might*. Hal Richardson might very well ground and shred all of her nerves!

Chapter Eighteen

Floating in over the hospital helipad, Kelly set the AStar down to the left of Roan's aircraft and watched as a team of medical staff rushed toward her with a gurney. The team in the rear of her aircraft worked quickly to make the handoff with the precision and timing that only came only from experience. The nurse had already hopped out of the helicopter, joining his partner as they headed inside with the hospital staff. Kelly imagined they'd be sharing vitals and other crucial information to help direct the emergency medical care for the downed pilot and the injured skier. Her gaze jumped to the other gurney being wheeled into the building. Two women followed as a team whisked the stretcher through a set of double doors and quickly out of sight.

Roan's voice crackled in her ear. "Kelly, do you copy?"

"Copy."

"Let's get these birds back to their cage."

"Roger that," she replied, and waited for him to take the lead. The snowfall here in the village was light and steady, posing none of the visibility and wind problems they'd encountered up top. Kelly glanced out her door, through her front windshield, then pulled her controls into motion, lifting the aircraft in an easy, gentle swing up and off from the ground. The flight back to the airport would take all of five minutes.

Five minutes and she'd be face-to-face with one Roan Phillips. A squiggle of nerves raced through her belly. With the high-adrenaline rescue behind them, they needed to talk. She needed to talk. Only...what would she say? What *could* she say?

*Roan, I had a breakdown. I lost it. But no worries, I re-
covered and I'm good to go. How about we keep that scene
between friends?*

Kelly scowled. No pilot wanted to hear that crap. Not
from themselves and not from another pilot. *No excuses.* That
was her motto. That would be Roan's. Spewing her breath out
in a ragged sigh, she thought, *No, this is something I'm going
to hear about, and on Roan's terms.* That's how she'd handle
it if the roles were reversed. She could only hope the man
would show a little compassion, like she would.

Wouldn't she?

Flying over the edge of town, Kelly was met by a sea of
upwardly turned faces. Without exception, the chest-
pounding thump of a low-flying helicopter drew everyone's
attention. Was it a medical emergency? Military? A movie
being filmed? Curiosity was curiosity, and almost everyone
was intrigued by the sound of a swift-moving helicopter, including her. She remembered well the days spent hanging out
at the local FBO, waiting on her dad, watching choppers
come in and take off. She loved the roar of engines as the
sound reverberated through her body. She loved the smell of
fuel and engine oil, the sight of chopping blades. Her friends
thought she was weird, but she didn't care. They didn't care
about helicopters. Not the way she did.

Sweeping up and over the offices of the local Silver
Creek newspaper, she sailed over a warehouse retailer and a
small chain hotel, gradually banking toward the airport. Within minutes, the FBO for Summit Aviation Services came into
view across the tarmac. Maintaining her distance from Roan
as he slowed, she watched for other aircraft as she filed in on
her landing zone, the area marked by a big yellow H inside a
circle. Roan would likely want the AStar in the hangar, which
meant she would have to set down on a landing pad, a mova-
ble platform that could be used to roll the helicopter inside
once the blades were strapped and secured. Roan would leave
the Augusta outside, expecting to return for Walsh and the
others.

Roan set his helicopter down and Kelly followed. Flipping switches and dialing back instruments, the whine of engines slowed markedly as she began the process of powering down. Out her window, she saw Roan doing the same. Her pulse quickened. Helmet on, aviator glasses in place, he reminded her of a swashbuckling pirate in the sky, an ace pilot with a thirst for freedom and endless skies. She swallowed, her attention snared by a few guys heading out from Summit Aviation Services to assist with securing the aircraft.

Twenty minutes later, Kelly followed Roan into the FBO. Stopping by the flight desk, he grabbed a flight case and asked the guy behind the counter, "Mind if I use the office?"

"Help yourself."

Roan turned to Kelly. "Got a minute?"

Her heart jumped. Running a hand through her hair, she nodded and steeled herself for the inevitable. *The talk*. Apparently it was happening right now.

Roan walked into a nondescript room with nothing inside but a metal-framed desk cleared of everything but phone, pen and pad of paper, a black leather chair, a single potted plant in a corner, and a map of Silver Creek on the wall. Kelly walked in and instantly felt tension squeeze into the room. Roan closed the door and stepped over to the desk but rather than walking behind it, he seemed to change his mind and dropped a hip to the edge. He crossed his arms and peered at her with a pensive gaze. "Wanna explain what happened up there?"

"Not really."

Roan waited through the pause. They both knew she would tell him. It was only a matter of time. Kelly turned away and circled around the chair. How did one explain a breakdown? Was it a breakdown? Maybe it was only a tiny break—a hiccup in an otherwise uneventful performance. One that could be considered normal.

Perfectly normal under the tenuous weather circumstances. Other than the near misses with the mountain and the heli-skiing pilot, the second of which had not been her fault and the first of which she had negotiated with stellar calm, it had been an uneventful rescue. Kelly shrugged and turned back toward Roan. "I don't know."

"You don't know, or you don't feel like talking about it?"

She stared at him and replied evenly, "Both."

It was the truth. She didn't know and she sure as heck didn't feel like talking about it. She was here because she had no choice. The facts on the ground gave her no choice.

The lines around Roan's dark eyes softened, lending a sweet comprehension to his features, as if he were seeking an intimate confidence between friends. "Kelly, we both know something happened up there. If you're planning on hiding it, you must know that Sean and his team couldn't have missed it."

She rolled her eyes and turned her back on him. He was stating the obvious. The suspicion in Sean's gaze had been glaring. He thought she'd been losing it. She hadn't—not completely—and she had finished the operation to prove it, but there was no denying the look he had seen in his eyes.

But at least she had finished her mission on a positive note. Her performance had been nothing less than a successful search and rescue operation. The downed pilot was safely in the hospital. Walsh had extra boots on the ground to assist in his search for Canyon. That should say something about her competence. Unfortunately, the episode couldn't simply be erased. Flipping her gaze to the ceiling, Kelly debated. How much could she admit and still retain her right to fly?

The rules were quite clear. PTSD had to be reported. Any episode, present or past, had to be reported. The FAA had a duty to maintain safety in the skies, and it was their job to weed out unfit pilots. Unstable pilots. Crazy pilots.

Taking a deep breath, Kelly crossed her arms over her chest and turned back to face Roan. "Seeing that chopper go down brought back some bad memories for me, okay? They were fleeting, but they were intense. That's it. That's all that happened."

Roan's expression hardened. "You thought they shot Jack down...whoever 'they' are. It sounded like you believed you were back in the middle of combat."

"Yes, well, a year or so back I witnessed one of my friends getting shot down. It pissed me off and today it all came back, I guess. But it's no big deal, Roan. I got over it and got on with the job. I have pages of successful flights recorded to prove it. I'm fine."

Pulling his back ramrod straight, Roan smacked his hands to his knees and drilled her with a wary gaze. "Are you?"

"Yes. You saw how I performed today. I flew through some pretty incredible crap, picked up the injured pilot and flew him to safety, same as you did with the skiers. I don't see the problem."

"The problem is that PTSD can sneak up on you. It's a nasty condition that if left untreated, can eat away at your soul. It'll take a piece of you every day until it whittles you down to nothing, killing you in the process—and not only you, but everyone close to you." Roan held her in his gaze. "Is that what you want? Is that how you want to walk away from an otherwise impeccable career?"

"Of course not," Kelly snapped, surprised by the vehemence in his voice. It wasn't the reaction she'd expected. It was too personal, as though Roan had a crystal ball and was peering into her future, predicting a horrible outcome. And what did he know about her career? Sure, she'd graduated with honors, flew more Apache combat hours than most women dreamed of and was recognized by top brass for her achievements, but he wasn't privy to that information. He knew nothing about her career other than what she'd told him.

Ambivalence pushed in from all sides. And why was he saying nice things to her? Was this his way of softening her up so she'd gush like a wet sponge? No way. She wasn't copping to anything, though it was kind of hard to push back against him when he was currently playing nice. Dropping her arms to her sides, Kelly walked across the office and spewed, "I just don't like giving in to the weakest part of me, allowing it to control me. It's not who I am," she added, trying to sound detached and unaffected. "Can you understand that?"

"What part? Your emotions?"

Yes, she wanted to say, but the way he asked the question sounded like he was mocking her. Roan was a man. He didn't understand that women were often classified according to their emotions. Men were allowed more leeway when it came to anger, resentment, bitterness, and even sadness. They could feel strong emotion and then bottle it away for a later day, a more convenient time. She did the same. As a soldier, a pilot, she had to. For a soldier, it was a matter of survival. War was hell on the psyche and an individual had to cope, adjust to life on the battlefront. For a pilot, it was part of the job. If a pilot couldn't put a clamp on fear and panic, flying through storms and mechanical failures could be deadly.

Most women might allow their emotions to flow far and wide, but not her. Kelly preferred the man's outlook on the subject. Including grief. "My emotions will not have control over me."

"But they do. It's the same for you and for me. We can't escape the reality."

"I disagree."

"Well, don't." Roan stood abruptly and stepped near her. Very near. "I've got enough experience in the matter for both of us."

Kelly suddenly felt cramped. Restricted. Her heart began to pound.

"Don't do this to yourself," he said, his voice quiet, his eyes heated. "You obviously haven't dealt with the loss or it wouldn't be haunting you the way it is."

"Haunting is a strong word," she muttered, struck by the scent of him standing so close. A faint mix of sweat and co-

logne, it was distinctly male and defied her every attempt to
ignore him. It felt strange to be this close to him, challenging
the boundaries of personal space.

Roan's gaze darted back and forth across hers. "Talk to
me. What happened up there?"

"I slipped back into a moment in time, that's all."

"It must have been a really strong moment in time to
pull you back so completely."

Kelly gulped. "It was."

"Tell me about it..."

"It was like any other day...we were out on a combat
mission, hunting the bad guy."

Roan peered at her, his lashes black as ink, his skin
smooth and damn near perfect in complexion. But it was the
emotion lingering deep in his dark gaze that drew her in, en-
tangling her thoughts like they'd been caught in a web of his
making. "We came under hostile fire," she uttered, falling
back through recall. "One of our choppers was hit."

"And it crashed."

She nodded, tugging at her lower lip with her teeth as the
memories surged...Guy Flannigan's face, the spit of gunfire,
the subsequent fireball. "We tried to provide cover but had to
get out before we went down too."

"Was the enemy's position unexpected? Is that why you
were caught off guard?"

Caught off guard. Kelly's mind swirled back through
time, the day coming into focus like a digital replay. "A sand-
storm came out of nowhere. We couldn't see...we couldn't
maneuver. We were sitting ducks at that point and had to get
out."

"Not a pleasant proposition for an Apache fighter pilot."

"No," she murmured. Her head fell forward and she was
overcome by a deep and penetrating ache. "It wasn't. It
sucked." Kelly folded her arms over her chest, squeezing until it hurt more than the memories.

Roan placed a finger to her chin, tilting it up to face him. "It wasn't your fault. There was nothing you could have done to save them."

Kelly stilled. No one had ever said those words to her. She'd always been told to grieve the loss, to mourn the fellow soldier and move on. You honored him by completing the mission. What they didn't understand, what they couldn't begin to fathom, was the pure and unrelenting guilt she felt over letting Guy down. He would be alive today if she had seen that fanatic on the ground swing his weapon toward Guy. If she had nailed the enemy fighter with a round from her gunner. But she hadn't. She had missed it. Totally and completely.

And Guy Flannigan was dead.

A tear spilled from her eye and Roan wiped it free. "It's not your fault. War sucks. It's hell and good people die."

Very good people, she agreed. *Amazing people.*

"But you can't win them all," he continued softly, his voice but a breath between them. "No matter how great a pilot you are—and you are one of the best I've ever flown with—you can't win them all. Life doesn't work that way." Roan lowered his gaze. "It never has and it never will."

The sadness sliced her in two. She appreciated the sentiment, but this loss was unbearable. It couldn't be reduced to an axiom. It was guttural. Life-changing.

"You have to deal with this before it destroys you, Kelly. Please...for me. Don't let this write your epitaph."

Chapter Nineteen

Roan Phillips pulled Kelly into his arms and hugged her. He hoped she didn't take it the wrong way but it was the only thing he could do when faced with such tortured pain. And there was no mistake about it: Kelly was torn up inside over the memory of a downed chopper, and the pain was fresh. Visceral. When he felt her arms slip around his waist and squeeze him firmly, he pressed his head against hers and something inside him softened. *That's right, Kelly. Let go. Let it all go...*

Closing his eyes, Roan marveled at how the connection felt warm and easy, not awkward or strained. It felt natural, her body fitting against his as though they were made for one another, for this. The thought struck hard. Kelly Jones was a good-looking woman. From the first day she'd walked into the Summit Aviation Services FBO, he'd wanted to know who she was and how he could get close to her. When he realized she was there to see him for flight instruction, he quickly put a cap on his desire and stuffed it away. Roan had a strict policy of "no fraternizing" with his students. Personal relationships interrupted his objectivity as a flight instructor and had to be avoided at all cost.

But now, holding her in his arms, all those feelings came rushing back to him. Desire streamed through his veins as he pictured the curve of her legs as she strode across the asphalt, muscles as well defined as a man's yet perfectly suited for her petite figure. She moved with confidence, determination. Then she'd slid off her aviator sunglasses as the two were introduced. Recalling the spark in her gaze when she realized he would be her instructor amused him even now. Pleasurable thoughts coiled around his limbs, filling him with renewed want. He and Kelly could make a good team. He'd been tough on her in training because he wanted the best from her. Not simply "enough to get by," but the best. Only the best.

She had it in her. She was a skilled pilot, able to do everything he asked and then some. He'd seen it again today. It was a miracle that her chopper hadn't gone down with Jack's, but it hadn't. She'd handled her bird with the reflexes of a pro. And holding skid to the mountain in blizzard conditions? Roan wasn't sure if even *he* could have managed that feat, let alone under emotional duress. Lingering in his thoughts of her, he knew Kelly was one of a kind—in the sky *and* on the ground. But she was hurting right now and needed to know it was going to be okay.

Which made it all the more difficult for him to report her conduct. Not that she had done anything wrong—nothing within her power to control—but they both knew what it would mean for her flying career. She'd have to get a psychiatric evaluation. She'd have to prove she wasn't vulnerable to any more episodes—a miracle in itself—and then maybe, just maybe she could get signed off by a doctor with a status of "recovered." It was her only hope of getting her FAA medical certificate reinstated. Without it, she couldn't be a part of SAR.

She couldn't fly, period.

Roan rubbed a hand up and down her back and said, "This isn't the end of your flying career." When she tensed, he immediately regretted bringing it up—but if she had hope, if she believed there was a possibility that she could maintain her ability to fly, wouldn't that be a good thing? "It isn't," he insisted. "I've heard of lots of pilots regaining a clean medical certificate and getting back to the business of flying."

Kelly pulled away and cool air swiftly filled the space between them. "You know that's not an easy prospect."

"Not easy but it is a possibility. The FAA has been forced to make all kinds of concessions for medical conditions to allow pilots to regain the right to fly."

"Mental disorders are not at the top of that list."

"You have to talk with someone before anyone can make that diagnosis."

"You and I both know that any psychiatrist will mark me. And not only will they mark me, they'll probably try to push drugs on me."

The death knell. Any pilot taking anti-psychotic meds would certainly be listed on the no-fly list. But that hadn't happened...yet. Nothing had happened yet. Not officially, anyway.

Roan held her by the shoulders and said, "PTSD is a serious condition that needs to be addressed. You don't want to live with this stuff popping into your brain at any random moment. You want to be in control. You want to dictate the terms of this dis—"

Roan didn't finish the sentence. He couldn't. "Disorder" sounded so clinical, so final, as though he'd already checked the box for her.

Shrugging free from his hold, Kelly cleared her throat and replied, "I'll deal with it, Roan. I'll talk to someone."

But I'm not going to make it public. He heard the next statement as if she'd said it aloud, only it wasn't an option. She knew it. He knew it. "You know I have to report it."

Distress cut through her gaze as she stared at him wordlessly.

Roan felt the same shards shredding his own stomach. "If it's any consolation, there's no one I feel safer flying with than you. I'd let you fly me anywhere." The smile he was hoping to see from her never materialized and, instead, a tear pushed from the corner of her eye. It cut him to the core. "Don't lose hope, Kelly. You can't give up. There is a light at the end of this tunnel, I promise you."

"Easy for you to say."

"Not really. My uncle came back from Desert Storm and battled alcoholism until the day he died, and why? Because he refused to get help. He turned bitter and angry and it tore my mother's life in two." That, along with Roan's brother's death. But adding him to the equation would serve no purpose. Kelly's demons came from her own combat experience. From *her* loss. "The trauma my uncle experienced during combat was bigger than he could handle on his own but he refused to see it that way. He wouldn't listen to the people closest to him. Like you, he said he could handle it." Roan paused. "He never did. The alcohol killed him."

Kelly's gaze snapped sideways and she wiped her eye. "I'm sorry to hear about your family, Roan. It's hard for some people, I get that, but I don't drink. I don't take drugs—I'm clean. I won't fall prey to substance abuse, if that's what you're worried about."

Roan frowned. If only avoiding substance abuse were so easy. When the pain became too great to bear, the pain relievers followed. When the prescriptions ran out, alcohol and illegal drugs weren't far behind. And while he'd never experienced it himself, Roan understood that it was one of the most difficult places to be: caught between escaping the pain of life and escaping the pain of addiction. Neither was an easy prospect. "I'm worried about *you*, Kelly. That's what I'm worried about."

Kelly stilled. Seemed she didn't have a comeback for that one.

Roan's cell phone rang. Grabbing it, he peered at the screen. "Wade—what's up?"

"What's your status on weather? Should I send a team up on snowmobiles?"

"Did Walsh call? Did they find Canyon?"

"No, but I want to get ahead of the situation. If you're grounded for the next several hours, I want to get an SAR team en route. Now."

"Gotcha. Let me check the radar and I'll call you in two."

Roan ended the call.

Kelly quickly asked, "Did he hear from Walsh?"

Sadly, the moment of tenderness had passed. Roan shook his head. There was no word on Canyon. And no commitment from Kelly that she had accepted what needed to be done about today. But she couldn't brush this incident out of her way and keep charging forward. It had to be addressed. He would make sure of it.

But now wasn't the time. "Wade wants to get an SAR team up one way or another," he told her. "If I can't fly, he wants to send the snowmobiles."

Without another word, he walked out of the office and headed for the computer equipment. Circling the desk, he dropped to a seat and brought up the radar screen. He grumbled loudly. "C'mon!"

"What is it?" Kelly asked, suddenly leaning near his shoulder.

"The system is only on top of us—nowhere else!"

"What are the odds..." she murmured.

"Pretty good, around here," he mumbled, acutely aware that her face was inches from his. Despite holding her in his arms, their bodies melded as one, it felt odd to be close to her in this environment. With her hand on the desk, she placed her other hand to the back of his chair. So close, he could hear her breathing.

Roan slid the computer mouse across the desk, clicking through several screens and clearing his voice. He commented, "Looks like we're going to get snow for hours."

"But the winds might die down, at least enough for us to fly through it."

Us. His chest tightened. Had Kelly missed something in their conversation? There wasn't going to be any "us." Not for a while, anyway. Maybe not ever.

Roan turned and found himself staring into her eyes at extremely close range. Kelly pulled back, but not far. "Kelly—"

"Yes?" she asked, her lips hovering apart.

"You can't go back up. Not with me. Not as lead pilot."

"But Roan—"

"Please," he urged quietly, careful not to draw attention from others in the room. "Don't make this any harder than it has to be."

With her gaze moving back and forth across his, Kelly appeared ready to argue her case, but she simply dropped the subject. "I get it."

"Do you?"

She nodded but didn't look at him.

"I don't want this to come between us." Between us. The words sounded like he and Kelly had a thing, which they didn't, but could they? Roan suddenly found himself eager to know. *Could they*?

Kelly's gaze churned with question.

Was she thinking the same thing? Roan's heart kicked. Was she considering the idea?

"I hear you," she replied, a thin veil of nerves evident in her voice as she pushed up from the desk. She strode across the room, headed for the refrigerator. Yanking open the door, she pulled out a bottle of water, twisted the cap open, and chugged like she hadn't had a drink for days.

Roan got up and walked over. "What do you want me to do?"

"Forget it ever happened. Understand that it was brief, had no lasting repercussions on my performance, and let it slide. Once. Just this once. If it happens again, I'll report it. I'll seek out a psychiatrist and let them have their way with me."

Roan crossed his arms over his chest and cocked a brow. "Really?"

Kelly scowled, the muscles in her rattlesnake-jaw jumping. "You know what I mean. I'll let them ask their questions and play their mind games. Promise."

There was no hint of the personal nature their conversation had taken earlier or the proximity their bodies had enjoyed. His had enjoyed, anyway. There was no mention of surprise or disgust. Kelly glossed over it like it never happened. Must be something she was pretty good at, he mused. "Is that what you really want me to do?"

She hesitated, as though unsure whether or not she could trust him. "Yes."

"Even if it goes against my better judgment?"

Kelly placed a hand to his arm, the spot heating quickly. "I'm asking you to trust *my* judgment."

"Over mine."

"Is this going to be a standoff?"

Roan shook his head. In an instant of clarity, he said, "I don't want to fight with you. I'm only trying to do what's best for you. Because I care about you." Strangely, he realized that he cared a lot. Not only athletic and attractive, Kelly was tough, smart, a capable pilot, and most everything Roan wanted in a woman. The two of them could have some good times, in the air and on the ground.

But rather than dwell on the stuff he wanted to do with her, he had to contend with the stuff standing between them. Like the truth, and her reaction to the truth. It gave him pause. Swallowing back a sudden lump in his throat, Roan said, "Someone really important to you must have gone down in that chopper for you to carry the guilt over their death every day. That's a pain I wouldn't wish on anyone. It tears people up—from the inside out. But I can't carry the load for you, nor can I ease it for you. You and only you can make that decision." Inhaling deeply, he expelled a sigh, fighting off a slew of things he wanted to say, things he wanted her to hear. Instead, he kept it simple and handed the ball back to her. "You have a fantastic future ahead of you. Don't let one day in your past trip you up when you least expect it. Pilot error kills, Kelly. It kills you and it kills others. Think about that."

Chapter Twenty

McIntyre Walsh checked the GPS reading, looked around the snowy terrain, and declared, "We need to move west, search that section of trees."

Goose nodded. "You think he could have made it that far?"

Walsh looked uphill, back toward the area where the avalanche had hit, about three hundred yards east from where they currently stood, then back toward the line of trees up ahead. Pellets of snow hammered, dropping visibility, though a distant wall of trees was discernible. Not branches or shadows, only massive clumps of white and green. "Canyon didn't disappear. He had to go somewhere. I checked the slope directly downhill from the slide and got nothing."

"You don't think he's buried?" Sean asked.

Walsh grunted. "He could be, but I think we would have located his beacon by now."

"If he had time to turn it on."

A flash of anger lit into Walsh. "He'd have time. Canyon's no neophyte when it comes to avalanches. He would have flipped that switch first thing."

"You're probably right," Goose replied. "This ain't his first rodeo."

No, Walsh agreed silently. And he'd be damned if it was going to be his last.

Walsh trudged through the snow with a determined step, consumed by a rare helplessness. He cursed the weather. New drifts of snowfall had filled the path they'd forged on their way to the downed chopper, making it even harder to maintain an organized search pattern. Backtracking wasn't productive. They needed to cover new ground, fresh ground, not waste their time searching the same terrain over and over again. Panting from exertion, Walsh resisted the urge to lick the freezing moisture around his nose and mouth. It would only serve to chap his lips, a complication he could do without at the moment. Same as the snow. Usually the stuff of a heli-skier's dreams, it proved a hindrance at the moment. The black dog barreled through the snow, seemingly oblivious to the discomfort Walsh was feeling.

"One way or another, Rugby will find him," Sean remarked.

One way or another. Walsh didn't like the implication but accepted the reality. Called "avy dogs," Rugby was one of many animals specially trained to pick up the scent of humans buried alive by avalanche. At this point, if Canyon was buried, they wouldn't find him alive. They'd simply find him. And Rugby would be instrumental in that process.

"I'm not ready to give up on him yet," Walsh stated flatly. "He could be lying somewhere in the snow, or, for that matter, skiing down the mountain."

"True."

Rugby bounded off-trail and Sean whistled. The dog froze, spun around, and charged back toward the men. "C'mon, boy. We're moving farther down the mountain before we start searching."

Peering at the dog's snow-encrusted black body, Walsh asked, "Did he pick something up?"

Sean chuckled. "Nah. He's just starting his search-traverse a little too soon."

"Maybe, maybe not," Walsh replied. "Canyon could be anywhere, as far as I'm concerned."

"We covered a pretty good distance hiking up here to hook up with that chopper. You don't think Canyon would actually be this far, do you?"

"I don't know what to think." At this point, it was the raw truth. Walsh was coming up empty and he didn't like it.

Pressing forward in silence, his face felt like a sheet of ice. The tip of his nose and his lower cheeks were singed by cold to the point of pain. Even his leg muscles were feeling the pain, but he wasn't about to slow down. There was too much ground to cover, too much time lost and his buddy needed him. *No man left behind.* Sean might be right about the condition in which they'd find Canyon, but Walsh was bringing him home. Today. One way or another, he wasn't leaving this mountain without his friend.

Leading the way toward the bank of trees, he cupped gloved hands to his mouth and shouted, "Canyon! Canyon, can you hear me?"

Rugby made a beeline for the trees then raced in and around their enormous girths, furiously sniffing at the ground. The dog was trained to detect the scent of a body buried in snow as deep as fifteen feet. It was also trained to work quickly, covering two and a half acres in thirty minutes, while twenty humans using avalanche probes would take four hours to cover the same. It was an amazing feat, and it explained why Rugby was so high energy. The dog had a job to do, and a job to do quickly.

Dodging in and out of the section of trees, Rugby sniffed the ground as he ran, not stopping in any one place. Walsh worked to keep him moving in the right direction—back to his original search area, the most probable place they'd find Canyon. After estimating the speed the skiers had been moving and the trajectory of travel including possible deviations, Walsh came up with a likely "landing zone" farther downhill. If they failed to find Canyon there, they would head back up the mountain to the area where Hal and the others had gone down. Despite the fact that a beacon search had turned up nothing, it was ground zero.

Rugby stopped suddenly. His ears perked and he looked straight down the perimeter line of trees. *Did he have something?*

The men exchanged a hopeful look. "Do you think he's on to something?"

Sean shrugged.

The dog bolted and Walsh's heart jumped. "Where the hell is he going?"

"That's not protocol," Goose said.

Walsh hadn't thought so, either. These dogs were supposed to traverse an area quickly, but they were to skim every square foot of the area, not bolt yards off course. Even the sharpest nose wasn't going to pick up anything at the pace the dog was running now. He was sprinting full speed.

"Do something!" Walsh shouted at Sean. "It's your dog—he should listen to you!"

Sean yelled, "Rugby! Hold up!"

Walsh spewed several obscenities and charged after the animal. *So much for their secret weapon.*

"Sorry, Walsh!" Sean called after him. "I don't know what got into him!"

"Well, something set a fire under his paws," Walsh grumbled under his breath in gusts of steamy exhalations. At least he could still see the dog. Leaping over large mounds of snow, the dog cut left around a huge boulder. Make that past tense. Walsh couldn't see the dog anymore and could only hone in on the spot where the animal had ducked out of sight.

"Rugby!" Goose called from behind him.

Walsh didn't bother waiting for the SAR members, figuring the two could use his tracks to keep up with his location. At the moment, he was more intent on catching up with that dog and getting him back on track. "Rugby!"

Walsh joined the others in yelling after the dog, as though the animal would listen to him over his handlers. Sean was Rugby's owner and primary handler, but Goose worked with the dog on a regular basis, too. Hell, as Sean's roommate, he lived with the animal!

Jogging after the dog amid shouts that pierced the quiet, Walsh began to lose stamina as he neared a dark boulder. At least forty, maybe fifty feet in height, its base was covered in a pile of white. Around him, tree branches were fat with snow, the accumulation so heavy it looked as though the branches could break under the weight. Peering into the winter forest, Walsh searched for any sight of the dog. His black body should be easy to spot.

Walsh's heart pounded. There he was, about twenty yards in, running circles around something on the ground. *Had he found something*?

Sean and Goose caught up with him, both spying the same thing. "Rugby!" Sean shouted. "What have you found, boy?"

"I can't make it out from here," Goose said, his labored breath billowing through the furious snowfall. The dog dropped to the ground and rolled around on its back, all four paws kicking up into the air. "Maybe it's a dead animal."

Wrong scent.

"Crap," Walsh muttered. He had once had a yellow Lab that had a knack for rolling in the first carcass he found, covering his body with the scent. The vet said it had something to do with primal instinct. Wild dogs used the trick to hide their scent while on the hunt. The only thing his dog Max ever hunted was his food bowl. Walsh felt a sudden pang of loss. His ex-wife had given Max away while Walsh had been on tour of duty with the Marines. Right before she filed for divorce, she dumped the dog. *Witch.*

Walsh carved old regrets from his heart and set his mind back to the task at hand. There was no way he was giving up on Canyon. He grunted. Or Rugby, for that matter. "Didn't the dog know what scent he was tracking?"

"Of course he does," Sean replied defensively. "But that doesn't mean he isn't distracted by other scents."

"Are you telling me a dead animal is enough to deter him from his duty?"

"Shouldn't," Sean murmured, sounding almost as let down as Walsh felt.

From the corner of his eyes, movement caught Walsh's attention. He whipped his head toward the dog. "What the—"

An arm reached up from the ground and grabbed onto the dog's neck.

Walsh's heart stopped. Goosebumps rippled across his skin.

Sean and Goose followed his gaze and Walsh took off toward the dog. Adrenaline fired through his arms and legs, his ski boots feeling no different from a pair of hiking boots as he sprinted toward the animal. Ducking beneath a branch, he leapt over forest debris and rocks until he came to a hard stop. "*Sonofa*—" Standing over the dog, his breath heaving from his chest, Walsh couldn't believe his eyes. "Canyon?"

"I was beginning to think you weren't going to make it," he replied weakly.

"Me?" Walsh blurted, shock winding deep into his brain as he tried to make sense of what he was seeing. Canyon was flat on his back, helmet and goggles in place as though he were taking a nap. In the middle of the forest. Walsh dropped to a knee and pushed the excited dog from licking Canyon's face. "How the hell did you get here?"

Canyon returned a half-smile. "I flew."

"What?"

Sean and Goose came running up and stopped short. They muttered in unison, "*Canyon*?"

Walsh grinned broadly. "The one and only."

"Son of a gun," Goose erupted. "Am I glad to see you!"

"Back at ya, Goose," he replied faintly. "Thanks for coming."

"Good job, Rugby!" Sean moved next to his dog and vigorously scratched the fur around its ears.

"I can't believe you made it this far out of the ski zone," Goose said.

Canyon dropped his hand to the ground and explained, "When the avalanche hit, I tried to dodge it, and I went over a cliff. I hit a boulder and it stopped me cold."

Registering the facts, Walsh quickly recalled the massive rock at the edge of the forest and glanced over Canyon's inert body. That was a boulder he wouldn't want to hit. "Are you okay? Is anything broken?"

"Probably, but I can't be sure. The collision knocked the wind out of me but I might have experienced a concussion, too. My ribs are bruised and my back..." He groaned. "My back is hurt, though I can't tell you the extent of it."

Walsh placed a hand to his chest. "Don't move."

"As you can see, I haven't budged from this location."

"Good thing," Goose said. "As it is, we're lucky to have found you at all. If it wasn't for Jack's chopper going down, Walsh and I wouldn't have come this far."

Canyon's expression changed. "Jack went down?"

"Yeah," Sean replied. "He and Kelly had a near mid-air collision. He went down, she didn't."

"Damn... Is he okay?"

"We think so," Walsh told him. "But why didn't you call for help? I tried your cell but you didn't answer."

"It was crushed when I hit the rock." Canyon reached into his coat pocket and revealed the mess of metal and glass. The screen was shattered.

Walsh took it from him. Examining the cell phone, he said, "Yeah, I'd say that's a total loss."

"Has anyone called Katharine?"

"Yes," Walsh replied. Canyon's eyes closed beneath his goggles and Walsh's heart wedged into his throat. He could imagine what his pal was thinking. They would be the same thoughts that would go through his own head with regard to Lisa. "I'll call her right now and let her know you're okay."

"Thanks, buddy."

Sliding the backpack from his shoulder, Walsh unpacked a thermal blanket and, with Sean and Goose's help, wrapped it over Canyon's body. They'd need a spine board up and heli-evac, but with the weather still raging, could they settle for a snowmobile?

"We're gonna need air support," Goose said, as though reading Walsh's thoughts. "There are several pretty steep sections between here and base." His gaze landed on Canyon. "A snowmobile might be able to navigate it, but he wouldn't be able to handle the ride."

Walsh wasted no time in making the call. Wade answered on the first ring. "We found Canyon."

Chapter Twenty-One

Wade's stomach fell into his boots. *Thank God.*

"What is it?" Katharine rushed to his side, her red-rimmed eyes pooling with tears.

"They found Canyon."

She clung to Wade's arm. "Is he okay? Does Walsh know if he's okay?"

"What's his condition, Walsh?"

"Not exactly sure," he replied and relayed the details Canyon had given him. "But we need a chopper up here. Is that a possibility?"

"He's going to be all right?" Katharine asked, more a statement of hope than a question. "He's okay, right?"

Wade nodded, doubting he could send Roan up, though he wasn't about to deliver that news until he was certain. "Let me call Roan."

"Great," Walsh said. "Get back to me when you know something. In the meantime, I've got Sean and Goose up here and we'll see to Canyon until help arrives."

Wade ended the call and told Katharine, "They found him, which means yes, he's okay." Her slender hands were wrapped tightly around his arm and gave him pause. Covering her hand with one of his own, he said, "He's going to be fine, Katharine. Canyon is going to be fine."

"Oh, thank heavens!"

At the quiver in her voice, Wade realized she was shaking. "He's okay, Katharine. Everything's going to be okay." Wade refused to elaborate on any possible back injury. It would only serve to upset her and there was no need for that until they had something definitive.

Katharine nodded but said nothing as tears streamed down her cheeks. Cody was by her side, apparently sensing that something had changed.

It pained him to see her like this, but the fact that they had found him alive was good news. Step two was getting him down. "I've got to call Roan," he said. Leaving Katharine to find solace in her dog, he dialed the number. The pilot picked up in seconds. "Roan, we found Canyon."

"Yes! Where is he? Is he okay?"

Wade explained the location, offering a cursory response to his physical condition, then asked, "What's our status with getting another chopper up there?"

"Status confirmed."

"Roan, check the radar. Canyon can sit tight if need be, now that he has Walsh and the guys with him. I don't want you going up under hazardous conditions."

"Roger that. I'll call you right back."

Wade ended the call.

"How long before they arrive at the hospital?" Katharine asked. "Should I leave now to meet them?"

He held her in his gaze. "Yes, that sounds like a good idea. Adele is already there and it will be good for you to be around friends." More importantly, in the event the team met with disaster on the way down, Katharine wouldn't have a front row seat to the action. A ripple of tension wound through the muscles in his neck and shoulders. This rescue wasn't over yet. They'd lost one helicopter to this storm. They could easily lose another. "I'll call you when I have a better estimate of time for his arrival."

Katharine nodded. Wiping tears from her eyes, she brushed stray strands of hair from her face, cleared her throat, and said, "Thank you, Wade. Thank you for everything."

"Don't thank me. It's those SAR members that did all the heavy lifting." The comment brought a smile to her face and for that, Wade was grateful. "Would you like a patrol car to drive you over?"

"Could they? Adele dropped me off but she's at the hospital and I have no way of getting there, other than a cab."

"Absolutely. Let me make a phone call and we'll get you and Cody over to Silver Creek Medical Center on the double."

Roan ended the call with Wade and hurried back to the computer. Not bothering to sit, he grabbed the mouse and slid it across the desk, pulling the radar up on the screen to check the conditions—conditions he knew had not changed in the five minutes since he'd last checked. Scrutinizing wind speed and direction, the forecasted precipitation, and estimated flight path, Roan saw nothing but trouble.

Canyon can sit tight, if need be, now that he has Walsh and the guys with him.

On impulse, Roan called Walsh. Wade had been vague on details, details Roan needed to make his decision. If Canyon was seriously injured, he needed medical care sooner rather than later, and Roan was his fastest method of transport.

Walsh answered and Roan wasted no time. "What's Canyon's condition?"

"It's like I told Wade," he said. "Couple of bruised ribs, possible broken back. We can't run him down on a snowmobile. We need chopper support. Can you help?"

The words lodged deep in his brain. *Possible broken back. Can't run him down on a snowmobile.* Translated: dragging him down behind a snowmobile could worsen the damage and potentially cause paralysis. No way. There was no way they could risk it.

Staring at the radar, Roan made a gut check. It would be rough, but he could do it. He had to go. He wasn't leaving Canyon up there any longer than absolutely necessary.

His friend needed him.

"What's going on?" Kelly asked.

Roan ignored her plea for information and said to Walsh, "I'm coming up. Text me your GPS coordinates and give me fifteen, maybe twenty minutes."

Kelly searched his gaze. "Roan? Are you serious?"

"Canyon's down with a possible back injury," he said, ending the call.

"Oh no..." Her eyes rounded and the concern in her gaze mirrored the emotion tearing through his midsection.

Oh yes—and it was up to Roan to get him down to safety.

"I'll go with you," she said.

"No. I'm going alone." Not trained in the mechanics of search and rescue operations, all Kelly could do to assist matters was fly, and flying was *not* what she needed to be doing right now.

"But Roan," she pressed. "I can *help* you."

Pausing, he looked her square in the eye, battling the torrent of thoughts and emotions that churned through him. The hurt in her gaze was clear. Instinct urged him to address it, but there was no time. Kelly was a distraction he didn't need right now—on so many levels—and he would have to leave it at that. "I'm going," he told her firmly. "You're staying."

Kelly watched as Roan left the building. A heavy weight settled in her chest. He was flying back up the mountain without her. End of story. The logical side of her understood his reasoning. It was true. The weather would prove enough of a challenge for his flight. Add the weight of five men and a dog and he'd be running heavy as it was. There was no room for her, even if he wanted to include her. Kelly heaved a sigh. But the emotional side of her knew his answer wouldn't have changed if he'd been carrying one man and a dog. Roan didn't want her in the air with him. Period. She was a liability.

The heaviness moved from her chest, pushing into her stomach with a crushing sensation. This was not who she was. She was a pilot, a team player. She should be in the thick of it—flying, assisting—taking part in the mission. But she wasn't. Couldn't. Because she had proven herself unfit to fly, in his eyes. Kelly turned, walked toward the refrigerator, and stopped. She wasn't hungry or thirsty. Realizing she held an empty water bottle in her hand, she tossed it into a garbage can next to the sofa. With a glance toward the television, and a glance toward a table littered with flying and golf magazines, she had no other option but to sit here and wait.

Only she had no desire to sit here and wait. She had no desire to do anything.

Casting her gaze out through the windows, she saw Roan and one of the Summit Aviation Services employees begin to prep the K2 for flight. *Pilot error kills, Kelly. It kills you and it kills others.* Is that what he thought of her? Did he really think she'd lost all of her ability to fly after one slip-up?

I don't want this to come between us. Recalling those words, the sweet slip of his voice when he said them, it almost sounded as though he had feelings for her, as though the two of them were something more than flight instructor and student. But Roan had never given her any indication that he was interested in her personally. It had always been about the lesson, the hovering lesson.

Curiosity percolated. Had something changed?

As soon as Kelly considered the idea, she brushed it away as nonsense. Roan was a straight shooter. He didn't play games like some men she knew. He played it straight—like Guy had always done. He liked something, he told you. He didn't, you heard about it. Suddenly, the brunt of this morning's incident slammed into her. She had lost it because she'd been reliving the day she lost Guy Flannigan.

Heartbeats fluttered in her chest. Closing her eyes, Kelly tried to shut out an instantaneous flood of images from that day, the fiery explosion, the subsequent news about the torched remains. She couldn't think of him right now, yet she couldn't erase the images storming through her mind. Guy had been an amazing pilot. He'd handled his Apache with a skill she respected, handled her with an honesty she longed for. Guy had always looked out for her. He told her what she needed to hear, not what she wanted to hear. He kept her honest. He kept her striving to be her best. He'd been her first love, her only love. Thinking about the man who was no longer, she felt a deep ache wind through her heart.

She had been his wingman, his air support, and she had failed him.

How could she have let him down? How could she have failed him so miserably and completely?

Storming out of the FBO, Kelly hurried to her truck. Covered by a film of filthy grime, the red short-bed was parked behind the building and blanketed by a layer of freshly fallen snow, yet the dirt was unmistakable. Only in Colorado had she seen cars look disgustingly dirty for months on end.

As she strode across the blacktop, cold air stung her cheeks and nose. The low whine of helicopter engines came to life as she pulled a key fob from her pocket and pressed a button. The lights on her vehicle flashed twice and the locks popped loudly. There would be no relief from the chill inside the cab, only a reprieve from prying eyes and curious stares. Kelly jumped in, slammed the door closed behind her, and gunned the engine to life. She didn't put the truck into gear. She just sat, inundated with memories and images she wanted nothing to do with.

Roan was right about one thing: it *had* been someone important in her life that caused the flashback. Someone very important.

Tears sprang to her eyes and she gripped her steering wheel. Hard. Now those memories—feelings, longings, old wants and desires that would forever go unfulfilled—were threatening to jeopardize her flying career. She'd been the cause; she'd been left empty by the outcome. Roan's face punctured her thoughts and Kelly screamed. "Stop!" She smacked the wheel and shouted at the top of her lungs, "What do you want me to do? I *failed*, okay?! I was trained to handle stressful events and I caved. I fell apart!"

Kelly had no idea who she was speaking to—screaming at—and it didn't matter. The action of shouting felt good. Similar to opening a shaken can of soda, the eruption was quick and complete and it felt good, releasing a tension she hadn't realized ran so deep.

"I don't know what you want from me," she yelled, energy waning with every breath. "I don't know what else I can do..."

She'd left the military. She'd moved to a new state. She'd started a new life. What more could she do? What more was there possibly left for her to do in order to move on with her life? It wasn't like she could erase the memories from her mind. She couldn't pretend it never happened.

Kelly froze. Staring out her windshield, her eyes glazed over. But that's exactly what she had asked Roan to do.

What do you want me to do?

Forget it ever happened.

Steam billowed from beneath her truck as she sat fixated on the thought. *Forget it ever happened.* How did one do that? How did an intelligent person forget what they saw, what they heard, what they knew to be true?

The thunder of blades filled her chest, reverberated through her body. Kelly's attention darted to the FBO. Roan was seconds from liftoff. Soon he would be in the air, mountain-bound, on his way to save Canyon—save the day—and she would be sitting here. Alone. Yearning swamped her, filled every nook and cranny of her heart and soul.

No. Don't leave me here. Please, don't leave me behind.

Tears rolled down her cheeks as she watched the helicopter lift from the ground and gently swing toward the right, toward town. Heartstrings shriveled into knots. Kelly had no place to go. No place to go except down. Leaning forward, she craned her head to watch the Augusta until the last bit of tail boom disappeared from sight. She wasn't going up with him, might never go up again. Because she was going down—down, down, down.

Chapter Twenty-Two

Gaining altitude as he flew over the town of Silver Creek, Roan clipped into his mic as he glanced uphill. Clouds shrouded the peaks, warning that the storm was still in full swing. Not what he wanted to see, but everything he expected to see. "Delta three-eight to base. Do you copy?"

"Base, copy."

"I'm en route to Walsh, ETA twenty."

"Copy that. I'll call Walsh and let him know to expect you."

"Roger," Roan replied, and ended the communication.

No more details were necessary. He knew what needed to be done.

As he cruised over the crowded streets below, Roan's thoughts returned to Kelly. The look in her eyes when he told her she wasn't coming pulled at him. But there was no way she could come, not with Sean, Walsh, Goose, and Canyon on board. And the dog. Roan couldn't forget Rugby—after all, the Lab was responsible for finding Canyon. No, flying that many passengers was mathematically impossible.

Kelly would understand. She was no rookie. He wished it hadn't felt personal, as though it was a direct rejection after her incident earlier. It wasn't. Not at all. It was a matter of safety.

Forget that it ever happened. Roan wasn't surprised that she'd asked him to keep the episode to himself. He'd had a friend once who asked him to do the same thing. *Hey, keep this between us, bro.* Only that time it had been a matter of a bad breakup. The guy was going crazy over a girl that had left him, had a complete meltdown in front of Roan to the point where he thought the guy was going to hurt himself. Roan told him to get help, that it wasn't the end of the world. The guy's reply?

You know what that will do to me—I'll lose my certificate.

Roan couldn't argue the point. Fighting to get a clean bill of health for the FAA could be a long and arduous battle, and it hadn't been the first thought on his mind when he'd suggested getting help. Which was a shame. They were human. Emotional. Sometimes life got sticky and there was no reason pilots shouldn't be allowed to get help when dealing with it. Things were getting better, but it was still a fight. The fact remained that pilots with any hint of medical instability were marked. It was that simple. Sometimes, it was for good reason. Airline pilots with suicidal tendencies could take hundreds of people down with them. PTSD could interfere with clear and level-headed thinking should crisis strike. As a flight instructor, he looked for those two core characteristics in every student: clear and level-headed thinking. The statistics were all too familiar to him. More than mechanical issues, weather, or hostile fire, pilot error was the leading cause of plane crashes, both civilian and military.

It was one of the reasons Roan took his position as a trainer so seriously. No one could put a number on the accidents prevented. They could only count the number of aircraft destroyed, the number of lives lost. Kelly needed to face the truth. She was hurting inside. Watching her friend go down in that chopper was eating away at her, that much was obvious. If she didn't get help, the torment would only continue. But if he didn't report what he knew and let the authorities decide, the secret would eat away at *him*.

It was something he couldn't live with.

As he neared the mountain ridge, Roan shifted his focus to the mission. He had a job to do and that's all he was going to think about. He could deal with Kelly and her issues when he returned. Taking a wide sweep over the resort village, Roan banked left and headed straight up, sailing over a mix of evergreen and bare aspen, trees that appeared more like toothpicks than trees without their leaves. Between them, huge swaths of groomed white snow were cut out, skiers appearing like ants scurrying down a hill. It was peak season on the slopes and people were taking full advantage. Same as his friends.

Roan thought about his friend Canyon. According to Wade, they'd found him completely by chance. After hitting a rock. Roan winced. Well, the guy did ride bulls for a hobby. Maybe it wasn't that much different from getting bucked off the hind side of a bull, he mused, imagining Canyon writhing on top of a two-thousand-pound meaner-than-a-snake ballbuster. The image drew a smile to Roan's lips. He'd watched Canyon ride a few rodeos and the guy was good. Crazy, but good, and earning a lot of money that he donated right back to Wainwright Ranch.

Roan's heart squeezed at the thought of Wainwright. Katharine would have been a mess if anything had happened to Canyon. She wasn't from Colorado, and from what he could tell seemed more "delicate socialite" than "rough-and-tumble cowgirl." He never thought her Canyon's type and, in the beginning, didn't give the relationship three months. But the pair was proving him wrong. They'd been together for over six months now, and they were showing no signs of quitting. In fact, Roan wouldn't be surprised if Canyon popped the question and made it official.

With every foot of rising elevation, the weather deteriorated, pulling Roan's thoughts from his musings. "Still looks like crap," he muttered aloud, tracking the coordinates Walsh had supplied as he scanned the landscape below. Situated near a line of trees, the target zone wasn't far from Jack's downed chopper. If Roan remembered correctly, there was a narrow strip of land where he could set down. Fairly steep, it would be risky but doable. If only he had a crew, he could lower a line.

Unfortunately, he was riding solo on this one. Syncing with the constant drum of rotor blades, Roan steadily moved his gaze back and forth, sweeping the terrain for sign of them.

Canyon would be hidden from sight beneath the trees, but one of the guys would stand out by the perimeter and vector him in. Roan only needed to get close. The guys could grab a spine board and transport Canyon to him.

Glimpsing a spot of red against the backdrop of white, Roan pitched left, securing a better view out his right window. Was that an SAR jacket?

Yes. Whoever it was waved. A gust of wind lifted the chopper sharply. Roan quickly recovered position and released a tight sigh. This might be tougher than first thought. With a steady hand, he lowered the chopper, forcing an angry swirl of snowflakes that dropped visibility to zilch. Roan worked from instinct. Feeling his way through the maneuver, he knew his blade span, could see the angle of the slope as he got closer. The SAR member kept his distance as Roan brought the chopper down, his rotor blades perilously close to the mountain as the skids kissed the ground. "Crap!"

Roan lifted and hovered, his blades furiously whipping the snow beneath him. His man on the ground held a hand over his face but didn't change position. He was waiting. Because he knew Roan, and knew Roan wouldn't give up. Checking the vicinity once again, he moved slightly backward and re-tried the maneuver. The bird shifted restlessly beneath him. Unable to anchor on hard ground, he dubbed it close enough.

A man ran towards him. The rear cargo door opened and a howl of icy air swept into the cabin. Goose Wilcox climbed in, giving a thumbs-up.

Breath Roan hadn't realized he'd been holding escaped in a rush. "Goose!"

Not like the man could hear him, but it felt good to say his name as he watched him scramble across the back and grab the spine board. He exited the aircraft as quickly as he'd entered and jogged cumbersomely toward the forest. Roan lifted from the ground, preferring to wait airborne as opposed to on the ground. Too many things could go wrong, including

ONLY WITH YOU 173

one slice of rotor blade into mountain rock whereby it would be "operation expiration."

Estimating the time it would take to secure Canyon for transport, Roan decided to lift higher. When he saw them emerge from the forest, he'd drop back down. "Delta three-eight to base, do you copy?"

"Copy, base."

"The guys are prepping Canyon for the ride now. I'd give them about five to ten and then we're heading down."

"Roger that. Hospital has been alerted and staff is expecting your arrival."

"Ten-four."

"Kelly's here and wishes you Godspeed."

Roan quelled a rush of nerves. "Kelly's there?"

"Yes."

Roan didn't know what to say. Why would she be at the police station? Had Wade called her? Was she keeping tabs on the rescue mission? She had started the operation with him... It made sense that she'd want to know the outcome.

"Let us know when you're en route."

"Roger," he murmured, his thoughts torn between the scene below and Kelly, more specifically everything she represented at the moment, both good and bad.

Chapter Twenty-Three

"Thanks," Kelly said, standing next to Wade as he ended the radio contact with Roan.

"No problem," he replied, curiosity spinning in his dark eyes. "Now what was it that you wanted to talk to me about?"

Dressed in a full suit and tie, Chief Wade Davis appeared utterly formal and foreboding to her. One of her father's closest friends, he was a good-looking man, had always been kind to her, but he was nonetheless intimidating. He reminded her of a commander she worked under while on active tour. He was a fair man and one for whom she held tremendous respect, one she had worked hard not to disappoint. Same held true for Wade.

Kelly spied the radio mic and a torrent of reservation swirled hot in her gut. "Is this a good time to talk? Maybe I should come back."

Wade sharpened his gaze on her. "We're not out of the woods, yet, but if you have something to say, say it. I'll tell you when I can't listen anymore."

Taking a deep breath, Kelly steeled her resolve and said, "I think I have PTSD."

Wade returned a quizzical gaze. "You think? As in you're not sure?"

She nodded. "I had a flashback during the flight this morning. I confused time and place, thought I was under fire, and, well, it could have cost me the mission. I could have jeopardized lives today and I can't accept that."

"Slow down," Wade said, his deep voice calm and reassuring. "I think you'd better start from the beginning. You're talking about the SAR mission for the heli-skiers?"

"Yes sir."

Wade paused, his gaze swirling with comprehension as he seemingly connected the dots. "Does this have anything to do with when Roan thought you went down and asked if you were okay?"

"Yes." Pressure pushed into her gut. "Jack's chopper went down and that's when it all came back to me."

Wade lowered a hip to his desk and sank his weight into it. He didn't appear angry or accusatory, more concerned. "Talk to me, Kelly. Tell me what's going on."

Tears pricked her eyes, butterflies swarmed her midsection, but she refused to let them undermine her. She was a soldier, an Apache combat pilot. She didn't cry. She was tough, strong—strong enough to face the consequences for her actions. "It happened during a combat mission," she began, looking directly into Wade's eyes, eyes that held familiarity and trust. This man was her friend. He was a longtime friend of her father's and practically family. If there was anyone she could confide in, it would be Wade.

Kelly told her story. She didn't leave out any details, no matter how personal or how painful, and she explained what had happened, how she felt about it, and her fears going forward. "I want to be a part of this team. I don't want to lose my license to fly with SAR because of one incident. It isn't fair."

Wade peered at her, a poignant sadness filling his brown eyes. "Combat stress is the worst kind of stress, Kelly. Watching a friend die in combat, feeling powerless to help but feeling responsible because you were there, that's tough. Really tough. Nobody will blame you for your reaction. Nobody."

"The FAA will," she protested.

"They won't, not in the long run. Not if you take the time to deal with it, they won't."

Kelly bit her lower lip and fought back a swell of anxiety. "We both know how this works. They'll label me as a psychiatric case. They'll insist on extended counseling and it will take me years to get a clean certificate." It was a stigma she'd wear around her neck like an albatross forever.

"The FAA is learning that PTSD is not a career-ending disorder. With proper treatment, it can be overcome. From what you're telling me, this is your first episode."

She nodded.

"Then it might be something a few counseling sessions can overcome. You might not have a chronic case, but step number one is figuring out what you're dealing with and going from there—not making assumptions about what the FAA will or will not do."

"Except that I already saw an Army shrink right after it happened."

Wade furrowed his brow. "One time isn't enough, Kelly. From what you said, this person was close to you, right? Or did I miss something?"

Kelly hesitated. She hadn't divulged exactly how close, but she nodded. "Yes. We were close."

"Then honor his memory by dealing with the loss. The FAA doesn't have to know anything more specific about your condition until you know it yourself. Take some time, get your head right, and then decide. If the counselor thinks you have a severe case, deal with it at that time. But you might be surprised by what you hear."

Kelly wanted to believe him. She wanted to cling to any scrap of hope he could offer, but the cynic in her wasn't so sure. Flying meant everything to her. It was her whole life. If the FAA grounded her, she'd *really* lose her mind, making the episode from this morning look like a walk through the park.

Wade lifted away from the desk and placed his hands on her shoulders. "Let me help you. I'll make some phone calls and we'll get through this process together."

"Yes sir," she murmured. "Thank you."

"Why don't you go and spend the rest of the day with your old man." Wade winked. "I bet he'd appreciate the company and I know he has one heckuva good ear."

Kelly nodded. Her father. Yes, she'd need to speak with him. He, above all people, would understand what she was going through and know better than anyone what she could do to continue flying and keep mentally healthy. After her mom left, her dad had gone through an emotionally rough time, during which he sought the help of a marriage counselor. Not because he thought he could make his wife stay. He couldn't. Alicia Jones hated Army life, hated that her husband seemed to prefer flying over her, hated the repeated deployments that left her alone to care for their child—so one day, she up and left the family. And of all the times she could choose to leave him, she had decided to do it while he was on tour, unceremoniously dumping her daughter with his mother. She claimed he'd abandoned her.

A total copout. Kelly knew her father had done nothing of the kind. He served his country, loved his family, and kept the faith. Her mother was the one who abandoned the family, not him. Kelly remembered well the feelings of abandonment she had endured at being discarded like a worn doll, a used toy no longer desired by its owner. Except she wasn't a doll, she was a human being. The fact that her own mother had been able to leave her with such ease had been imprinted on Kelly's heart forever. *Unwanted.*

And Kelly resented her for it. With every fiber of her being, she resented the woman and broke all contact with her. She and her dad were the only family she needed. He was her all, and she was his. If anyone had told her to give up flying, Kelly would have told them to go pound sand. But not him. He didn't fight it, only sought to understand exactly what had happened so that he could move on and not repeat the mistake.

Mistake. Kelly's insides curdled. It hadn't been *his* mistake. It had been his wife's.

Shaking the sudden animosity from her mind, Kelly inhaled deeply, squared her shoulders and said, "Thanks again, Wade. I appreciate you hearing me out."

"Anytime, sweetheart. I'm always here for you." He smiled, and the tender affection in his gaze nearly undid her.

Katharine Wainwright sat rigid in her chair, one of many lined up against the wall in the surgical waiting room. She clutched her designer purse, opened the center section and spied her phone. Should she call Wade? It had been over an hour since she'd left the police station. Had something gone wrong? Would he call her if it had?

Seated next to her, Adele spoke softly, "He's okay, Katharine. I'm sure you'll hear something soon."

Katharine's gaze darted to her side. "Are you a mind reader now?"

Adele placed a hand over Katharine's. She smiled, and her dark eyes held a knowing gaze. "You've reached for your cell phone eight times since you've been sitting here. I know you want to call, but no news is good news, remember?"

Flicking a gaze toward Lisa and Kinsley, seated in chairs opposite her and Adele, Katharine asked, "Is that how you're coping? You haven't heard a word about Hal's condition, yet you're counting on no news being good news?"

"I trust his physicians. They'll let me know when there's news to share."

"She's right, Katharine," Lisa spoke up. "Canyon is in good hands. If anyone can get him down that mountain safely, it'll be Walsh and Roan."

"There are two others with him," Katharine said. "Sean and Goose?"

"Both great guys," Adele confirmed.

Katharine knew Sean. He owned a black Lab that worked with Canyon's dog, Buck, on search and rescue operations, and she had come to like him very much. Goose was a stranger to her, other than meeting at an SAR barbecue last fall. Roan and Walsh were Canyon's best friends, men he trusted with his life. She knew Lisa was right, but unwinding the knot of tension in her stomach was easier said than done. Katharine looked to Kinsley. She appeared as worried for her boyfriend as Katharine was for Canyon. "How are you holding up?"

Kinsley shrugged. "I'm hanging tight. Like Adele said, I trust the doctors. They know Grant's history and have treated him for a long time. They'll let me know when they can."

She was so matter-of-fact, Katharine thought, and much more stoic. It was a character trait she envied at the moment. Try as she might, she couldn't shake her worry. She had no idea what to expect. How did Canyon get separated from the group? Why hadn't he used his cell phone to call for help? If they hadn't found him with others, something awful must have been the cause.

Turning her thoughts outward, she tried to focus on something other than her anxiety. "It's amazing you weren't caught up in the avalanche, Lisa."

"Sure is. If it wasn't for Walsh and his uncanny sense for danger, I would have been right smack in the middle of it! In fact, I was about to ski down when he told me to stop."

"Unbelievable," Katharine replied, latching onto Lisa's bright smile, willing it to loosen her mood.

"I'm amazed by how quickly it all happened," Kinsley said. "One minute we were skiing, the next we were bowled over by a pummel of snow. Grant was nowhere to be seen so we began a frantic search."

"That must have been so scary," Katharine said, realizing Canyon had also been nowhere to be seen, which would have compounded their fear. It was a good thing that she hadn't been up there with them, because she would have lost it altogether!

"It was definitely that," Kinsley agreed. Turning to Lisa, she added, "Actually, I've never been so scared in my life, as knowing Grant was buried under the snow and we had to find him."

"But find him, we did," Lisa said.

Kinsley stilled and looked to her friend. "If it hadn't been for you performing CPR, he might not have made it."

Lisa waved off the comment. "You would have done the same thing. I just hopped into action a little quicker."

Kinsley broke the glance and her voice fell away. "I don't know. I took the course after we started dating, just in case he ever had a heart attack...but when the time came to perform, I was in shock."

Katharine understood exactly what Kinsley meant. Knowing what to do in an emergency and acting upon that knowledge could be two very different things. She'd learned that firsthand. When Frank Dillard had tried to kidnap her after his embezzlement was discovered, she'd been stunned to the point of inaction. She couldn't think straight, let alone act. If it hadn't been for Canyon and Roan, she would have been dumped off in Mexico, leaving Frank to get away scot-free. Her gaze moved to Lisa. She didn't flinch when crisis hit. Katharine remembered Canyon telling the story about how Lisa and Walsh had met, when the girl had proved she was an expert when it came to Crisis Management 101. A killer stalked her, forced her off a cliff, rendered one leg immobile, then tried to shoot her, and she still persevered in her goal to get down the mountain alive. Katharine shuddered. Walsh had been with her, but still. Canyon said Lisa had been a real trooper.

Lisa's cell phone rang and Katharine's gaze zapped it like a fly. *Was it news about Canyon?*

"Hello?" Lisa answered, then looked to Katharine and the others. She gave a thumbs-up gesture. "Great news."

Katharine leaned forward in her seat, hanging from Lisa's facial expressions. What was great news?

"I'll let her know." Ending the call, Lisa announced, "That was Walsh. They're en route to the hospital and expect to be here in about ten minutes."

"Oh, thank God!" Katharine sputtered, her heart pounding erratically. "He's okay? Canyon's okay?"

"Walsh didn't get into details. He just said to let you know. You can meet them at the helipad if you'd like." Lisa stood and Katharine stood with her. "I'll take you."

Chapter Twenty-Four

Hands dug deep into the pockets of her parka, Kelly walked the cobblestone streets of Silver Creek. A flurry of snowfall sprinkled passersby, littering hair and wool caps with fluffy white flakes. Some slogged through the streets dressed in full ski gear, helmets secured snuggly on their heads, ski boots pounding heavily as they walked. Others were dressed for a casual day of shopping or sightseeing, chic in their expensive leather boots and scarves wound tightly around their necks. Meandering among them, Kelly felt out of place. She'd never been one for skiing. She didn't see the point in traversing hill after hill, riding a lift up so you could do the same thing all over again. It seemed boring to her. She was a runner. She liked a change in scenery, liked the way her body felt when she found a rhythm and sank into it for the long haul, immersing herself in the sights and scents. Occasionally she trained at the gym, sweating through the latest workout rage, Crossfit. She enjoyed it because it tested her limits, challenged her muscles and made her feel strong. Powerful.

It was the same way flying made her feel. Soaring high above the clouds, moving at incredible speeds, it gave her a sense of control. She felt alive, as if there were no limits except those she placed upon herself. Flying was in her blood. She lived and breathed it, like her father.

Spend the rest of the day with your old man.

Kelly slowed. She hadn't called him. Wade was right. Her dad would know what to do. He'd be able to guide her on how to proceed, how to handle the emotions she was feeling and what to do next, but she hadn't called him. She didn't want to face him, not yet. She needed time to organize her thoughts, and walking through town gave her time to think. Strategize. Decide the best way to break the news.

From a distance came the familiar rumble of rotor blades. Her heart stopped. Reflexively, Kelly looked up and turned in the direction of the sound. Seconds later, the expected helicopter sailed overhead. Several heads around her turned as well, peering up into the sky, their expressions overcome by curious stares. Seemed everyone wanted to know why a helicopter would be flying so close to town. Only Kelly knew the reason. It was Roan en route to the hospital. Silver Creek Medical Center was located half a dozen blocks from where she stood and Roan probably couldn't get there fast enough. He had an urgent delivery—one Canyon Laredo.

Kelly's heart tripped. She hoped he was okay. She hoped everyone was going to be okay after their ordeal this morning. It had to have been traumatic for them. She'd never experienced anything like it herself, but according to Roan, these kinds of situation weren't uncommon around here. They had dozens each season, and skiers had to be prepared.

His friends *had* been prepared, she mused soberly. It's probably what saved their lives.

Watching Roan put distance between them, a deep longing settled in Kelly's heart. Roan was an incredible guy with a great group of friends. Loyal to the bone, trained to perfection, his skills were sterling and so was his reputation. The compassion he had shown her back at the FBO was more than she had expected but rang true to his personality. Kelly knew a lot of guys who would have let their ego step in and rule the day, but not Roan. He allowed his heart to lead.

Allowing her gaze to drift, the hustle and bustle around her blended into one mass of blurred scenery, a sea of no particular face, no one place. For a moment, she floated between time and space. She should call her dad, but she wasn't ready. Soon. Soon, she'd call him and confess everything.

She wanted to call Roan, but she couldn't imagine what she'd say to him or why she'd say it. The most important words had already been spoken. Hadn't they?

Nerves skirted through her belly. A crazy thought had been circulating through her brain ever since she'd left the police station. She and Roan. Together. Heartbeats raced as she centered on the thought. *Is that so crazy?* If it wasn't, why did the thought of them together unsettle her so much?

Was it Guy? Was she still holding onto him after all this time?

Kelly didn't know the answer. She didn't know what to do or what to think. It was too confusing. One minute she was steeped in longing for Guy, the next, Roan. What was wrong with her brain? What was wrong with her mind that she couldn't think straight?

Dialing back into the scene around her—the people, the tempo—Kelly kicked back into step. *Walk*, she told herself. *Walk it off and the rest will come*.

In one fluid maneuver, Roan set the Augusta down on Silver Creek Medical Center's helipad, then signaled to his SAR team that it was safe to unload. Same as before, a hospital crew was waiting to transport patients from rooftop to operating room or wherever Canyon's injuries warranted. Katharine Wainwright stood among them, her gaze pinched as she watched and waited. Behind Roan, the door slid open, allowing a brisk wind to whip through the cabin. To Roan it was a welcome sweep of fresh air. Much like the stress he'd felt moments before, the flurry of snowfall was a mere hint of the conditions he'd left behind, melting as soon as it hit the spot marked H.

Seated next to him, Walsh reached to remove his headset. "Thanks for the ride."

Roan smiled. "Glad I could be of service."

"Thank Kelly for me, too, will you?"

"Sure thing," he replied automatically, instantly filled with thoughts of her, the damage he was about to inflict upon her flying career, the sadness he'd witnessed in her dark-eyed gaze when all he wanted to do was see her smile. He wanted to hold her in his arms and reassure her that everything was going to be okay. But he couldn't. Because it might not be.

Pausing, Walsh held Roan's gaze for a long moment. "Is everything okay?"

"What do you mean?"

"I mean, your tone just took a nosedive."

"I'm fine," he said, and tried to shake the thoughts from his mind.

Walsh grunted. "Could have fooled me," he replied, removing his headset. Quickly pushing out of the helicopter, he joined his team as the medical staff wheeled their gurney to the helicopter. Rugby hung back but not too far, shadowing his master's every movement.

Leave it to Walsh to keep it short and sweet, Roan mused. The man didn't waste words. Not when it came to emotion, anyway. Turn him loose on a SAR mission and he'd unleash a litany of directives and instruction and talking non-stop as he and his team coordinated search efforts.

Katharine hovered just beyond the blade span, her eyes trained on Canyon as Sean and Goose eased him out the rear and onto the awaiting gurney. She couldn't hide the fear in her eyes even if she tried. Roan understood. Canyon was in bad shape. At this point they had no idea the extent of his injuries, only that they were enough to immobilize him. And that was saying something. Canyon was used to being bucked off bulls, and he was tough enough to bust his butt and get clear of their horns. To see him stopped cold by a skiing accident was not easy. He'd seen his fair share of falls and had always walked away. One thing Roan was certain of was that Katharine would remain by his side for the duration. She was that kind of woman and they were that kind of couple.

She rushed to the gurney the second it cleared the blades and grabbed Canyon's arm. The team stopped, allowing her to lean down and kiss him, then resumed their pace quickly and surely. Katharine cupped a hand over her mouth and

Walsh pulled her to him. It was a hug between friends, between two people concerned about their loved one. Contact broke as quickly as it had started and the two hurried to catch up with the others.

Watching the activity progress, Roan waited for Goose. Once Canyon was handed off and the hospital staff was briefed on his condition, Goose would need a ride back to his car at the airport. Sean and Rugby could take a bus back to the gondola.

Counting the seconds as Goose jogged back toward the chopper, Roan could only think about touching base with Kelly. Walsh had it pegged. Roan wasn't okay. He needed to talk to her. He needed to tell her how he felt and help make things right for her. As much as he wanted to forget what happened, he couldn't. Not in the air and not on the ground. Hot stabs of desire fired through him as thought about Kelly. There was no denying his feelings for her. They were complicated, but they were real.

Goose jumped into the left seat and closed the door with thumbs up. Roan powered the engines and lifted off, dipping the nose to the left as he headed for the airport. It would be a short flight from here and once landed, he'd call Kelly. Unless she was still there, which he doubted. But maybe. His pulse quickened. Maybe. In ten minutes, he'd know. Ten minutes.

Sailing over town, this bird couldn't move fast enough.

Kelly dropped to a seat on a low-profile stone wall. Bordering a cobblestone path than led to an elegant hotel, an exterior lined with balconies boasting slope side views, it was situated near the gondola and several restaurants with iron tables and chairs for al fresco dining. Still early, only half the tables were currently occupied, but Kelly had learned that once the *après* ski crowd hit there would be standing room only. It was the time of day when lifts closed, ski school lessons ended and skiers discarded skis and poles, stripped off their heavy gear and sought food and drink and music.

Glad for the early hour, Kelly wanted nothing to do with the merriment and festivities. She wanted to sit. And think. Organize her thoughts. Once she told her dad what happened, he would want to talk. He'd want to counsel her on the best way forward. His advice would be good. It would be solid. Only it wasn't a conversation she was ready to have. Not yet.

The cold penetrated her jacket, chilling her backside. Ambivalence bathed her heart. She wanted to talk to Roan. She wanted to let him know how much she appreciated him, how much it meant to her that he had taken the time to share his personal experience with her. His uncle had died an alcoholic. Kelly shuddered, and her was attention drawn to a group of women seated a table. Enjoying an afternoon of leisure, they had glasses of red wine all around. Alcoholism wasn't a fate Kelly was concerned for herself. She didn't even like the taste of alcohol. But she wasn't immune to the need for escape, one that had adversely affected Roan and his family.

Because I care about you. Kelly moved her gaze from the women, back to the anonymity of the mass of skiers congregating around the gondola. Strangely, those were the words that kept ringing in her ears. It had felt so intimate when Roan said them, so genuine. She didn't want to misread his intentions. If she mistook his feelings for her beyond friendship, she'd look the fool. The complete and total fool. But foolish was not how she felt at the moment. Staring at a couple of skiers walking passed, a man and woman, hand-in-hand, Kelly was acutely aware of a shift happening inside her. She hadn't had feelings for anyone since Guy. No one.

But Guy Flannigan was gone. There was no going back, no hitting replay. It was over. He would forever be a part of her, but he was her past. A sharp ache suddenly wound through her trailing ribbons of grief. Their relationship had been a slice in time, a piece of the pie. She had loved Guy. She had loved him with all her heart, but he was no more. He was nothing but a memory—a memory she would cherish, but one she had to move to the back of her mind. If she ever wanted to love again, and that was her core problem. She couldn't love again until she let go of Guy.

Kelly's pulse fluttered. If she were going to be brutally honest, she'd have to admit that Roan reminded her of Guy in many ways. Confident and capable, he was also sincere and down to earth. He wasn't cocky or condescending but instead, compassionate and kind. Well, not all the time. Roan razzed her to be sure, but it had never felt mean-spirited or insulting. It had been more rivalry and challenging. Roan pushed her because he wanted more from her, more of what he believed she held inside. It was a compliment. A vote of confidence.

Kelly's phone vibrated. The sensation startled her. Reaching inside her coat, she looked at the caller ID and her pulse jumped. Roan Phillips. With a shaky hand, she answered, "Hello?"

"Kelly, it's Roan. Where are you?"

She looked around, as though she'd forgotten. "Near the gondola."

"What are you doing?"

"I'm, uh..." She felt a warm flush in her cheeks. "I'm sitting."

If Roan thought she had lost her mind, he gave no indication. "Can I come see you?"

Heartbeats battered her ribs. "Sure. I'll wait."

"I'll be there in ten."

A shiver raced up her spine. Ten minutes. Roan would be here in ten minutes.

Chapter Twenty-Five

Kelly sat. Nerves ramped up, her mind raced as she contemplated Roan's intentions in coming to talk to her. It was most likely about her episode, the notorious "incident" as she now thought of it. Losing her license to fly posed a slew of problems, not only professionally but also personally. What would she do for a living? Would her father suggest she move back to Tacoma? Would he want her near him as she battled personal demons? What would she do if she stayed?

Silver Creek was a beautiful place. The resort town was littered with upscale boutiques and hotels, five-star restaurants and gourmet candy shops. It looked like a piece of Europe had been plucked from abroad and inserted into the mountains of Colorado, blending Old World elegance with the raw spirit of the American West. From the rugged landscape to the luxurious accommodations, this village appealed to thrill-seekers like Canyon Laredo and his friends, epitomized the strength and determination of people like McIntyre Walsh and his girlfriend, and indulgently embraced the utterly wealthy.

Even the drive to get here was gorgeous, which was saying something. Kelly hated to drive. But the winding highway leading into town had been cut through a section of mountain exposing striations in sediment that had been embedded in the red rock thousands of years ago. In some areas the rock face was steep and covered by evergreen, the highway tagged by a creek running alongside it, while in others the landscape swept gently away from the road, giving home to horse pastures and cattle grazing. Kelly never saw any wildlife on her drive in, but Roan assured her it was plentiful. Colorado took her breath away, but without flying, what would she do?

Glancing around, Kelly pondered her alternatives. Wait tables like the staff rushing in and around the outdoor café? Act as a lift operator and swipe electronic readers over jackets registering tickets of skiers as they filed past?

Idling on a group of ski instructors patiently leading children from one end of a moving sidewalk to the other, the leaders struck her as ducks waddling in a row behind their mamas. Kelly couldn't ski, didn't want to wait tables. She couldn't imagine herself in any of those roles. She was a pilot. Pure and simple. She flew helicopters for work and for play. Some people might like to hang out on the slopes all day, but not her. She wanted to be flying over them, cruising at speeds of one hundred knots or more!

From across the expanse of diners and milling guests, the gold rim of Roan's aviator sunglasses snared her focus. Riveted, she watched him scan the faces of people lingering about the patios, the gondola. Her breath caught. He seemed like a man with a purpose.

Kelly tamped down a rush of angst. Lifting up, she raised a hand and gave a small wave to catch his attention. Roan spotted her. Detouring around the fenced-in dining area, he headed straight toward her.

She gulped and dropped back to her seat. *Show time*.

"Hey," Roan called out before he slowed to a stop. He looked around, as though trying to figure out why she was sitting here. "Aren't you cold?"

A chill rippled across her shoulders. "No."

Roan lowered to a seat on the wall beside her. He glanced around once more and said, "Thanks for waiting."

No biggie. Not like she had any other place to go. Her pulse quickened. At least, no place else she *wanted* to go. "No problem," Kelly replied casually, pressing back the current of nerves ricocheting through her abdomen. "How's Canyon?"

"Not sure. He has a possible back injury, but we won't know anything until he gets some X-rays. Walsh is going to call me when he knows something."

"Oh," she replied, a sudden sinking feeling in her chest. She'd seen her share of back injuries during her tour of duty and inwardly cringed. Some of the soldiers had regained their ability to walk but others had not, relegated to permanent wheels. She hated to think of Canyon in the same predicament because of a skiing accident. In war, one expected casualties. In recreation, one did not. "Was he able to move his arms and legs?"

"Yes. It was the pain that concerned him most. Canyon's hurt himself a few times and knows what kind of pain is okay and what kind is not so okay. I think he was a little nervous. From what he said, he hit a rock pretty hard on his way down."

Kelly paused. "A rock?"

"Yep. He tried to outrun the avalanche and ended up going off the edge of a cliff, sideswiping a huge boulder."

"Wow." Kelly grimaced. "I bet that hurt."

"I'm sure it did. We're hoping it's only a massive bruise that's causing him pain, but we won't know until the doctors take a look at him." Roan shifted his knees toward her, then looked down. He removed his sunglasses. Blinking against the flat light, he rubbed the bridge of his nose. "Listen, I wanted to talk to you about today." He glanced askance. "We were interrupted earlier and we left it—"

She raised a hand. "I told Wade."

"You did?"

Visibly shocked, he stared at her, as if it was the last thing on earth he had expected her to do. Probably because that's how she had left it with him. *Forget it ever happened.*

Kelly felt bad for asking him to hide the fact in the first place. It wasn't fair. "You were right," she said. "I have to deal with it, not hide from it."

"I think you made the right decision," he said quietly, approval softening the shock in his gaze. "You'll be better off in the long run."

Kelly knew he was referring to the hopefully short-term struggle she'd have with her medical certificate. It was something she didn't want to think about but would eventually have to face. There were no guarantees. It would be her against the government bureaucracy and most people knew how that matchup typically ended. The little guy lost. "I want you to know that I appreciate you trying to help me. It was so unexpected, and I guess I acted a bit rash."

"Unexpected that I'd try to help?"

She shrugged. "Sorry. I don't know what I was thinking. Guess I was just freaked out."

"You didn't freak out. Not exactly," he said with a slight smirk. "You reacted the same way any other pilot would have reacted. You know the ramifications." His gaze grew serious. "But knowing them and accepting them are two very different things."

She nodded. "That they are."

"You're taking responsibility and that's what matters."

"Yeah..." Kelly sighed. Roan understood what she was facing. With him in her corner, she felt a little better. At least she wouldn't go through it alone.

"Can I ask you something?" He peered at her, a mix of curiosity and suspicion churning in his gaze. "The person you lost in combat, is it something you can talk about?"

Her heart pushed into her throat.

"I mean, I'm getting the feeling that maybe it was more than a friend..."

Her throat locked. Staring into Roan's eyes, his dark, sensitive, openly caring eyes, Kelly couldn't speak. Not the first word.

"You don't have to talk about it, if you don't want to. I understand."

When he looked away, she felt like a window of opportunity was closing—a window she wanted left open. Placing a hand to Roan's arm, she swallowed over the painful lump in her throat and murmured, "No, it's okay."

He wanted to know the truth. He'd sensed there was more to the story and had asked her directly. After the compassion he'd shown her today, it was the least she could do;

be honest. Tell him the truth. If she had any chance of getting past it, she had to talk about it. Her stomach tightened. *No matter how difficult*. "His name was Guy Flannigan," she confessed softly.

Comprehension registered swiftly in Roan's eyes.

She wasn't sure if he was upset or not, but he'd asked, and she was going to answer. Setting hands to her thighs, she squeezed her legs, wading through memories of Guy. His image was sharp, clear, details she could summon at will. To this day, Kelly could recall every line in his face, every curve of muscle, the nuance in his gaze. His smile was quick and strong, his touch tender and loving. Everything about Guy remained crystal clear in her mind's eye. And that was the problem. His memory burned bright and was tinged by regret. Tears threatened, but she held them in check. Roan was waiting.

"We were in a relationship." Kelly paused, debating how much she should reveal about the man who had once meant everything to her. There'd been a day when she couldn't imagine her life without him. But that day was gone. "Guy was a great pilot, a wonderful man, and he was...he was..."

The love of my life. Kelly looked away, torn between recall and reality. There had been no one like Guy. Not now, not ever. He'd been in his own league, personally and professionally. It didn't detract from Roan in any way, only set the bar high. She peered at Roan. Very high. "He was very important to me and I feel like it was my fault that he was hit, that his chopper went down. I feel like if I had done things differently, he wouldn't be dead."

There. She expelled a sigh. She'd said it.

Roan waited for her to continue, but when she didn't, he said simply, "It wasn't your fault, Kelly. You have to believe that."

"You weren't there." It was her generic reply, the one she'd relied on over the years to ward off sympathy, but it was also true. Roan hadn't been there. He didn't know. Nor did the guys in her unit, nor did the staff at the military hospital. Only her gunner had been there. And he'd never mentioned a word about it. Never tried to say nice things and let her off the hook. He just dealt with it. Guy Flannigan and his gunner were dead. He and Kelly had to abort. End of story.

"I know you," Roan said, pulling her back into the moment. "You're an amazing pilot. You fly a chopper like it's an extension of your body, like it's your right hand. You fly by instinct and you're not afraid of anything. If I flew combat and could choose anyone as my wingman, I'd choose you."

Tears burned in her eyes.

"Walsh thinks the same, you know. He said he'd share a foxhole with you any day of the week."

The image of her and Walsh sharing a hole in the ground during combat unwound the knot in her chest. Walsh was definitely a fighter. And a Marine. That man could survive anywhere, under any conditions. According to Roan, Walsh had actually lived on a mountain around here for a year—alone—because he didn't trust people. It wasn't a stretch for her to believe it. That was the kind of man Walsh was. Guy couldn't have managed it. He needed to be around people.

Inhaling deeply, Kelly looked past Roan and replied, "Well, that's saying something, I guess."

"It is. It's saying a lot. You hit a rough patch up there today. It happens. But you'll move on. You have a great future ahead of you." Roan dropped his gaze and reached for one of her hands. "I hope I can be a part of it."

The hairs on the nape of her neck stood on end as she did a double-take at the move. Through her thin leather gloves, she could feel the warmth of his bare skin as he pressed her hand between his. "Roan..." she sputtered.

"I have feelings for you, Kelly."

She stared wordlessly. *Feelings?*

"I know I've never said anything." A half-smile pulled at his mouth. "I kinda have this strict rule about dating students."

But now that she wouldn't be able to fly...

"Do you think it's a possibility?" Roan asked. "I mean, are you, do you still—" He dropped the question abruptly.

Seemed he didn't know how to ask the obvious question. Was Kelly too hung up on a past relationship to begin a new one with him?

Guy was someone she couldn't forget. If losing sight of reality this morning because of his memory didn't convince her of that, nothing would. But Roan was asking her to move forward. *Could* she move forward?

Peering into Roan's expectant gaze, Kelly realized she wanted to. The incident from this morning made her realize that there was more to her relationship with Roan than student and instructor. More that she wanted, and more that he wanted. It stirred a desire that she had long thought dead. And she was far too young to feel dead inside.

Doubt whittled at her. Was it too soon? Kelly didn't know the first thing about Roan's personal life, other than what he'd revealed to her today about his uncle. An eager curiosity began to build inside of her. Was Roan seeing someone?

But that wouldn't make sense, she thought instantly, not if he was asking to begin something with her. Kelly reeled in her emotions like a spool rewind. Roan was a good-looking guy. There was no way he'd remain single for long.

"Kelly?"

"Yes?" she blurted awkwardly.

Confusion seized his features.

"I mean, *yes*, I'm able to, I'm okay to—"

Roan laughed and shook his head. "We're not very good at this, are we?"

Kelly burst into laughter, the pressure released on her emotions like a locomotive blasting its exhaust cap. "No, I guess not."

He smiled and squeezed her hand. "How about we take it slow, huh? One day at a time."

"Yes," she replied, her gaze drawn to the billows of warm breath escaping from his mouth. Roan was someone real. Very. He was a real live, breathing, hot-blooded male. Startled by how quickly her thoughts detoured into intimate territory, Kelly savored a private smile. Maybe she would be okay. Maybe she *could* get over Guy and deal with the events of his death.

Guy Flannigan was another time, another place. They were details that didn't need telling. She'd been a different woman back then, with goals and a future that had since changed. Not that she would ever forget him, but at least she could put the past behind her and continue with the job of living.

Looking into Roan's face, his brown eyes staring into hers, Kelly thought yes, she could do this. She did have residual feelings for Guy, but she couldn't let them prevent her from moving forward with someone new. Part of her had always feared that hooking up with anyone else would be her way of plugging a hole, paving over a wound created by loss. But Roan felt different. He felt like that someone new. Not a substitute but his own man, a man whom she could love.

Chapter Twenty-Six

"How is he, doctor?" Katharine locked onto Canyon's hand as he lay on the hospital bed, his body filling the narrow mattress. The connection felt solid, warm, unlike the room. White walls, white sheets, the room exuded none of the understated elegance of the police station, or post office, or the airport...or any other public space in Silver Creek, for that matter. Generally, the buildings embodied the richness of the town, the robust spirit of natural rock and warm woods, the gorgeous scenery depicted by local artists and sculptors. But not the Silver Creek Medical Center. The appointments here were minimal, basic, except for the sleek machinery in the room. Katharine was not medically astute, but she recognized expensive technology when she saw it—digital monitors and colorful touchscreens. She'd actually invested in some of the companies branded onto the equipment sitting in this room.

Canyon's physician stood on the opposite side of the bed. Chart in hand, he flipped through several pages, then tucked the file under one arm. Clasping hands together, he dropped them to rest in front of him. He didn't appear to be much older than Canyon, which had initially concerned Katharine, but she deferred to Adele's counsel. If she said this doctor was the best in his field, then so be it. Katharine could overlook the fact that he looked like a recent graduate and would rely on his expertise, which Adele assured Katharine was vast. She'd also overlook his flirtatious smile and the dancing grin in his engaging green eyes. The man was confident. Katharine would take that as a good sign.

"You're a lucky man," Dr. Gordon said to Canyon. "You're going to walk away from this thrill ride with nothing more than some cracked ribs and a few pulled muscles."

Canyon rolled his gaze toward the doctor. "My back feels a lot worse than a few pulled muscles."

"I'm sure it does. You must have been skiing at a pretty good clip when you grazed that boulder. I'm afraid the bruises you sustained will be with you for a while. Your left side's a lot worse than the right."

"That's where I hit and bounced off." Canyon chuckled. "That rock won't forget me anytime soon."

Katharine squeezed his hand. "Canyon, how can you joke about this? You could have been killed!"

"No harm, no foul."

"*Canyon...*"

The doctor raised a brow as he watched the exchange.

Canyon returned a sheepish smile. "I'm sorry, sweetheart. It's nothing more than my way of getting back on the bull. I can't let it beat me. You can understand that, can't you?"

"You mean to tell me you're planning on going heli-skiing again?!"

"Would you be mad?" Canyon asked.

"Furious!" She slid a glance to their hands and mumbled, "However, I doubt that's going to stop you."

"You can't stop living," he said, lifting himself up. Canyon winced sharply and dropped back to the bed. "Now come down here and give me a kiss. I can't seem to meet you halfway."

Katharine groaned loudly to make sure that everyone in the room read her displeasure without confusion but obliged, leaning over to peck his cheek.

Canyon quickly turned his head and caught her on the lips. "Gotcha!"

With an exaggerated roll of her eyes, she said, "You're incorrigible."

"And I'm all yours."

"Yes," she replied, a swift relief flooding through her. Katharine was grateful for that fact. Canyon was the love of her life. If that meant she'd have to endure a future of nervous worry when he sought adventures, then that was the life she'd chosen. Maddening or not. Tamping back a swell of angst, she gushed, "I'm going to see to it that you don't move for a month!"

"A month?" Canyon looked to the doctor. "Tell her I don't need to be tied to the corral for a month."

Dr. Gordon grinned. "A month might be overstating it, but I'd definitely put you out of commission for the foreseeable future. Come back and see me in two weeks and we'll reevaluate then."

Canyon moaned.

"Count your blessings," Katharine told him. "Hal is going to be out for a lot longer than you."

Canyon rolled his head to the side. "He's going to be madder than a wet hen about it, too. How's he going to get around?"

"Don't worry. Adele will take care of him."

"With a restaurant to run?"

"She'll tie him to a post if she has to, same as I'll do to you if you don't sit still and let your body heal."

Canyon laughed softly. "See what I'm up against, doc?"

"I see that you're in very good hands." Shooting Canyon a knowing smile, Dr. Gordon retreated toward the door. "Call my office in a few weeks and I'll see what I can do for you then."

Canyon waved him off. "Thanks, doc."

"Yes, thank you, doctor. We appreciate everything you've done."

"My pleasure."

As Dr. Gordon walked out of the room, Canyon pulled Katharine nearly on top of him. "Now come here and keep me warm, pretty lady."

"Canyon! Your ribs!"

"My ribs are fine. This isn't my first rodeo, you know."

She smirked. "Very funny."

"Knock, knock," Adele said, rapping her knuckles against the open door. Eyeing Katharine's awkward position, she quipped, "Shouldn't you two wait until you get home for that?"

Katharine stood at once and pulled her hand from Canyon's. "Yes." Flicking a glance toward him, she added, "But I seem to be having some trouble convincing the patient."

"Want me to send Hal down? Maybe he could talk some sense into him."

"Not a chance," Canyon shot back. "I'm going home to sit by a warm fire with my woman. Besides, Hal's going to be as ornery as a goat."

"You're not kidding!" Adele laughed and cupped a hand to her forehead. "He's already complaining because they won't give him any crutches."

"No?" Katharine asked, surprised.

Adele shook her head. "No movement, no crutches. Zero," she said flatly. "They want him off his feet until his bone sets."

"Wow," Canyon said. "That's gotta hurt."

Adele frowned. "It does."

Katharine dropped her gaze and said, "Don't think you're going dancing anytime soon."

"Not even a slow one?" he asked, dragging out his request as he reached for her.

"No," she replied, but she obliged the kiss he was seeking. Soft and sweet, the sensation of his lips invited Katharine to linger, to enjoy the mere feel of him. Canyon was alive and that was all that mattered.

"You two never quit," Adele said.

"Why should we?" Canyon tossed back.

"You shouldn't. But I didn't come here to talk about your love life." She turned to Katharine. "I'm going to run home before heading back to the restaurant. Would you like me to give you and Cody a ride home?"

Reminded that her poor baby was stuck in a car in the parking garage, Katharine hesitated. "Well, Cody would prefer his warm bed to a cold car but—"

"Go," Canyon urged her. "They're not going to let me out of here anytime soon."

"Isn't Dr. Gordon releasing you today?"

"Yes, but the paperwork alone will take over an hour. Take Cody home and come back for me."

"Are you sure?"

"I'm sure." Canyon squeezed her hand. "Just don't forget to come back for me. I have no intention of spending the night here." He winked. "I have a fire to look forward to, remember?"

A rush of pleasure streamed through her. "I remember."

"I do want to stop in and check on Grant before we leave," Adele said. "Lisa went to see him and I told her I'd meet her there."

"Where is he?"

"They're monitoring him on the cardiac floor."

Katharine's pulse tripped. "Is he going to be okay?"

"From what I understand, yes. But he has a history of heart trouble so they want to err on the side of caution and keep him overnight."

Canyon's gaze filled with concern. "Walsh said they had to dig him out of the snow after the avalanche hit."

Adele nodded. "Lisa performed CPR but seemed to feel he would pull through without issue."

"He took a pretty big hit," Canyon said.

Adele nodded. "They're concerned but continue to hope for the best."

Katharine felt the sudden need to check in with the women herself. She didn't know Kinsley very well but felt like they were kindred spirits after sharing the same crisis. Leaning over Canyon, she kissed his cheek, relishing the familiar scent of him. "I'll see you later," she whispered.

"Give them my best, will you?"

"I will. And I'll check on Buck, too." These days, Canyon's dog usually hung out at the ranch with Cody, but she hadn't thought to bring him with her. One dog was enough to manage, even on a good day—let alone during a time of panic.

"And will you call Roan for me?" Canyon asked.

"Of course."

Canyon laughed. "Without my cell phone, I can't do a darn thing on my own!"

"I'm sure you'll have a new phone set up by tomorrow," Adele commented. "It'll give you something to do."

"Me?" Canyon scoffed. "I have more than enough to occupy my time without the added pain of programming a new phone."

Glancing to Adele, Katharine asked, "How about I stop and pick one up on my way back?"

"Black," he replied. "I want black this time and not silver. And don't get me the newer model. It's too big. Make sure they have an old one or don't get one at all."

Katharine patted his hand. "Yes, dear."

Adele laughed. "Talk about ornery! Since when do you care about what your phone looks like?"

"Since the love of my life decided I needed the latest and greatest and took it upon herself to acquire it for me." Canyon looked directly at Katharine. "I don't need the latest and greatest. I need functional."

"Functional," Katharine repeated. "Yes, you are a man of few needs, aren't you?"

"I am. You, the dogs, the kids, my rodeos. Done."

Adele laughed. "There's for summing up a life in four squares!"

Katharine laughed with her and it felt good. Really good. Today had been a tough day, harder than she had imagined possible. Not knowing if Canyon was dead or alive had hurt her deeply. It had caused her to think ahead and envision her life without him—what it would be like, feel like.

It had felt horribly empty. Canyon filled her world with an enthusiasm she hadn't had working in New York City. The investment business filled her days with details and challenges, drive and ambition, but not enthusiasm. Which was strange. Katharine had loved her life in New York. She had thrived on making deals and mergers, creating hedge funds and battling corporate raiders. But now it seemed a hollow existence. Working for the sake of money no longer fulfilled her; it couldn't compare with the satisfaction she derived from working with Canyon and the children of Wainwright Ranch. This was an existence that set roots. It was a life filled with love and compassion. How she had ever survived dancing to the beat of the world's financial center was something Katharine could no longer explain. Her life in Colorado felt right. Certain.

Heartbeats fluttered in her chest. The thought of losing it scared it her to death.

"I love you," Katharine said to Canyon, steeling her voice against a flurry of nerves, then followed Adele out of the room.

Katharine and Adele walked into the hospital room on the cardiac floor where Kinsley and Lisa sat in chairs that flanked Grant's hospital bed. Covered by layers of white sheets, he sat propped up by two pillows with a tube attached to one arm. His eyes were closed, his skin pale but not deathly hued. Beneath his cotton hospital gown, Katharine could see wires attached to electrodes on his chest, whereby monitors above him recorded his rhythm as a steady bounce of lighted display. She hated to see a man like this. It made him appear vulnerable, weak. Canyon had looked at odds in his bed, but had lost none of his virility in the setting. Grant, on the other hand, looked as though he needed round-the-clock care and attention.

"Hi, Adele," Lisa said brightly.

"Hi. Where's Walsh?"

"He went with Goose to get his car."

"Good idea. How's the patient?"

Grant's eyes fluttered open and he replied, "He's good."

Good? Katharine wondered and shared a skeptical glance with Adele. Did he really know?

"Glad to hear it," Adele said, easily rolling over any doubts or concerns. "You put a scare into us, Mr. Powell."

A small smile tugged at his mouth. "I'm sorry."

Kinsley reached for his hand and said, "A big scare."

Grant's smiled faded. He turned his head slowly to look at her. "I'm going to be fine."

"I know, but that doesn't mean you didn't have me guessing there for a while."

"I still can't believe it..." Grant murmured. "That thing came out of nowhere. I've heli-skied almost a dozen times and never encountered an avalanche before."

"Hal says they can sneak up on you," Adele noted. "It's why I say helicopters and skiing don't mix."

Katharine emitted a nervous chuckle. "I'm with you."

"It's part of the deal," Lisa said affably. "With adventure sports, you run the risk that your adventure gets a little *extra* risky."

Katharine balked. "A little? It's amazing no one was killed up there!"

"Probably why you sign your life away in legal waivers," Kinsley replied wryly. "Add in a check for thousands of dollars and it's part of the appeal for those thrill-seeker types." She hitched her head toward Grant, adding, "They can't get enough of it."

"Does that mean you're not going up with me again?"

"You're seriously going to chance those extreme conditions again?" Katharine balked. "After everything that's happened?"

A faint smile returned, more knowing than anything. "Avalanches are one in a million."

"Uh, not exactly," Lisa said tentatively, as though uncertain whether or not she should explain the realities to them.

Kinsley slid a glance toward Lisa. "He knows better. He thinks he's pulling a fast one over me, but he's wrong."

Adele set hands to hips and asked, "Today was your first time heli-skiing, wasn't it?"

"Yes."

"Will it be your last?" Katharine asked.

"No." Kinsley sank back into her chair and said, "I can't give up over one bad run. Wouldn't be fair to the sport."

"That's my girl," Grant said, evidently ready for another run himself.

Which was insane. Katharine thought they were all insane.

Lisa smiled. "The thrill isn't supposed to be from fear of an avalanche and a 'Will I survive or not?' mentality. It's the thrill of skiing virgin powder. It's totally bomb!"

Katharine crossed her arms over her chest. "Thanks, but I'll seek my thrills another way."

"You and me both," Adele agreed and walked to the foot of Grant's hospital bed. "Anyway, I'm glad to see you're okay. Hal was concerned."

Grant's gaze clouded. "I'd go and see him, but it seems we're both bed ridden at the moment."

"You'll have plenty of time to stop by the house and see him this week. He won't be going anywhere for a while."

Grant laughed softly. "So I hear..."

"I think that sounds like a great idea," Kinsley chimed in. "Because no matter what your doctor tells you, you're going to take it easy for the next several days, minimum."

Offering no protest, he replied, "Yes, ma'am."

Adele smiled. "I'm glad to see that you're showing more sense than Hal." She shook her head but didn't sound too upset and proposed, "I'll check my ingredients at the restaurant and whip up something nice for you boys."

Grant groaned loudly. "Now you're talking my language."

"Mine, too!" Lisa chimed in. "Can Walsh and I join you?"

Adele laughed. "Absolutely." Turning to Katharine, she said, "We'd better get going. Sounds like I have work to do!"

Chapter Twenty-Seven

Roan's heart swam with a strange new pleasure. Kelly was open to a relationship with him. After months of dodging his feelings for her, avoiding the constant impulse to touch her during their lessons or make a flirtatious remark, he could now pursue his desire. But Guy Flannigan had clearly been important to her and he'd be wise to keep that in mind.

No problem, Roan mused. He would take it slow. Whatever had been between them was no longer. The man was dead. Roan winced inwardly. A death Kelly felt responsible for. She wasn't, of course. If there was one thing he knew, it was that she would have done everything in her power to save a man in battle. He could feel it in his bones. Kelly was good. Damn good. He hadn't been kidding when he'd said he'd want her as his wingman in combat. Walsh hadn't been kidding when he'd said he'd share a foxhole with her. Kelly Jones was that kind of woman. If her fellow soldier hadn't been saved, he couldn't be saved. It was that simple.

It was an issue they'd face together. Moving forward, if she was diagnosed with PTSD, Roan would be there for her. If she lost her license to fly, he'd help her get it back. But those were goals for another day. Right now, he wanted to check in on Canyon.

Roan turned to Kelly. "Wanna go to the hospital with me? I'd like to check in on my buddy and make sure he's okay."

"Canyon?" she asked.

"Yeah."

Kelly dropped her gaze to their entwined hands. For a second, Roan feared she was going to pull away. But she didn't. "I was going to go see my father..."

Her father. To tell him what had happened. "Oh, I'm sorry. I wasn't thinking. Don't let me stop you, then," Roan dodged quickly. "I don't want to interfere with you and your dad."

She smiled, the move coy and flirtatious and totally unlike her. "You're not very good at this, are you?"

"What?"

"Girls."

The word struck him as odd, the polar opposite of the woman who had uttered it. So much so that he didn't know what to say.

Kelly burst out laughing. "Don't tell me you've never taken up the offers from those adoring female students of yours!"

"No," he replied, instantly feeling stupid. "I told you, I don't date students."

"Do you date anyone?"

"Of course," he snapped. "I date all the time!" He didn't, but *she* didn't have to know that. He was too busy flying to spend his time chasing women. Didn't make him some kind of loser, he mused sourly.

"Wow." She shook her head. "This should be fun."

It should be, but suddenly their conversation was becoming anything *but*. "Listen—"

Kelly raised a hand. "I'll go to the hospital with you."

"You will? What about your dad?"

"He can wait. I was only going to see him because I thought my life was over."

"And it's not?"

She grinned broadly. "No." Squeezing his hand, she leaned over and kissed him.

Directly on the lips. Stunned, he stifled a gasp. The feel of her mouth on his was shocking—unexpected—in the most exhilarating and mind-reeling sort of way. Roan immediately kissed her back, leaning into the connection as he probed the warm sensation building between them. It obliterated the cold pinching his ears and nose, wiped out the crowd around them.

He could feel nothing but Kelly—and a sharp rise of want. Kelly pulled back but Roan reached up and grabbed the sides of her head tenderly. He wasn't ready to let go of this. Not yet. She emitted a guttural sound and softened, allowing the slip of his lips over hers.

Pleasure exploded inside him. This was going to be good, really good—but not here. Not in front of the prying eyes of strangers. Roan jerked away abruptly and stood. "Let's go."

"To the hospital?"

"For now, yes," he replied, purposely vague as thoughts raced through his mind, feelings rushed through his body. While he enjoyed the surprise in her gaze, he wanted time to think about his next step. Contemplate the "how, where, and when" of this new relationship.

Do you date anyone?

Roan savored a private smile. *Oh yes*. Now more than ever.

Roan strolled into Canyon's hospital room with Kelly by his side, startled to see Canyon sitting on the edge of the bed. He wasn't laid out in a hospital gown and wired for sound as Roan had expected him to be, but instead, the man was wearing the same ski pants and turtleneck Roan had transported him to the hospital in. The only thing he was missing was his ski jacket, but that lay tossed over a chair next to him. Shouldn't he be under a doctor's care still? It was only a few hours ago that he'd careened full-speed into a rock!

"Hey, Canyon," Roan said light-heartedly, exchanging a questioning gaze with Kelly. "How's it going, buddy?"

"Great. Did Katharine call you?"

"She did."

"So you know the deal."

"She gave me the spiel while I was on my way over, but I wanted to come and see for myself." Roan glanced over Canyon's body from head to toe and settled on his face. The guy didn't look like he'd just tapped the door of Heaven. He wasn't covered in bruises, nor was he scratched up or gouged. Instead, he looked more like a man passing through for a patient visit. "For a guy who almost ate it, you don't look too bad."

Canyon chuckled. "It was a rough morning, but thanks to you two," he replied with an audible wince, "I made it without incident."

"Without incident?" Kelly blurted in disbelief. "Is that what you call crashing into a rock and nearly breaking your back?"

Canyon laughed and covered his ribs with a hand. The other hand hitched a thumb in her direction. "Who dragged in Miss Sunshine?"

Roan smiled, amused by the commentary, but didn't utter a word.

"More like Miss Reality," Kelly spit back. "You could have been killed!"

"Now you sound like my girlfriend."

But she wasn't. Roan suppressed a grin. She was his girlfriend, though it was a bit too soon to open *that* can of worms. "Well, I'll vouch for her concern. You definitely had us worried, but I'm glad to see you're okay. Ya know... I almost didn't make it back up for you."

"I have full faith and confidence in you, Roan. I wasn't worried for a minute."

"Seriously," Kelly put in, swapping a stunned look with Roan. "The weather was crap. The helicopter was almost grounded."

Canyon shrugged. Settling on Kelly, a glint of amusement flashed in his gaze. "I knew you two would come back for me eventually."

Kelly stiffened. It was subtle, but Roan caught it. She hadn't been allowed to go back for him. But where Canyon missed her tension, he seemed to be picking up on a different wavelength in the room. A hint of comprehension crept into his gaze. Seemed he sensed something had changed. Roan's pulse caught. Was it that obvious?

He'd razzed him about it enough times, suggesting Roan should hook up with the "new blood" in town before someone else did. Resisting the urge to tell all, Roan shook the thoughts from his head. Eventually Canyon would learn the truth. Sliding a gaze toward Kelly, Roan thought, *They all will*.

Walsh and Lisa walked into the room and stopped short. "Someone having a party they forgot to tell me about?" Walsh cracked.

Both Walsh and Lisa still had their ski gear on. As usual, Lisa sported pink, while Walsh was clad entirely in black. The color definitely gave him a dangerous bend, Roan mused, underscoring the odd green of his eyes. Against his deeply tanned skin, the sea-green color jumped out as though sucking in your every last secret. Funny, but secrets weren't something Roan normally concerned himself with—until Kelly.

"No party," Roan replied quickly, instinctively wanting to spill his news but deciding it was better to wait. Standing in the middle of a hospital room with his best friends didn't seem quite the right time. This should be about them and their ordeal, not him and his new...his new...

Roan looked at Kelly to fill in the blank and, instantly, thoughts of their kiss popped into his mind. Drawn to her mouth, he was overcome by an urge to kiss her. A very strong urge. Swallowing hard, he simmered in thoughts of her. Kelly was hot. *Very* hot.

"That was some pretty decent flying up there," Walsh said to Kelly, sailing smoothly over the undercurrent in the room. A man of few words, the ones he did speak carried heavy weight.

Kelly cocked her head as though about to object, but replied with a quiet "Thanks."

Walsh moved his attention to Roan, then the others, as if checking to see if anyone else in the room picked up on her hesitation. He was right to wonder. It wasn't like Kelly to hem. "Without you two," Walsh went on, "we would have been spending the night, something this guy might not have handled well."

Canyon bucked at the slight. "Me? I could have stayed up there for days."

Walsh grunted and looked between Roan and Kelly. "On a good day, maybe, but not incapacitated."

Canyon swept open palms over his body. "Who are you talking about being incapacitated? I'm fine, head to toe."

"We didn't know that."

Canyon laughed, trying not to grab his midsection as he did so. "Would've figured it out soon enough."

"Kelly was amazing up there," Roan said. "How she didn't go down with Jack is beyond me."

Walsh nodded and hitched hands to his hips. "Sign of a combat pilot used to flying in difficult situations."

Kelly's eyes glistened with a sheen of tears as they treaded sensitive territory. Roan's heart pricked with outrage. She had nothing to feel bad about. She'd recovered because of incredible skill and presence of mind. Her PTSD episode had been a hiccup in an otherwise stellar performance. Out of nowhere, Roan was flanked by guilt. Why hadn't he signed her off to fly SAR before now?

Shards of guilt stabbed him. Because he had wanted to keep her under his instruction. It wasn't pretty and nothing he'd cop to, but truth be told, a part of him had wanted to keep her close by not signing her off. Once he did, she wouldn't need him anymore. He'd be lucky to see her at all, since most SAR flights were solo operations. It wasn't often they'd need two choppers in the air for a rescue mission.

Then again, he could have asked her out on a date. Stealing a glance at the woman by his side, Roan avoided Kelly's mouth and focused on her jaw. Her angular, rattlesnake-like jaw, the one she could use to snap a comeback with a viper's speed and precision. Nerves shimmied through his gut as he wondered how many men were tough enough to risk *that* rejection. Roan laughed at himself. He wasn't sure if he'd make that list or not, suddenly glad he didn't have to find out. Their connection began naturally, as naturally as two people meant for each other could find one another—through shared experience. Good, bad, or ugly, crisis brought people together. In his case, Roan felt good about it. Witnessing Kelly's PTSD episode gave him a window into her soul, allowed him a peek at the delicate woman behind the façade of the combat pilot. The sensitive woman who pulled at his heartstrings, the sexy woman who drew lustful thoughts from him—the take-charge woman about to reveal him for the smitten fool that he was!

"Roan?" Canyon prodded, brow raised in amusement.

Registering his name with a noticeable delay, he turned to Canyon. "What?"

"Is there something you wanted to tell us?"

Walsh smirked. Lisa giggled.

Roan felt a hot rise to his cheeks. "What?" Involuntarily, he looked at Kelly, who was chuckling under her breath. "Great. Is it that obvious?"

Canyon cocked his head with a grin. "To your friends, it is." He laughed. "And to think I thought you had rules against this sort of thing. Is this what you really do during your lessons?"

"No," Roan denied fiercely. "It just happened when we—"

Walsh raised a hand. "How about we save the details for a beer?"

"Save what for a beer?" Katharine asked, walking in on the group.

"Nothing." Canyon laughed and doubled over holding his ribs. "Nothing we know of—yet, anyway!"

Roan wasn't sure he liked them making fun at his expense. Even Kelly seemed to be joining in. Nice, considering she was the cause of it all!

Kelly slapped a hand to Roan's shoulder and shook her head with a smile. "Definitely not very good at this."

Roan begged to differ, but trapped between the amusement of his friends and his embarrassment at being caught red-handed with feelings for a student, defending himself would only make him look silly. "Give me time," he told her with a sly wink. "I'll show you exactly how good."

Chapter Twenty-Eight

Sitting on the hood of her pickup truck, Kelly lifted her face to the sun and immersed herself in the sensation of facial skin baking. The thin denim of her jeans soaked in the rays, too, as did her bare arms. Dressed in a cotton tank, she had a denim jacket rolled in her bag for later. Colorado's summer days were warm but the evenings turned cool. Right now there wasn't a cloud in the sky and the sun felt intense, almost burning, but in a good way. It made her feel alive, at one with the world around her.

The booming chop of rotor blades hammered the air. Like heavy artillery rounds, the sudden sound thundered through her body as the helicopter swooped overhead. Pleasure filled her as she anticipated a flight with Roan. He was picking her up and the two of them were flying to Red Rocks for a concert. Her all-time favorite alternative band was playing and she couldn't wait to hear them. And from what Roan had said, the venue was amazing. It was a naturally formed geological open-air amphitheater unlike any other place in the world, courtesy of Mother Nature's architectural genius.

The site consisted of two three-hundred-foot monoliths, Ship Rock and Creation Rock as they were known, that provided acoustic perfection for any performance. The dramatic red sandstone towers had been in existence for millions of years, home to generations of animal and plant life. Roan said dinosaurs had probably walked by the towers and scratched their backs across them. The image brought a smile to her face. Pterodactyls had probably flown through the skies above, too, darting in and around the dinosaurs, taunting them like unwanted insects. Roan was kind of a nerd when it came to geological stats, though he always tried to make it sound fun. Not exactly what she expected from an ace helicopter pilot, but then again Roan was unexpected in so many ways.

Leaping down from her truck, Kelly hit the ground and her heart raced as she caught the glint of his sunglasses through the windscreen of his black chopper. Roan had proven he was a man among boys, a man who would stand by her side through good times and bad and never let her down. And Kelly had hit some bad times. Admitting her PTSD episode had been harder than she had imagined, giving way to feelings of failure and incompetence, the likes of which she had never known. At one point, she had considered returning to Washington with her father, but Roan wouldn't let her. He insisted that she needed to stay and fight her way back into the cockpit no matter how slim the odds seemed that she would prevail.

The FAA had advised her that she might be able to regain her certificate if she could demonstrably prove that she had dealt with Guy's death and had moved on without lasting negative effects. A mental health professional had to sign off on her evaluation and attest to the fact that she could handle the stress of flying solo under difficult circumstances. Then and only then would the FAA evaluate her individual case. Working in her favor was the fact that she didn't experience recurring nightmares, exhibited no substance abuse, and had finished her one SAR mission with a successful outcome. From the beginning, Roan had been a huge part of the equation. With the patience of a saint, he held her hand, looked her in the eye, and told her to press forward when every fiber of her being wanted to turn and run.

It was a good thing. Because of him, she had managed to stick it out and, to her surprise had received a six-month special issuance from the FAA. It wasn't a hundred-percent reinstatement, but it was a start. The day she received word had felt like the first day of the rest of her life. *She could fly*. For the time being, anyway. The certificate carried limitations, but with time, she'd be free as a bird to fly whenever and wherever she pleased. Roan promised her it would include flying with SAR.

Hovering just outside the Summit Aviation Services FBO, Roan brought the chopper down in a slow descent. Honing in on his figure, she felt excitement skitter through her pulse. Roan was the reason. He was the reason she was healing, the reason she would fly again. Old wounds still ached, but they were losing their power to unravel her. It had been a tedious process, talking about things she didn't want to talk about, re-living moments she wanted desperately to forget, but she was persevering. Because of Roan. Kelly jogged around the chain-link fence and headed straight for him. She would never forget Guy Flannigan, but for the first time in her life, she was beginning to see her future with a new man. Roan spotted her and waved. Kelly waved back. That new man was Roan Phillips.

Ducking as she approached, Kelly steeled her senses against the piercing whine of the engine and popped open the passenger door. Grabbing the metal frame, she placed a boot heel onto the foot pad and pulled herself up and in, snapping the door to a close behind her. A rush of warmth surged into her cheeks as Roan flashed her a smile, leaning over for a quick kiss. Strange, how six months together didn't dim the heat of his kiss. Her heart still pounded like it was the very first time. But that was Roan. He was fresh, unexpected—and hot. Kelly giggled as her thoughts went instantly to the previous night. *Very* hot.

She reached up for the headset and pulled it on. Adjusting the mic to her mouth, she said, "Hey."

"Hey yourself. You ready for a good time?"

She grinned, beaming at him like a schoolgirl. "Always."

"Good. Because I have a surprise for you."

"A surprise?" she asked, her stomach suddenly sinking into her seat as Roan lifted off. Crossing her arms over her chest, she resisted the natural urge to handle the controls.

He nodded but didn't say another word.

Kelly dropped her gaze to the tarmac as they quickly ascended. Roan wasted no time, banking over the hangar and heading east. "What surprise?" she pressed.

"If I told you, it wouldn't be a surprise."

Curiosity churned and she wanted to demand to know what he had planned, but at the same time, she loved that he kept her guessing. It was another one of his better features. Roan always kept one step ahead of her—or at least tried—and she loved it. She loved that he wasn't predictable or boring. Even his geological discussions were entertaining.

"Canyon invited us to the Wainwright Ranch barbecue this weekend," Roan said, his voice small and distant over the aircraft comms as it competed with the loudness of the engine. "Wanna go?"

"Sure. I enjoyed the last one. Maybe the kids will let me help them harvest their corn."

"Maybe."

Kelly ignored the skepticism in his voice. Roan wasn't into gardening; he was a cheeseburger kind of guy. But not her—she loved the idea of Katharine's ranch for terminally-ill children and loved even more the idea of them working their own vegetable garden. Kelly had never been exposed to gardening as a kid but thought it was a brilliant idea. A health nut, she believed every child should learn to eat more fruits and vegetables. Organic produce, all the better. Between Katharine's garden and Canyon's henhouse, the kids had it made—except for the fact that they were battling serious illnesses.

Kelly's heart fell. The kids were so precious and their attitudes so positive, one would never know the pain and stress of their young lives. They worked the ranch without complaint, even hiked through the mountains. One visit to Wainwright Ranch put Kelly's entire situation into perspective. Hers was similar in that it was an illness, but one from which she could fully recover. Hanging with the kids reminded her to count her blessings.

Settling in for the flight, Kelly skimmed the horizon. The terrain was flattening and growing spotty with brush. As they flew east, the land lost its rich hues from red clay and lush evergreen-covered slopes, but it was still beautiful. In the distance she could see the first inklings of skyscrapers. The Red Rock Amphitheatre was located outside of Denver, and Roan said the views of the city were incredible. Kelly couldn't wait for the concert and could barely contain her curiosity about the surprise. *What could it be?*

As though reading her mind, Roan looked over and said, "No guesses? I'd think you'd be chomping at the bit to know what I have planned for you."

"I can wait," she said, refusing to take his bait. Roan wasn't going to tell her, no matter how many times she asked.

He chuckled. "Aw, you're no fun."

"You only want me to ask so you can taunt me!"

He mocked, "Me? How can you say something so cruel?"

"Because I've come to know you, Mr. Phillips, and I know how that mind of yours works."

Roan shook his head. "No fun, that's what you are. No fun."

Kelly thought otherwise but was proud of herself for not hurling a litany of questions at him in hopes of breaking his secret wide open. She wanted nothing more than to pry it out of him, but she could wait. She'd have to. Besides, as the ground below became more populated, she knew her surprise would have to be revealed soon.

Roan pointed out their destination and Kelly's gaze zeroed in on the spot. She could see two distinct rock tower formations and felt a quick rush. They stood out easily against the drab beige hills. As they flew closer, she began to make out the terraced seating between the two rocks, converging at a simple covered stage at the bottom. It looked too simple to be capable of such stellar acoustics. Instinctively, she scouted for a landing pad. "Where are you setting down?"

He winked. "You'll see."

Soaring over the stage, the aircraft banked left, and she saw a large commercial bus in the parking lot, the kind that bands used to travel across the country. Shiny black, it had a neon-green stripe swirled along its side. The windows were blackened, guaranteeing the occupants complete privacy. She imagined the band members inside and excitement pumped through her.

Roan circled overhead and remarked, "That's the band's bus."

"I see that," she replied, looking for a place they could set down. "Where are you landing?"

"I figured I'd park right next to them."

She gaped at him. "Do you think that's a good idea?" Kelly doubted the band would want them that close. "I mean, they probably have security to prevent that sort of thing."

"We're good."

Roan's hands worked the controls, lowering the chopper to the ground. She eyed the space between the chopper and bus. He wasn't kidding. He was putting the aircraft within shouting distance. Ambivalence tore through her. Make that *talking* distance.

"You sure about this? I mean, I don't want to get thrown out of the venue before the concert even starts!"

The helicopter touched down. "You won't. They're expecting us."

"What?"

Roan grinned. "You have a private meeting with the band before the concert."

"I do not."

"Surprise!"

Breath escaped her. Her gaze flew to the bus, then back to Roan. "Are you kidding me?"

"I'd never kid you about something so important." He nodded his head in the direction of the bus. "There they are now."

She whipped her head toward the bus and, sure enough, the lead singer was standing there, the green coloring in his short-cropped hair shimmering in the late-afternoon sunlight. He was waving. Her heart stopped. *This was really happening*. The guitar player showed up in the doorway behind him and Kelly wanted to bust Roan with a bear hug. She turned to him. Adrenaline pulsed through her limbs. "How did you do this?"

"A buddy of mine flies for them. I asked a favor and he made it happen."

Kelly stared at him. "I can't believe it. I can't believe you did this for me!1"

"They're your favorite, aren't they?"

"My number-one all-time favorite!"

"Well, then you'd better hurry before they get the wrong idea!"

She sat stunned, mouth agape. "You're not coming?"

"Oh, I'm coming, all right." He laughed. "I'm cashing in on this one big time, but I have to tie down the chopper, first."

"Oh, yeah..."

"Don't worry. I'll do all the work. You run along and have fun—but not too much. You're still my date for the evening."

She erupted with a laugh. A silly, foolish, embarrassed laugh as she registered what he meant. "I'm no groupie, Roan. It's not like I'm going to walk on board their bus and forget you exist."

"I know. You're just a woman crazy-excited to see her favorite band...a woman who's too nervous to get out and actually meet them."

"What? I am not!"

"It's written all over your face. You're afraid to get out."

"I'm getting out all right, you watch." But not before she let him know how much she appreciated the gesture. Kelly leaned over and cupping a hand to his chin, kissed him full on the lips. Soft and lingering, she took her time. Roan was right about one thing: she was paying up big time for this one, and she would happily do so for every future surprise he had in store for her. There was no chance she'd forget she was his date.

No chance. Kelly Jones only had eyes for Roan Phillips.

# # #

The End

Roasted Red Pepper Hummus

2 whole red peppers, sliced with seeds removed
2 cups fresh chickpeas, cooked (1 - 15 oz, can
chickpeas)
1/4 cup tahini
1 large lemon, juiced
2 cloves garlic, minced
2 TBSP olive oil
1 tsp ground cumin
1/2 tsp salt
1/4 cup bean liquid or water

Roast red peppers until golden brown. Remove from oven and allow to cool. In a food processor, combine tahini and lemon juice and blend until smooth, about 30 seconds. You can use the entire lemon, peel and all (without seeds), though the result will be a strong lemony flavor. Your choice!

Next, add peppers, garlic, olive oil, cumin and salt and process 30 seconds. Scrape sides and process 30 seconds longer or until fully blended. Add chickpeas and process until smooth, 1-2 minutes. You might want to alternately stop and scrape sides throughout this process.

If hummus is thicker than you prefer, add your reserved bean liquid/water accordingly. We prefer our hummus on the creamy side and added only a TBSP of liquid. Remove hummus from processor and enjoy!

Yield about 3 cups

For a delicious twist, use pesto instead of roasted red peppers. Better yet, how about sautéing the chickpeas in olive oil, garlic and cumin until aromatic prior to adding to the food processor. Yum. Curry would be a delightful addition, as well. Only your imagination limits your options with this recipe!

About the Author:

Dianne Venetta lives in Central Florida with her husband, two children and part-time Yellow Lab Cody-boy! An avid gardener, she spends her spare time growing organic vegetables, surprised by what she finds there every day. Who knew there were so many amazing similarities between men and plants? Women, life and love and her discoveries along the way provide for never-ending fun on her garden blog: BloominThyme.com. When she's not knee-deep in dirt or writing, Dianne also contributes garden advice to various websites.

You can also find her on twitter @DianneVenetta and facebook.com/DianneVenetta. Plus, learn how you can become a member of her street team, Bloomin' Warriors, where you'll be eligible for special discounts, advance excerpts, author swag and unique gift items throughout the year. For full details, be sure to check out her website, DianneVenetta.com.

Other novels by Dianne Venetta:
Mystery/Romantic Adventure Fiction
Silver Creek Series:
NOT WITHOUT YOU #1
BECAUSE OF YOU #2
ALL ABOUT YOU #3
ONLY WITH YOU #4

Mystery/Romance Fiction
Ladd Springs Series:
LADD SPRINGS #1
LADD FORTUNE #2
HOTEL LADD #3
LADD HAVEN #4
LOSING LADD #5
LADD CHRISTMAS #6

Romantic Women's Fiction
The Gables Trilogy:
JENNIFER'S GARDEN
LUST ON THE ROCKS
WHISPER PRIVILEGES

Women's Fiction
CONDEMN ME NOT

ONLY WITH YOU